Honour
Thyself

www.daniellesteelbooks.co.uk

Also by Danielle Steel

* Published outside the UK under the title PASSION'S PROMISE

For more information on Danielle Steel and her books, see
her website at www.daniellesteel.com

DANIELLE STEEL

Honour Thyself

CORGI BOOKS

TRANSWORLD PUBLISHERS
61–63 Uxbridge Road, London W5 5SA
A Random House Group Company
www.rbooks.co.uk

HONOUR THYSELF
A CORGI BOOK: 9780552154741

First published in Great Britain
in 2008 by Bantam Press
a division of Transworld Publishers
Corgi edition published 2009

A CIP catalogue record for this book
is available from the British Library.

Addresses for Random House Group Ltd companies outside the UK
can be found at: www.randomhouse.co.uk
The Random House Group Ltd Reg. No. 954009

The Random House Group Limited supports The Forest Stewardship
Council (FSC), the leading international forest certification
organisation. All our titles that are printed on Greenpeace approved
FSC certified paper carry the FSC logo. Our paper procurement policy
can be found at
www.rbooks.co.uk/environment

Typeset in 12/15pt Garamond by
Falcon Oast Graphic Art Ltd.
Printed in the UK by CPI Cox & Wyman, Reading, RG1 8EX.

2 4 6 8 10 9 7 5 3

To my mother, Norma,
who never read any of my books,
but was proud of me anyway, I hope.
To the challenging relationships
between some less fortunate
mothers and daughters, the missed opportunities,
the good intentions gone awry, and in the end
the love that carries one through, whatever
the story looked like, appeared to be, or was.
In all the ways that mattered to me at the time,
I lost my mother when I was six,
when she was no longer there to comb my hair,
so I wouldn't look silly at school.
We knew each other better as adults,
two entirely different women,
with such different views of life.
We disappointed each other often,
understood each other little,
but I give us both credit for trying and hanging in till the end.
This book is for the mother I wish I had had,
the one I hoped for every time we met,
the one who cooked pancakes and Swedish meatballs
when I was little, before she left,
for the one I'm sure she tried to be even after she did,
and finally with love, compassion, and forgiveness
for the one she was.
In her own way, she taught me to be the mother that I am.
May God smile on you and hold you closely,
may you find joy and peace.
I love you, Mom.

d.s.

'If you become whole,
everything will come to you.'

Tao Te Ching

Honour Thyself

1

It was a quiet, sunny November morning, as Carole Barber looked up from her computer and stared out into the garden of her Bel-Air home. It was a big, rambling stone mansion that she had lived in for fifteen years. The sunny greenhouse room she used as an office looked out over the rosebushes she had planted, the fountain, and the small pond that reflected the sky. The view was peaceful, and the house silent. Her hands had barely moved over the keyboard for the past hour. It was beyond frustrating. Despite a long and successful career in films, she was trying to write her first novel. Although she had written short stories for years, she had never published any. She had even tried her hand at a screenplay once. During their entire marriage, she and her late husband, Sean, had talked about making a movie together, and never got around to it. They were too busy doing other things, in their primary fields.

Sean was a producer-director, and she was an actress. Not just an actress, Carole Barber was a major star, and had been since she was eighteen. She had just turned fifty, two months before. By her own choice, she hadn't had a part in a movie for three years. At her age, even with her still remarkable beauty, good parts were rare.

Carole stopped working when Sean got sick. And in the two years since he'd died, she had traveled, visiting her children in London and New York. She was involved in a variety of causes, mostly relating to the rights of women and children, which had taken her to Europe several times, China, and underdeveloped countries around the world. She cared deeply about injustice, poverty, political persecution, and crimes against the innocent and defenseless.

She had diligently kept journals of all her trips, and a poignant one of the months before Sean died. She and Sean had talked about her writing a book, in the last days of his life. He thought it was a wonderful idea, and encouraged her to start the project. She had waited until two years after his death to do it. She had been wrestling with writing it for the past year. The book would give her an opportunity to speak out about the things that mattered to her, and delve deep into herself in a way that acting never had. She wanted desperately to complete the book, but she couldn't seem to get it off the ground. Something kept stopping her, and she had no idea what it was. It was a classic case of writer's block, but like a dog with a bone, she refused to give up and let it go. She wanted to go back to acting eventually, but not until she wrote the book. She felt as though she owed that to Sean and herself.

In August, she had turned down what seemed like a good part in an important movie. The director was excellent, the screenwriter had won several Academy Awards for his earlier work. Her costars would have been interesting to work with. But when she read the script, it did absolutely nothing for her. She felt no pull to it at all. She didn't want to act anymore unless she loved the part. She was haunted by her book, still in its fetal stages, and it was keeping her from going back to work. Somewhere deep in her heart, she knew she had to do the writing first. This novel was the voice of her soul.

When Carole finally started the book, she insisted it wasn't about herself. It was only as she got deeper into it that she realized that in fact it was. The central character had many facets of Carole in her, and the more Carole got into it, the harder it was to write, as though she couldn't bear facing herself. She had been blocked on it again now for weeks. It was a story about a woman coming of age and examining her life. She realized now that it had everything to do with her, the life she'd led, the men she'd loved, and the decisions she had made in the course of her life. Every time she sat down at her desk to write it, she found herself staring into space, dreaming about the past, and nothing wound up on the screen of her computer. She was haunted by echoes of her earlier life, and until she came to terms with them, she knew she couldn't delve into her novel, nor solve its problems. She needed the key to unlock those doors first, and hadn't found it. Every question and doubt she'd ever had about herself had leaped back into her head with the writing. She was suddenly questioning every move she'd ever made. Why? When? How? Had she been right or wrong? Were the people in her life actually as she'd seen them at the time? Had she been unfair? She kept asking herself the same questions, and wondered why it mattered now, but it did. Immensely. She could go nowhere with the book, until she came up with the answers about her own life. It was driving her insane. It was as though by deciding to write this book, she was being forced to face herself in ways she never had before, ways she had avoided for years. There was no hiding from it now. The people she had known floated through her head at night, as she lay awake, and even in her dreams. And she awoke exhausted in the morning.

The face that came to mind most often was Sean's. He was the only one she was sure about, who he had been, and what he meant to her. Their relationship had been so straightforward and clean. The others weren't, not to that degree. She had questions in her mind about all of them but Sean. And he had been so anxious for her to write the book she had described to him, she felt she owed it to him, as a kind of final gift. And she wanted to prove to herself that she could do it. She was paralyzed by the fear that she couldn't, and didn't have it in her. She had had the dream for more than three years now, and needed to know if she had a book in her or not.

The word that came to mind when she thought of Sean was *peace*. He was a kind, gentle, wise, loving man, who had been only wonderful to her. He had brought order to her life in the beginning, and together they had built a solid foundation for their life together. He had never tried to own or overwhelm her. Their lives had never seemed intertwined or entangled, instead they had traveled side by side, at a comfortable pace together, right until the end. Because of who he was, even Sean's death from cancer had been a quiet disappearance, a kind of natural evolution into a further dimension where she could no longer see him. But because of his powerful influence on her life, she always felt him near her. He had accepted death as one more step in the journey of his life, a transition he had to make at some point, like a wondrous opportunity. He learned from everything he did, and whatever he encountered on his path, he embraced with grace. In dying, he had taught her yet another intensely valuable lesson about life.

Two years after he had gone, she still missed him, his laughter, the sound of his voice, his brilliant mind, his company, their long quiet walks together along the beach, but she always had the feeling that he was somewhere nearby, doing his own thing, traveling on, and sharing some kind of blessing with her, just as he had when he was alive. Knowing and loving him had been one of her greatest gifts. He had reminded her before he died that she still had much to do, and urged her to go back to work. He wanted her to make movies again, and write the book.

He had always loved her short stories and essays, and over the years she had written dozens of poems to him, which he treasured. She had had all of them bound in a leather folder several months before he died, and he had spent hours reading them over and over again.

She hadn't had time to start the book before he died. She was too busy taking care of him. She had taken a year off to spend time with him, and nurse him herself when he got really sick, particularly after chemo and in the last few months of his illness. He had been valiant till the end. They had gone for a walk together the day before he died. They hadn't been able to walk far, and they had said very little to each other. They had walked side by side, holding hands, sat down frequently when he got tired, and they had both cried as they sat and watched the sunset. They both knew the end was near. He had died the following night, peacefully, in her arms. He had taken one last long look at her, sighed with a gentle smile, closed his eyes, and was gone.

Because of the way he'd died, with such elegant acceptance, afterward it had been impossible to be overwhelmed with grief when she thought about him. As best as one could be, she was ready. They both were. What she felt in his absence was an emptiness she still felt now. And she wanted to fill that void with a better understanding of herself. She knew the book would help her do that, if she could ever get a handle on it. She wanted to at least try to measure up to him, and the faith he'd had in her. He had been a constant source of inspiration to her, in her life and her work. He had brought her calm and joy, and a kind of serenity and balance.

In many ways, it had been a relief for her not to work in films for the past three years. She had worked so hard for so long that even before Sean got sick she knew she needed a break. And she knew that time off for introspection would eventually bring deeper meaning to her acting as well. She had made some important movies over the years, and had been in some major commercial hits. But she wanted more than that now, she wanted to bring something to her work that she never had before. The kind of depth that only came with wisdom, seasoning, and time.

She wasn't old at fifty, but the years since Sean got sick and died had deepened her in ways she knew she would never have experienced otherwise, and she knew that inevitably that would show on the screen. And if she mastered it, surely in her book as well. This book was a symbol of ultimate adulthood for her, and freedom from the last ghosts of her past. She had spent so many years pretending to be other people through her acting, and appearing to be who the world expected her to be. Now was the time in her life when she wanted to be unfettered by other people's expectations, and finally be herself. She belonged to no one now. She was free to be whoever she wanted to be.

Her years of belonging to a man had been over long before she met Sean. They had been two free souls, living side by side, enjoying each other with love and mutual respect. Their lives had been parallel, and in perfect symmetry and balance, but never enmeshed. It was the one thing she had feared when they got married, that it would get complicated, or he would try to 'own' her, that they might somehow stifle or drown each other. That had never happened. He had assured her it wouldn't, and had kept his promise. She knew that her eight years with Sean were something that only occurred once in a lifetime. She didn't expect to find that with anyone else. Sean had been unique.

She couldn't imagine herself falling in love, or wanting to be married again. She had missed him for these past two years, but had not mourned him. His love had sated her so totally that she was comfortable now even without him. There had been no agony or pain in their love for each other, although like all couples, they'd had resounding arguments now and then, and then laughed about them afterward. Neither Sean nor Carole was the kind of person to hold a grudge, and there wasn't a shred of malice in either of them, or even in their fights. In addition to loving each other, they had been best friends.

They met when Carole was forty, and Sean was thirty-five. Although five years younger than she was, he had set an example for her in many ways, mostly in his views about life. Her career was still going strong, and she was making more movies than she wanted to at the time. For so many years before that, she had been driven to follow the path of an ever-more-demanding career. They met five years after she had moved back to Los Angeles from France, and she'd been trying to spend more time with her children, always pulled between her kids and increasingly alluring movie roles. She had spent the years after her return from France without a serious involvement with a man. She just didn't have the time, or the desire. There had been men she'd gone out with, usually for a brief time, some of them in her business, mostly directors or writers, others who were in different creative fields, art, architecture, or music. They had been interesting men, but she'd never fallen in love with any of them, and was convinced she never would again. Until Sean.

They had met at a conference they'd both gone to, to discuss the rights of actors in Hollywood, and had been on a panel together about the changing role of women in films. It had never bothered either of them that he was five years younger than she was. It was completely irrelevant to both of them. They were kindred spirits, regardless of age. A month after they met, they had gone to Mexico together for a weekend. He had moved in three months later, and never left. Six months after he moved in, despite Carole's reluctance and misgivings, they were married. Sean had convinced her it was the right thing for both of them. He was absolutely correct, although at first Carole had been adamant about not wanting to get married again. She was convinced that their careers would somehow interfere and cause conflicts between them, and impact their marriage. As Sean had promised, her fears had been unfounded. Their union seemed blessed.

Her children had been young then, and still at home, which was an added concern for Carole. Sean had none of his own, and they had none together. He was crazy about her two children, and they had both agreed that they were too busy and wouldn't have had time to give to another child. Instead they nurtured each other, and their marriage. Anthony and Chloe were both in high school when she and Sean married, which was part of her decision to marry Sean. She didn't like setting the example of just living together with no further commitment, and her children had cast a strong positive vote for the marriage. They wanted Sean to stick around, and he had proven to be a good friend and stepfather to both of them. And now, much to her chagrin, both her children were grown up and gone.

Chloe was in her first job, after graduating from Stanford. She was the assistant to the assistant accessories editor for a fashion magazine in London. It was mostly prestige and fun, helping with styling, setting up shoots, doing errands, for almost no pay and the thrill of working for British *Vogue*. Chloe loved it. With looks similar to her mother's, she could have been a model, but preferred to be on the editorial end, and she was having a ball in London. She was a bright, outgoing girl and was excited about the people she met through her job. She and Carole talked often on the phone.

Anthony was following in his father's footsteps on Wall Street, in the world of finance, after getting an MBA from Harvard. He was a serious, responsible young man, and had always made them proud. He was as handsome as Chloe was pretty, but had always been a little shy. He went out with lots of bright, attractive girls, but no one important to him so far. His social life interested him less than his work at the office. He was diligent about his career in finance, and always kept his goals in mind. In fact, very little deterred him, and more often than not when Carole called him on his cell phone late at night, he was still working at his desk.

Both children had been deeply attached to Sean, and to their mother. They had always been wholesome, sensible, and loving, despite the occasional mother–daughter skirmish between Chloe and Carole. Chloe had always needed her mother's time and attention more than her brother, and complained bitterly when her mother went on location for a movie, particularly during high school, when she wanted Carole around, like the other mothers. Her complaints had made Carole feel guilty, even though she had the kids fly out to visit on the set whenever possible, or came home during breaks in filming to be with them. Anthony had been easy, Chloe always a little less so, at least for Carole. Chloe thought her father walked on water, and was more than willing to point out her mother's faults. Carole told herself it was the nature of relationships between mother and daughter. It was easier to be the mother of an adoring son.

And now, on her own, with her kids grown and gone, and happy in their own lives, Carole was determined to tackle the novel she had promised herself to write for so long. In the past few weeks, she had gotten seriously discouraged, and had begun to doubt it was ever going to happen. She was beginning to wonder if she had been wrong to turn down the part she had declined in August. Maybe she had to give up writing, and go back to making movies. Mike Appelsohn, her agent, was getting annoyed with her. He was upset about the parts she kept turning down, and fed up with hearing about the book she didn't write.

The story line was eluding her, the characters still seemed vague, the outcome and development seemed to be tied in a knot somewhere in her head. It was all a giant tangle, like a ball of yarn after the cat played with it. And no matter what she did, or how intently she thought about it, she couldn't seem to sort out the mess. It was frustrating her beyond belief.

There were two Oscars sitting on a shelf above her desk, and a Golden Globe she'd won just before the year she'd taken off when Sean got sick. Hollywood still hadn't forgotten her, but Mike Appelsohn assured her they'd give up on her eventually, if she didn't go back to work. She had run out of excuses for him, and given herself till the end of the year to start the book. She had two months left, and was getting nowhere. She was beginning to feel panicked about it every time she sat down at her desk.

She heard a door open gently behind her, and turned with an anxious look. She didn't mind the interruption, in fact she welcomed it. The day before, she had reorganized her bathroom closets instead of working on the book. When she turned, she saw Stephanie Morrow, her assistant, standing hesitantly in the doorway of her office. She was beautiful, a schoolteacher by profession, whom Carole had hired for the summer, fifteen years before, when she first came back from Paris. Carole had bought the house in Bel-Air, accepted parts in two films that first year, and signed on for a year in a Broadway play. She got deeply involved in women's rights, had publicity to do for her movies, and needed help organizing her kids and staff. Stephanie had come to help her out for two months, and stayed forever. Fifteen years later, she was thirty-nine years old. She lived with a man, but had never married. He was understanding about her work and traveled a lot himself. Stephanie still wasn't sure if she ever wanted to marry, and was clear she didn't want children. She teased Carole and said she was her baby. Carole reciprocated by saying Stephanie was her nanny. She was a fabulous assistant, handled the press brilliantly, and could talk her way in or out of any situation. There was nothing she couldn't manage.

When Sean was sick, she had done everything she could for Carole. She was there for the kids, for Sean, and for her. She even helped Carole plan the funeral and pick the casket. Over the years, Stephanie had become more than just an employee. Despite the eleven years that separated them, the two women had become close friends, with deep affection and respect for each other. There wasn't an ounce of jealousy in Stevie, as Carole called her. She was happy for Carole's victories, mourned her tragedies, loved her job, and faced each day with patience and humor.

Carole was deeply attached to her, and readily admitted that she would have been lost without her. She was the perfect assistant, and as people did in jobs like hers, it meant putting Carole's life first and her own second, or sometimes not having a life at all. Stevie loved Carole and her job, and didn't mind. Carole's life was far more exciting than her own.

Stevie stood six feet tall, with straight black hair and big brown eyes, and was wearing jeans and a T-shirt as she stood in Carole's office doorway. 'Tea?' she whispered.

'No. Arsenic,' Carole said with a groan, as she swiveled in her chair. 'I can't write this goddamn book. Something's stopping me, and I don't know what it is. Maybe it's just terror. Maybe I know I can't do it. I don't know why I thought I could.' She looked at Stevie, frowning in despair.

'Yes, you can,' Stephanie said calmly. 'Give it time. They say the hardest part is the beginning. You just have to sit there long enough to do it.' For the past week, Stevie had helped her re-organize all her closets, then redesign the garden, and clean out the garage. And decide to redo the kitchen. Carole had come up with every possible distraction and excuse to avoid starting the book, again. She had been doing it for months. 'Maybe you need to take a break,' Stevie suggested, and Carole groaned.

'My whole life is a break these days. Sooner or later, I have to go back to work, either on a movie, or writing this book. Mike is going to kill me if I turn down another script.'

Mike Appelsohn was a producer, and had acted as her agent for thirty-two years, since he discovered her at eighteen, light-years before. A million years ago, she had been just a farm girl from Mississippi, with long blond hair and huge green eyes, who came to Hollywood more out of curiosity than real ambition. Mike Appelsohn had made her what she was today. That, and the fact that she had real talent. Her first screen test at eighteen had blown everyone away. The rest was history. Her history. Now she was one of the most famous actresses in the world, and successful beyond her wildest dreams. So what was she doing trying to write a book? She couldn't help but ask herself the same question over and over again. She knew the answer, just as Stevie did. She was looking for a piece of herself, a piece she had hidden in a drawer somewhere, a part of her she wanted and needed to find, in order for the rest of her life to make sense.

Her last birthday had affected her deeply. Turning fifty had been an important landmark for her, particularly now that she was alone. It couldn't be ignored. She had decided that she wanted to weave all the pieces of her together, in ways she never had before, to solder them into a whole, instead of having bits and pieces of herself drifting in space. She wanted her life to make sense, to herself if no one else. She wanted to go back to the beginning and figure it all out.

So much had happened to her by accident, in her early years particularly, or at least it seemed that way. Good luck and bad, though mostly good, in her career anyway, and with her kids. But she didn't want her life to seem like an accident, fortuitous or otherwise. So many things she'd done had been reactions to circumstances or other people, rather than decisions she'd actively made. It seemed important now to know if the choices she'd made had been the right ones. And then what? She kept asking herself what difference it would make. It wouldn't change the past. But it might alter the course of her life for her remaining years. That was the difference she wanted to make. With Sean gone, it seemed more important to her now to make choices and decisions, and not just wait for things to happen to her. What did *she* want? She wanted to write a book. That was all she knew. And maybe after that, the rest would come. Maybe then she'd have a better sense of what parts she wanted to play in movies, what impact she wanted to have on the world, what causes she wanted to support, and who she wanted to be for the rest of her life.

Her kids had grown up. Now it was her turn.

Stevie disappeared and reappeared with a cup of tea. Decaffeinated vanilla tea. Stevie ordered it for her from Mariage Frères in Paris. Carole had become addicted to it while she lived there, and it was still her favorite. She was always grateful for the steaming mugs of it Stevie handed her. It was comforting for her. Carole looked pensive as she put the mug to her lips and took a sip. 'Maybe you're right,' Carole said thoughtfully, glancing at the woman who had been her companion for years. They traveled together, since Carole took her on the set when she was making a movie. Stevie was a one-man band who made Carole's life smooth as silk, and enjoyed doing it for her. She adored her job, and coming to work every day. Each day was different, and a challenge. And it still excited her after all these years that she worked for Carole Barber.

'What am I right about?' Stevie asked, letting down her long limbs into the room's comfortable leather easy chair. They spent a lot of hours together in that room, planning things, talking things out. Carole was always willing to listen to

Stevie's opinions, even if she did something different in the end. Although most of the time, she found her assistant's advice to be solid, and valuable to her. And to Stevie, Carole was not only an employer, but something of a wise aunt. The two women shared opinions on life, and often saw things the same way, particularly about men.

'Maybe I need to take a trip.' Not to avoid the book, but maybe in this case to crack it, like a hard shell that resisted and wouldn't open any other way.

'You could go visit the kids,' Stevie suggested. Carole loved visiting her son and daughter, since they seldom came home anymore. It was hard for Anthony to get away from the office, although he always made time to see her in the evening when she was in New York, no matter how busy he was. He loved his mother. As did Chloe, who would drop everything to run around London with her mother to play and shop. She soaked up her mother's love and time, like a flower in rain.

'I just did that a few weeks ago. I don't know . . . maybe I need to do something completely different . . . go somewhere I've never been before . . . like Prague or something . . . or Romania . . . Sweden . . .' There weren't a lot of places left on the planet where she hadn't been. She had spoken at women's conferences in India, Pakistan, and Beijing. She had met heads of state around the world, worked with UNICEF, and addressed the U.S. Senate.

Stevie hesitated to state the obvious. Paris. She knew how much the city meant to her. Carole had lived in Paris for two and a half years, and had only been back twice in the last fifteen. Carole said there was nothing for her there anymore. She had taken Sean to Paris shortly after they were married, but he hated the French, and always preferred going to London instead. Stevie knew she hadn't been back now in about ten years. And she'd only been there once in the five years before Sean, when she sold the house on the rue Jacob, or actually in a small alley behind it. Stevie had gone with her to close the house, and loved it. But by then Carole's life had shifted back to L.A., and she said it made no sense to keep a house in Paris. It had been hard for her when she closed it, and she never went back again, till her only trip there with Sean. They stayed at the Ritz, and he complained the entire time. He loved Italy and England, but not France.

'Maybe it's time for you to go back to Paris,' Stevie said cautiously. She knew that ghosts lingered there for her, but after fifteen years, she couldn't imagine that they would still affect Carole. Not after eight years with Sean. Whatever had happened to Carole in Paris had long since healed, and she still spoke of the city fondly from time to time.

'I don't know,' Carole said, thinking about it. 'It rains a lot in November. The weather is so good here.'

'The weather doesn't seem to be helping you write the book. Somewhere else then. Vienna . . . Milan . . . Venice . . . Buenos Aires . . . Mexico City . . . Hawaii. Maybe you need a little time on the beach, if you're looking for good weather.' They both knew the weather wasn't the issue.

'I'll see,' Carole said with a sigh, getting out of her desk chair. 'I'll think about it.'

Carole was tall, though not as tall as her assistant. She was slim, lithe, with a still-beautiful figure. She worked out, but not enough to justify the way she looked. She had great genes, good bone structure, a body that defied her years, and a face that willingly lied about her age, and she had had no surgery to help it.

Carole Barber was just a beautiful woman. Her hair was still blond, she wore it long and straight, often tied back in a ponytail or in a bun. Hairdressers on the set had been having a ball with her silky blond hair since she was eighteen. Her eyes were enormous and green, her cheekbones high, her features delicate and perfect. She had the face and figure of a model, not just a star. And the way she carried herself spoke of confidence, poise, and grace. She wasn't arrogant, she was just comfortable in her own skin, and she moved with the elegance of a dancer. The studio that had signed her first had made her take ballet. She still moved like a dancer today, with perfect posture. She was a spectacular-looking woman, and rarely wore makeup. She had a simplicity of style that made her even more striking. Stevie had been in awe of her when she first came to work. Carole had only been thirty-five then, and now she was fifty, hard as that was to believe. She looked easily ten years younger than she was. Even though he'd been five years younger, Sean had always looked older than she did. He was handsome, but bald, and tended to put on weight. Carole still had the same figure she'd had at twenty. She was careful about what she ate, but mostly she was just lucky. She had been blessed by the gods at birth.

'I'm going to run some errands,' she told Stevie a few minutes later. She had put a white cashmere sweater around her shoulders, and was carrying a beige alligator bag she'd bought at Hermès. She had a fondness for simple but good clothes, especially if they were French. At fifty, there was something about Carole that reminded one of Grace Kelly at twenty. She had that same kind of elegant, aristocratic ease, although Carole seemed warmer. There was nothing austere about Carole, and considering who she was, and the fame she'd enjoyed for all of her adult life, she was surprisingly humble. Like everyone else,

Stevie loved that about her. Carole was never full of herself.

'Anything you want me to do for you?' Stevie offered.

'Yeah, write the book while I'm out. I'll send it to my agent tomorrow.' She had lined up a literary agent, but had nothing to send her.

'Done.' Stevie grinned at her. 'I'll man the fort here. You hit Rodeo.'

'I am *not* going to Rodeo,' Carole said primly. 'I want to look at some new dining room chairs. I think the dining room needs a facelift. Come to think of it, so do I, but I'm too chicken to get one. I don't want to wake up in the morning looking like someone else. It's taken me fifty years to get used to the face I have. I'd hate to turn it in.'

'You don't need one,' Stevie reassured her.

'Thanks, but I've seen the ravages of time in the mirror.'

'I have more wrinkles than you do,' Stevie said, and it was true. She had fine Irish skin that wasn't wearing as well as her employer's, much to her chagrin.

Five minutes later, Carole drove off in her

station wagon. She had driven the same car for the last six years. Unlike other Hollywood stars, she had no need to be seen in a Rolls or a Bentley. Her station wagon was fine with her. The only jewelry she wore was a pair of diamond stud earrings and, when Sean was alive, her plain gold wedding band, which she had finally taken off that summer. Anything more than that she considered unnecessary, and the producers borrowed for her when she had to appear to promote a film. In her private life, the most exotic piece of jewelry Carole wore was a simple gold watch. The most dazzling thing about Carole was herself.

She was back two hours later, while Stevie was eating a sandwich in the kitchen. There was an office nook for her, where she worked, and her main complaint was that it was much too close to the fridge, which she visited too often. She worked out at the gym every night to compensate for what she ate at work.

'Did you finish the book yet?' Carole asked as she walked in. She looked in much better spirits than when she left.

'Almost. I'm on the last chapter. Give me another half-hour, and I'll be all set. How were the chairs?'

'They were the wrong look for the table. The scale wasn't right. Unless I get a new table too.' She was looking for projects, and they both knew that she needed to go back to work, or write the book. Indolence wasn't her style. After a lifetime of working constantly, and now that Sean was gone, Carole needed something to do. 'I decided to take your advice,' Carole said, sitting down at the kitchen table across from Stevie with a solemn look.

'What advice?' Stevie could no longer remember what she'd said.

'About taking a trip. I need to get out of here. I'll take my computer with me. Maybe sitting in a hotel room, I can get a fresh start on the book. I don't even like what I've got so far.'

'I do. The first two chapters are good. You just need to build on that and keep going. Like climbing a mountain. Don't look down or stop until you reach the top.' It was good advice.

'Maybe. I'll see. Anyway, I need to clear my

head,' she said with a sigh. 'Book me a flight to Paris for the day after tomorrow. I don't have anything to do here, and Thanksgiving isn't for another three and a half weeks. I might as well get my ass out of here before the kids come home for that. It's the perfect time.' She had thought about it all the way home and made up her mind. She felt better now.

Stevie nodded and refrained from further comment. She was convinced it would do her good to get away, particularly to a place she loved.

'I think I'm ready to go back,' Carole said softly, with a pensive look. 'You can get me a room at the Ritz. Sean hated it, but I love it.'

'How long do you want to stay?'

'I don't know. Why don't you book the room for two weeks, so I have it. I thought I'd use Paris as a base. I actually do want to go to Prague, and I've never been to Budapest either. I want to wander around a little, and see how I feel when I'm there. I'm free as a bird, I might as well take advantage of it. Maybe I'll get inspired if I see something new. If I want to come home earlier, I can. And I'll stop in London and see Chloe for a couple of days on the way home. If it's close enough to Thanksgiving, maybe she'll want to fly back with me. That might be fun. And Anthony's coming out for Thanksgiving too, so I don't need to stop in New York on the way back.' She always tried to see her kids when she went anywhere, if they had the time and she did. But this trip was for her.

Stevie smiled at her, as she jotted down a note to herself with the details. 'It'll be fun to go to Paris. I haven't been since you closed the house. That was fourteen years ago.' Carole looked slightly embarrassed then. She hadn't made herself clear.

'I hate to be a shit. I love it when we travel together. But I want to do this one on my own. I don't know why, but I just think I need to get into my own head. If I take you with me, I'd rather talk to you than dig into myself. I'm looking for something, and I'm not even sure what it is. Me, I think.' She had a deep conviction that the answers to her future, and the book, were buried in the past. She wanted to go back now to dig up everything she had left behind and tried to forget long ago.

Stevie looked surprised, but smiled at her employer. 'That's fine. I just worry about you when you travel alone.' Carole didn't do that often and Stevie didn't love the idea.

'I worry too,' Carole confessed, 'and I'm lazy as hell. You've spoiled me. I hate dealing with porters and ordering my own tea. But maybe it'll do me good. And how hard can life be at the Ritz?'

'What if you go to Eastern Europe? Do you want someone with you there? I could hire someone for you in Paris, through security at the Ritz.' There had been threats over the years, though nothing recent. People recognized her in almost every country. And even if they didn't, she was a beautiful woman traveling alone. And what if she got sick? Carole brought out the mother in Stevie every time. She loved taking care of her and shielding her from real life. It was her mission in life and her job.

'I don't need security. I'll be fine. And even if they recognize me, so what? As Katharine

Hepburn used to say, I'll just keep my head down, and avoid eye contact.' They were both still surprised at how often that worked. When Carole didn't make eye contact with people on the street, they recognized her far less. It was an old Hollywood trick, although it didn't always work. But more often than not it did.

'I can always fly over if you change your mind,' Stevie offered, and Carole smiled. She knew that her assistant wasn't angling for a trip. Stevie was just concerned about her, which touched Carole's heart. Stevie was the perfect personal assistant in every way, always striving to make Carole's life easier and anticipate problems before they could occur.

'I promise I'll call if I run into trouble, get lonely, or feel weird,' Carole assured her. 'Who knows, I may decide to come home after a few days. It's kind of fun to just go, and not have any set plans.' She had been on a million trips to promote movies, or on location when she made them. It was rare for her to just take off like this, but Stevie thought it was a good idea, even if it was unusual for her.

'I'll keep my cell phone on so you can call me, even at night or at the gym. I can always hop on the next plane,' Stevie promised, although Carole was conscientious about not calling her at night. She had kept firm boundaries over the years, which went both ways. She respected Stevie's private life, and when Carole had one, Stevie respected hers. It had made working together that much better over the years. 'I'll call the airline and the Ritz,' Stevie said, finishing her sandwich, and going to put the plate in the dishwasher. Carole had long since reduced her housekeeping staff to one woman, who came in the mornings five days a week. With Sean and the kids gone, she didn't need or want much help. She rummaged in the refrigerator herself and no longer had a cook. And she preferred driving herself. She enjoyed living like a normal person without all the trappings of a star.

'I'll start packing,' Carole said as she left the kitchen. Two hours later she was finished. She was taking very little. Some slacks, some jeans, one skirt, sweaters, comfortable shoes to walk in, and one pair of high heels. She packed one jacket and a raincoat, and took out a warm hooded wool coat to wear on the plane. The most important thing she was taking was her laptop. She needed very little else, and maybe she wouldn't even use that, if nothing came to her while on the trip.

She had just finished closing her suitcase, when Stevie walked into her bedroom to tell her that the reservations had been made. She was on a flight to Paris in two days, and the Ritz had a suite for her on the Vendôme side of the building. Stevie said she would drive her to the airport. Carole was all set for her odyssey to find herself, in Paris, or wherever else she went. Whatever other cities she decided to travel to, she could make the reservations once she was in Europe. Carole was excited now at the thought of going. It was going to be wonderful being in Paris after all these years.

She wanted to walk past her old house near the rue Jacob, on the Left Bank, and pay homage to the two and a half years she had spent there. It seemed like a lifetime ago. She had been younger than Stevie when she left Paris. Her son,

Anthony, who was eleven then, had been delighted to come back to the States. Chloe had been seven and was sad to leave Paris and her friends there. She had spoken perfect French. They had been eight and four when they first went there, when Carole was making a movie in Paris. The film had taken eight months, and they had stayed on for two years after that. It seemed like a big chunk of time then, especially in young lives, and even to her. And now she was going back, on a pilgrimage of sorts. She had no idea what she'd find there, or how she'd feel. But she was ready. She could hardly wait to leave. She realized now that it was an important step in writing the book. Maybe going back would free her, and open the doors that were sealed so tightly. Sitting at her computer in Bel-Air, she couldn't pry them open. But maybe there the doors would swing wide open on their own. It was what she hoped.

Just knowing that she was going to Paris, Carole was able to write that night. She sat at her computer for hours after Stevie left, and was back at it the next morning when she arrived.

She dictated some letters, paid her bills, and did a last few errands. By the time she left for the airport the next day, Carole was ready. She chatted animatedly with Stevie on the way to the airport, remembering last details, of what to tell the gardener, some things she'd ordered that would arrive while she was away.

'What do I tell the kids, if they call?' Stevie asked as they reached the airport, and she took Carole's bag out of the station wagon. She was traveling light, so she could manage more easily on her own.

'Just tell them I'm away,' Carole said easily.

'In Paris?' Stevie was ever discreet, and only told people, even her children, what Carole told her she could say.

'That's fine. It's not a secret. I'll probably call them at some point myself. I'll call Chloe before I go to London at the end. I want to see what I decide to do first.' She loved the feeling of freedom she had, traveling on her own, and making decisions about her destinations day by day. It was rare for her to be that spontaneous, and do whatever she wished. It seemed like a real gift.

'Don't forget to tell me what you're doing,' Stevie chided. 'I worry about you.' Probably more than her kids did, who were sometimes less aware, although they loved her. Stevie was almost maternal toward her at times. She knew the vulnerable side of Carole that others didn't see, the frail side, the one that hurt. To others, Carole showed tranquility and strength, which wasn't always the case underneath.

'I'll e-mail you when I get to the Ritz. Don't worry if you don't hear from me after that. If I go to Prague or Vienna or somewhere, I'll probably leave my computer in Paris. I don't want to bother with a lot of e-mail while I'm away. Sometimes it's fun to just write on legal pads. The change might do me good. I'll call if I need help.'

'You better. Have fun,' Stevie said as she hugged her, and Carole smiled up at her.

'Take care. Enjoy the break,' Carole said, as a porter took her bag and checked her in. She was traveling first class. He did a double-take as he looked at her and then smiled as he recognized her.

'Well, hello, Miss Barber, and how are you today?' He was thrilled to meet the star face-to-face.

'Just fine, thank you.' She smiled back. Her big green eyes lit up her face.

'Going to Paris?' he asked, dazzled by her. She was as beautiful as she was on screen, and seemed friendly, warm, and real.

'Yes, I am.' Just saying it felt good to her now, as though Paris was waiting for her. She gave him a good tip, and he tipped his hat to her, as two of the other porters rushed up and asked for autographs. She signed them, waved at Stevie one last time, and then disappeared into the terminal in jeans, her heavy dark gray coat, and a large traveling bag on her arm. Her blond hair was pulled back in a sleek ponytail, and she slipped dark glasses on as she went inside. No one noticed her as she walked by. She was just another woman hurrying toward security, on her way to a plane. She was traveling Air France. And even after fifteen years, she was still comfortable in French. She'd have a chance to practice on the plane.

The plane left LAX on time, and she read a book she'd brought with her as they winged their way toward Paris. Halfway through the flight, she slept, and as requested, they woke her forty minutes before they arrived, which gave her time to brush her teeth, wash her face, comb her hair, and have a cup of her vanilla tea. She was in her seat, looking out the window as they landed. It was a rainy November day in Paris, and her heart leaped just seeing it again. For reasons she wasn't even sure of, she was making a pilgrimage back in time, and even after all these years, she felt as though she were coming home again.

2

The suite at the Ritz was as beautiful as she hoped it would be. All the fabrics were silk and satin, the colors pale blue and hushed gold. She had a living room and a bedroom, and a Louis XV desk where she plugged her computer in. She sent Stevie an e-mail ten minutes after she got there, while she waited for croissants and a pot of hot water. She had brought a three-week supply of her own vanilla tea with her. It was coals to Newcastle since it came from Paris, but this way she didn't have to go out and buy it. Stevie had handed it to her as she packed.

The e-mail said that she had arrived safely, the

suite was gorgeous, and the flight had been fine. She said it was raining in Paris, but she didn't mind. And she mentioned that she was turning off her computer and wouldn't be writing to Stevie again for a while, if at all. If she had a problem, she'd call on her assistant's cell. She thought about calling her children after that, but decided not to. She loved talking to them, but they had their own lives now, and this trip belonged to her. It was something she needed to do for herself. She didn't want to share it with them yet. And she knew they'd find it odd that she was wandering around Europe on her own. There was something faintly pathetic about it, as though she had nothing to do, and no one to be with, which was true, but she was comfortable about this trip. And she sensed now that the key to the book she was trying to write was here, or one of the keys at least. And she knew her children might worry about her, if they knew she was traveling alone. Sometimes Stevie and her children were more aware of her fame than she was. Carole liked to ignore it.

The croissants and tea arrived, delivered by a liveried waiter. He put the silver tray on the coffee table, already laden with small pastries, a box of chocolates, and a bowl of fruit, with a bottle of champagne from the manager of the hotel. They took good care of her. She had always loved the Ritz. Nothing had changed. It was more beautiful than ever. She stood at the long French windows, looking out at the Place Vendôme in the rain. Her plane had landed at eleven that morning. She had gone right through customs, and was at the hotel at twelve-thirty. It was one o'clock by then. She had the whole afternoon to wander around and see familiar landmarks in the rain. She still had no idea where she was going after Paris, but for the moment she was happy. She was beginning to think she wouldn't go anywhere, just stay in Paris, and enjoy the time there. It didn't get better than this. She still thought Paris was the most beautiful city in the world.

She unpacked the few things she'd brought with her, and hung them in the closet. She bathed in the enormous tub, and reveled in the thick pink towels, and then put on warm clothes. At two-thirty she was walking across the lobby, with a handful of euros in her pocket. She left her key at the front desk. The heavy brass tag on it made it too cumbersome to carry, and she never took a handbag when she went out walking. They always seemed like too much trouble to her. She dug her hands into her pockets, pulled up her hood, put her head down, and slipped quietly through the revolving door, and as soon as she got outside, she put on dark glasses. The rain had turned to mist by then and felt gentle on her face, as she walked down the front steps of the Ritz, and out into the Place Vendôme. No one paid any attention to her, nor recognized her. She was just an anonymous woman in Paris, going out for a walk, as she headed to the Place de la Concorde on foot, and from there she wanted to head toward the Left Bank. It was a long walk, but she was ready for it. For the first time in years, she could do whatever she wanted to in Paris, go wherever she chose. She didn't have to listen to Sean complain about it, or entertain her children. She didn't have to please anyone but herself. She realized that coming here had been the perfect decision. She didn't even mind the light November rain, or the chill in the air. Her heavy coat kept her warm, and the rubber-soled shoes she'd worn kept her feet dry on the wet ground. She looked up at the sky then, took a deep breath, and smiled. There was no more spectacular city than Paris, no matter what the weather. She had always thought the sky there was the most beautiful in the world. It looked like a luminous gray pearl now, as she looked past the rooftops as she walked along.

She walked past the Hotel Crillon and into the Place de la Concorde, with the fountains and statues, and traffic whizzing past them. She stood for a long time, soaking in the soul of the city again, and then set off on foot toward the Left Bank, with her hands dug into her pockets. She was happy she had left her handbag in her room. It would have been a nuisance to carry it with her. She felt freer this way. And all she needed with her was enough money to pay for a cab home, if she strayed too far from the hotel and was too tired to walk back.

Carole loved to wander in Paris. She always had, even when the children were small. She had taken them all over the city, to all the monuments and museums, and to play in the Bois de Boulogne, the Tuileries, Bagatelle, and the Jardins du Luxembourg. She had cherished their years here, although Chloe remembered very little of it, and Anthony had been happy to go home. He missed baseball, hamburgers, and milkshakes, American television, and watching the Super Bowl. In the end, it had been hard to convince him that life was more exciting in Paris. It wasn't, for him, although both children had learned French, and so had she. Anthony still spoke a little, Chloe none at all, and Carole had been pleased to find on the plane that she could still manage fairly well. She rarely had a chance to speak it anymore. She had applied herself while they lived there, and became completely fluent. She no longer was, but she still spoke it very well, with the expected *le* and *la* mistakes that Americans made. It was hard for anyone who hadn't grown up in the language to speak it flawlessly. But when they lived there, she had come pretty close, and impressed all her French friends.

She crossed to the Left Bank on the Pont Alexandre III, heading toward the Invalides, and then headed up the Quais, past all the antiques dealers she still remembered. She turned down the rue des Saint Pères, and wended her way toward the rue Jacob. She had come back here like a homing pigeon, and turned into the little alley where their house was. For the first eight months of her time in Paris, they lived in an apartment that the studio rented for them. It was small and cramped for her, both kids, an assistant, and a nanny, and eventually they had moved to a hotel briefly. She had enrolled the kids in an American school, and after the film was finished, when she decided to move to Paris, she had found this house, just off the rue Jacob. It had been a little gem, on a private courtyard, with a lovely garden behind it. The house had been just big enough for them, and had endless charm. The children's rooms and the nanny had been on the top floor with *oeil de boeuf* windows and a mansard roof. Her room on the floor below it had been worthy of Marie Antoinette, with huge, high ceilings, long French windows that looked out over the garden, eighteenth-century floors and *boiseries,* and a pink marble fireplace that worked. She had an office and a dressing room near her bedroom, and a huge tub where she took bubble baths with Chloe, or relaxed on her own. On the main floor there was a double living room, a dining room and kitchen, and an entrance to the garden, where they ate in spring and summer. It was an absolute beauty of a house, built in the eighteenth century for some courtesan or other. She had never learned its full history, but one could easily imagine it being very romantic. And it had been for her as well.

She found the house easily, and walked into the courtyard, as the doors were open. She stood looking up at her old bedroom windows, and wondered who lived there now, if they were happy, if it had been a good home for them, if their dreams had come true there. She had been happy there for two years, and then at the end very sad. She had left Paris with a heavy heart.

Just thinking back to that time, she could feel the weight of it even now. It was like opening a door she had kept sealed for the past fifteen years, and remembering the smells and sounds and feelings, the thrill of being there with her children, of making new discoveries, and establishing a new life, and then leaving finally to go back to the States. It had been a hard decision to make, and a sad time for her. She still wondered at times if she had made the right decision, if things would have been different if they'd stayed. But standing here now, she somehow felt she had done the right thing, for her kids, if nothing else. And maybe even for herself. Even fifteen years later it was hard to know.

She realized now that this was why she had come. To figure it out again, to be sure she had been right. Once she knew that, in her soul, she would have some of the answers she needed for the book. She was traveling backward on the map of her life, before she could tell what had happened. Even if the book was fictionalized, she needed to know the truth first, before she could spin it into a tale. She knew too that she had avoided these answers for a long time, but she was feeling braver now.

She walked slowly out of the courtyard with her head down, and bumped into a man walking through the gates. He looked startled to see her, and she apologized to him in French. He nodded, and walked on.

Carole walked around the Left Bank after that, looking into antiques shops. She stopped at the bakery where she used to take the children, and bought *macarons,* which she carried out in a little bag, and ate as she walked. The neighborhood was filled with bittersweet memories for her, which rushed over her like an ocean at high tide, but it wasn't a bad feeling. It reminded her of so much, and suddenly she wanted to go back to the hotel and write. She knew what direction the book should take now, and where she should start. She wanted to rewrite the beginning, and as she thought about it, she hailed a cab. She had been walking for nearly three hours, and it was already dark.

She gave the driver the address of the Ritz, and they headed toward the Right Bank, as she sat back in the cab, thinking about her old house, and the things she'd seen that afternoon as she walked. This was the first time she had wandered around Paris and allowed herself to think of those things since she left. It had been different when she'd come here with Sean, and the avalanche of grief she'd experienced when she'd come to close the house with Stevie. She had hated to give it up, but there was no point in keeping it. Los Angeles was too far away, she was working on one film after another back to back, and she no longer had any reason to come to Paris. That chapter was over for her. So she sold the house a year after she left. She flew in for two days, told Stevie what to do, and then went back to L.A. She hadn't lingered that time, but now she had nothing but time on her hands. And the memories didn't frighten her anymore. After fifteen years, they were too far back to do her any harm. Or maybe she was just ready now. Having lost Sean, she could face other losses in her life. Sean had taught her that.

She was lost in thought as they drove into the tunnel just before the Louvre, and got stuck in traffic. She didn't care. Carole was in no hurry to go anywhere. She was tired from the trip, the time difference, and her long walk. She was planning to eat an early dinner in her room, and work on her book before she went to bed.

She was thinking about the book as they advanced in the tunnel a few feet, and then came to a dead stop. It was rush-hour traffic, with people going home, others going out. At that hour Paris traffic was always bad. She glanced into the car next to her, and saw two young men in the front seat, laughing, and honking their horn at the car in front. Another young man stuck his head out of that car, and waved back at them. They were having a ball, and laughing hysterically about something, which even made Carole smile. They looked Moroccan or North African, and were dark skinned in a beautiful café au lait color, and in the backseat of the car next to her was a boy in his late teens, not sharing in their laughter. He looked nervous and unhappy about something, and for a long moment, his eyes met Carole's. It was almost as though he were frightened, and she felt sorry for him. The traffic in her own lane stayed stationary, but the lane next to her moved forward finally. The boys in the front seat were still laughing, and as they pulled away, the boy in the backseat jumped out of the car and began running. Carole was watching, fascinated by him as he ran backward through the tunnel and vanished, and just as he disappeared, she heard a truck backfire somewhere ahead of them. As she heard it, she saw both cars with the laughing young men turn into fireballs, as the entire tunnel reverberated with a series of explosions and she could see a wall of fire move toward them. Her mind told her to get out of the car and run, but almost as she thought the words, the cab door flew open and she could feel herself flying over cars, as though she had suddenly grown wings. All she could see was fire around her, the cab she had been in had disappeared, pulverized into oblivion along with other cars near them. It was like being in a dream then, she could see cars and people disappearing beneath her, other people were flying just like she was, and then she drifted gently down into total blackness.

3

There were dozens of fire trucks outside the tunnel near the Louvre for hours. The CRS, the riot troops, had been called in, in full battledress, with shields and helmets, carrying machine guns. The street had been closed off. Ambulances, the SAMU, and fleets of paramedics had arrived. The police were controlling onlookers and pedestrians, while the bomb squads looked for more bombs that had not exploded. And inside the tunnel there was a raging inferno, as cars continued to explode from the fire, and it was almost impossible to get people out. Bodies littered the tunnel floor, survivors moaned, and those who could walk, run, or crawl emerged, many with their hair and clothes on fire. It was a total nightmare, as news teams arrived for coverage of the scene, and to interview survivors. Most were in a state of shock. As yet, no known terrorist group had taken responsibility for it, but from everything people who'd been in the tunnel had described, it had clearly been a bomb, and more likely several.

It was after midnight when firemen and police told reporters they believed they had gotten all the survivors. There were still bodies trapped in vehicles, or among the wreckage and debris, but it would be several more hours before they could put out the fire, and extricate the bodies. Two firemen had died in the blaze, trying to rescue people, when yet more cars exploded, and several rescuers had been overcome by fumes and flames, as had paramedics who were trying to assist people, or tend to them where they were trapped. Women, children, men had died. It was a spectacle beyond belief, and many were brought out alive but unconscious. Victims were being sent to any of four hospitals, where additional medical personnel had been brought in to help them. Two burn centers were already over-crowded, and people burned less severely were being sent to a special unit on the outskirts of Paris. The rescue efforts had been extraordinary and impressively coordinated, as one of the news-casters said, but there was only so much they could do in the wake of an attack of that nature. It had presumably been done by terrorists, and the force of the bombs used had even taken out sections of the walls of the tunnel. It was hard to believe that anyone had survived, when one saw the fierce blackness of the smoke, and the fire still raging in the tunnel.

In the end, Carole had landed in a little alcove of the tunnel, which, by sheer luck, had protected her as the fire advanced. She had been one of the first to be found by the firefighters who went in. She had a gash on one cheek, a broken arm, burns on both arms and near the cut on her cheek, and a major head injury. When they brought her out on a gurney and turned her over to the SAMU, manned by doctors as well as paramedics, she was unconscious. They rapidly assessed her injuries, intubated her to keep her breathing, and sent her to La Pitié Salpêtrière hospital, where the worst cases were being taken. Her burns were far less severe than many of the others they'd seen. But the head injury was life threatening. She was in a deep coma. They checked her for some kind of identification, and found none. She had nothing in her pockets, not even money. But her pockets would have been emptied by the force of her flight through the air. And if she'd had a handbag, she'd lost it when she was blown out of whatever vehicle she was in. She was an unidentified victim, a Jane Doe in a terrorist attack in Paris. There was absolutely nothing on her to identify her, not even a key to her room at the Ritz. And her passport was on her desk at the hotel.

She left the scene in an ambulance, code blue, with another unconscious survivor who had come out of the tunnel naked, with third-degree burns across his entire body. Paramedics tended to them both, but it seemed unlikely that either patient would be alive when they got to La Pitié.

The burn victim died in the the ambulance. Carole was still alive, though barely, when they rushed her inside to the trauma unit. A team was standing by, waiting for the first casualties to arrive. The first two ambulances had already shown up with dead bodies.

The female doctor in charge of the trauma unit looked grim as she examined Carole. The cut on Carole's cheek was a nasty one, the burns on her arms were second degree, the one on her face seemed minor compared to the rest of her injuries. They called in an orthopedist to set her arm, but it had to wait until they assessed the damage to her head. CT scans had to be done immediately, and her heart stopped before they could even start them. The cardiac team worked on her frantically, and got her heart going again, and then her blood pressure dropped dramatically. There were eleven people working on her, as other victims were brought in, but for the moment Carole was one of the worst. A neurosurgeon came in to examine her, and they were finally able to get the CT scans done. He decided to wait to do surgery, she wasn't stable enough to survive it. They cleaned up her burns, her arm was set, she stopped breathing on her own, and they put her on a respirator. It was morning before things calmed down in the trauma unit, and the neurosurgeon evaluated her again. Their main concern was swelling to her brain, and it was difficult to assess how hard she had hit the wall or pavement in the tunnel, or how great the damage would be later on, if she survived. He still didn't want to operate, and the head of the trauma unit agreed with him. If surgery could be avoided, they preferred it, in order not to add to her trauma. Carole was holding on to her life by a thread.

'Is her family here?' the doctor asked, looking grim. He assumed they would want her to have last rites. Most of the families did.

'No family. We have no ID on her,' the head of the trauma unit explained, and he nodded. There were several unidentified patients at La Pitié that night. Sooner or later, families or friends would look for them, and their identities would be known. It was irrelevant at this point. They were getting the best possible care the city could provide, no matter who they were. They were bodies that had been shattered by a bomb. He had already seen three children die that night, within moments of being brought in, all three burned beyond recognition. The terrorists had done a dastardly thing. The surgeon said he'd be back to check on Carole in an hour. She was in the *réanimation* section of the trauma unit in the meantime, getting the attention of a full team, which was trying desperately to keep her alive and her vital signs stable. She was literally hovering between life and death. The only thing that seemed to have saved her was the alcove she'd been blown into, which had provided an air pocket for her, and a shield against the fire. Otherwise, like so many others, she would have been burned alive.

The neurosurgeon went to get some sleep at noon, on a gurney in a closet. They were treating forty-two patients from the bombing in the tunnel. In all, police at the scene had reported ninety-eight people injured, and they had counted seventy-one bodies so far, and there were still more inside. It had been a long, ugly night.

The doctor was surprised to find Carole still alive when he came back four hours later. Her condition was the same, the respirator was still breathing for her, but another CT scan showed that the swelling to her brain had not worsened, which was a major plus. The worst of her injury seemed to be located in the brain stem. She had sustained a diffuse axonal injury, with minor tears from severe shaking of her brain. And there was no way to assess yet what the long-term effect of it would be. Her cerebrum had also been impacted, which could ultimately compromise her muscles and memory.

The gash on her cheek had been stitched up, and as the neurosurgeon looked at her, he commented to the doctor checking her that she was a good-looking woman. He knew he'd never seen her before, but there was something familiar about her face. He guessed her to be about forty or forty-five years old at most. He was surprised that no one had come looking for her. It was still early. If she lived alone, it could take days for anyone to realize that she was missing. But people didn't stay unidentified forever.

The following day was Saturday, and the trauma unit teams continued to work around the clock. They were able to shift some patients to other units of the hospital, and several were moved by ambulance to special burn centers. Carole remained listed among their most severely injured patients, along with others like her in other hospitals in Paris.

On Sunday her condition grew worse, as she developed a fever, which was to be expected. Her body was in shock, and she was still fighting for her life.

The fever lasted until Tuesday, and then finally subsided. The swelling of her brain improved slightly, as they continued to watch her closely. But she was no nearer to consciousness than she had been when she came in. Her head and arms were bandaged, and her left arm was in a cast. Her cut cheek was healing, although it was going to leave a scar. Their worst concern for her continued to be her brain. They were keeping her sedated, due to the respirator, but even without sedation, she was still in a deep coma. There was no way to assess how great the damage would be to her brain long term, or if she would even live. She wasn't out of the woods yet by any means. Far from it.

On Wednesday and Thursday nothing changed, and she continued to cling to life by a thin thread. On Friday, a full week after she came in, the new CT scans they took looked slightly better, which was encouraging. The head of the trauma unit commented then that she was the only Jane Doe who had not been identified yet. No one had come to claim her, which seemed strange. Everyone else, whether dead or alive, had been identified by then.

On the same day, the day maid who cleaned her room made a comment to the head house-keeper at the Ritz. She said that the woman in Carole's suite hadn't slept there all week. Her handbag and passport were there, and her clothes, but the bed had never been used. She had obviously checked in, and then vanished. The housekeeper didn't find it unusual, since guests sometimes did strange things, like rent a room or a suite, to have a clandestine affair, and only appeared sporadically, rarely, or not at all, if things didn't work out as planned. The only thing that seemed odd to her was that the guest's handbag was there, and her passport was on the desk. Clearly, nothing had been touched since she checked in. Just as a formality, she reported it to the front desk. They made note of the fact, but she had booked the room for two weeks, and they had a credit card to guarantee it. Past her reservation date, they would have been concerned. They were well aware of who she was, and perhaps she never intended to use the room, but just keep it available for some unexplained purpose. Movie stars did strange things. She might have been staying somewhere else. There was no reason to link her to the terrorist attack in the tunnel. But they made a note on her account at the front desk (client has not used room since checked in). That information was, of course, not to be shared with the press, or anyone for that matter. They knew better than that. And her disappearance, if it was that, might well have to do with her love life, and a need for discretion, which was sacred to them. Like all fine hotels, they kept many secrets, and their clients were grateful for it.

It was the following Monday when Jason Waterman called Stevie. He was Carole's first husband, and the father of her children. They were on good terms, but didn't speak often. He told Stevie he had tried for a week to reach Carole on her cell phone, and had gotten no response to the messages he left her. And he had had no better luck when he tried her at the house over the weekend.

'She's away,' Stevie explained. She had met him several times, and he was always pleasant to her. She knew Carole had maintained a good relationship with him, because of their children. They had been divorced for eighteen years, although Stevie didn't know the details. It was one of the few things Carole didn't discuss with her. She just knew they had gotten divorced while Carole was making a movie in Paris eighteen years before, and she had stayed in Paris for two years after, with the kids.

'She has her cell phone with her, and it doesn't work when she's abroad. She left almost two weeks ago. I should be hearing from her soon.'

Stevie hadn't heard from her either since the morning she'd arrived in Paris, ten days before, but Carole had warned her that she would be out of touch. Stevie assumed she was either floating around, or writing, and didn't want to be disturbed. Stevie wouldn't dream of bothering her, and waited for Carole to contact her when she was ready.

'Do you know where she is?' He sounded concerned.

'Not really. She started out in Paris, but she was going to do some traveling on her own.' He wondered if she had a new romance, but didn't want to ask. It sounded like that to him. 'Is anything wrong?' Stevie suddenly wondered about the kids. Carole would want to know immediately if anything had happened to either of them.

'No, it's not important. I'm trying to make plans for Christmas. I know they're planning to spend Thanksgiving with her, but I wasn't sure what her Christmas plans were. I talked to Anthony and Chloe, and they weren't sure either. Someone offered me a house in St. Bart's over New Year's, and I didn't want to screw up her plans with them.' Particularly now, with Sean gone, the holidays with her children meant more to her than ever. And Jason had always been nice about it. Stevie knew he'd remarried briefly, and had two other kids, who now lived in Hong Kong with their mother and were in their teens. Carole had mentioned that he didn't see them often, only a couple of times a year. He was far closer to his children by Carole, and to her.

'I'll tell her to call you as soon as I hear from her. It shouldn't be long now. I expect to hear from her any day.'

'I hope she wasn't in Paris when that bomb went off in the tunnel. What a mess that was.' It had been all over the news in the States too, and an extremist fundamentalist group had finally claimed responsibility for it, which had caused an outcry in the Arab world too, who in no way wanted to be linked to the perpetrators of the attack.

'It looked pretty awful. I saw it on the news. I worried about it at first, but it was the day she got there. I'm sure she was cozily tucked into the hotel after the flight, and nowhere near it.'

Long-distance travel usually wore her out, and she often stayed in her room and slept the day she arrived.

'Have you tried e-mailing her?' Jason asked.

'Her computer is turned off. She really wanted some time to herself,' Stevie answered matter-of-factly.

'Where's she staying?' he asked, sounding worried. And he was getting Stevie upset too. She had thought of it, but told herself it was ridiculous to worry. She was sure that Carole was fine, but Jason's concern was contagious.

'At the Ritz,' Stevie said quickly.

'I'll call her, and leave a message.'

'She might be traveling, so you may not get an answer for a couple of days. I'm not too worried yet.'

'It can't hurt to leave her a message. Besides, I need to know about this house, or I'll lose it. And I don't want to take it unless the kids want to come down. It might be fun for them.'

'I'll let her know if she calls me,' Stevie assured him.

'I'll see if I can catch her at the Ritz. Thanks.'

He hung up then, and Stevie sat at the desk in her office, thinking about it. It seemed so unlikely that anything had happened to Carole, that Stevie was determined not to worry. What were the odds that she had been in the terrorist attack? About one in a hundred million. Stevie forced it out of her mind as she went back to work on a project she'd been doing, gathering information for Carole for some of her women's rights work. With Carole away, it was a good time for Stevie to catch up. The research she was doing was for a speech Carole was planning to make at the UN.

As soon as he hung up, Jason called the Ritz in Paris, and asked for Carole's room. They put him on hold, while they called her room to announce the call. She always had her calls screened by any hotel she was in. They came back on the line then, said she wasn't in her room, and referred him to the front desk, which was unusual. He decided to stay on the line and see what they had to say. A desk clerk asked him to wait for a moment, and then an assistant manager with a British accent came on and asked Jason who he was. The call was getting stranger by the minute, and he didn't like it.

'My name is Jason Waterman, I'm Miss Barber's ex-husband. And I'm a long-standing client of the Ritz. Is something wrong?' He was beginning to have a sick feeling in the pit of his stomach, and he wasn't sure why. 'Is Miss Barber all right?'

'I'm sure she is, sir. And this is rather unusual, but we've had a note from the head housekeeper about her room. These things happen, and she may be traveling, or actually staying somewhere else. But she hasn't used her room since she checked in. Normally, I wouldn't mention it, but the housekeeper was concerned. Apparently all of her things are there, as well as her handbag, and her passport is on the desk. There's been no sign of activity in the room for nearly two weeks.' He spoke in a hushed voice, as though divulging a secret.

'Shit,' Jason blurted out. 'Has anyone seen her?'

'Not that I'm aware of, sir. Is there anyone you'd like us to call?' This was very unusual.

Hotels like the Ritz did not tell people who called that the guest they were calling hadn't used their room in two weeks. Jason knew they must have been worried too.

'Yes, there is,' Jason answered his question. 'This probably sounds crazy, but could you check with the police, or the hospitals where the victims of the tunnel attack were taken, and just make sure there are no unidentified victims, either dead or alive?' It made him sick to say it, but he was suddenly worried about her. He still loved her, always had, she was the mother of his kids, and they were good friends. He just hoped nothing terrible had happened. And if it wasn't the tunnel attack, he had no idea where the hell she was. Stevie probably knew more than he did, and didn't want to divulge secrets. Maybe she'd been meeting some guy in Paris, or elsewhere in Europe. She was, after all, single again now, since Sean's death. But then why hadn't she used her room, or at least taken her passport and hand-bag? These things didn't happen, he told himself. But sometimes they did. He hoped she was shacked up somewhere, with a new romance, and not in a hospital, or worse. 'Would you mind calling around?' he asked the assistant manager, who immediately promised that he would.

'Would you be kind enough to leave me your number, sir?' Jason gave it to him. It was one o'clock in New York, and just after seven at night in Paris. He didn't expect to hear from him till the next day. He hung up, feeling uneasy, and sat at his desk, staring at the phone for a long time, thinking of her. His secretary told him the Hotel Ritz in Paris was on the line twenty minutes later. It was the same clipped British voice he'd spoken to before.

'Yes? Could you find anything out?' Jason asked, sounding tense.

'I believe so, sir, although it may not be her. There is a victim of the bombing who was taken to La Pitié Salpêtrière hospital. She is blond, approximately forty to forty-five years old. She is unidentified and has not been claimed.' He made her sound like lost luggage, and Jason's voice was a croak when he spoke.

'Is she alive?' He was terrified of the answer.

'She's in the intensive care unit, in critical

condition, with a head injury. She's the only unidentified victim of the bombing they have left. She also has a broken arm, and second-degree burns.' Jason felt sick as he listened. 'She's in a coma, which is why they've been unable to identify her. There's no reason to believe it's Miss Barber, sir. I would think someone would have recognized her even in France, since she's known worldwide. This woman is probably French.'

'Not necessarily. Maybe her face is burned. Or maybe they just didn't expect to see her there. Or maybe it's not her. I hope to God it's not.' Jason sounded near tears.

'So do I,' the assistant manager said in a gentle voice. 'What would you like me to do, sir? Should I send someone over from the hotel to have a look?'

'I'll fly over. I can catch the six o'clock flight. That will get me to Paris around seven A.M., and the hospital about eight-thirty tomorrow morning. Could you book me a room?' His mind was racing. He wished he could get there sooner, but he knew there was no earlier flight. He went to Paris often, and it was the flight he always took.

'I'll take care of it, sir. I truly hope it's not Miss Barber.'

'Thank you. I'll see you tomorrow.' Jason sat at his desk then, feeling stunned. It couldn't be. This couldn't have happened to her. It didn't bear thinking about. He didn't know what to do, so he called Stevie back in L.A. and told her what he'd heard from the assistant manager at the Ritz.

'Oh my God. Please God, tell me that's not Carole,' Stevie said in a strangled voice.

'I hope to hell it's not. I'm going over to see for myself. If you hear from her, call me. And don't say anything to the kids if they call. I'll tell Anthony I'm going to Chicago, or Boston or something. I don't want to say anything to them until we know,' Jason told her firmly.

'I'll fly over,' Stevie said, sounding frantic. The last place she wanted to be now was in L.A. On the other hand, if Carole was fine, Carole was going to think they were all nuts, when she and Jason walked in, as she arrived back at the Ritz from Budapest, or Vienna, or wherever she'd been. She was probably fine, and floating around in Europe somewhere, having a good time, with no idea that anyone was worried about her.

'Why don't you wait till I see what I find out there. The guy at the hotel is right, it may not be her. They probably would have recognized her if it is.'

'I don't know. She looks pretty simple without makeup and fancy hair. And they probably don't expect an American movie star to show up in a trauma unit in Paris. It may not have occurred to them.' Stevie also wondered if her face had been burned, which would explain their not recognizing her.

'They can't be that stupid, for Chrissake. She's one of the best-known female stars on the planet, even in France,' Jason snapped.

'I guess you're right,' Stevie said, sounding unconvinced. But then again, he wasn't convinced either, or he wouldn't be going there. They were just trying to reassure each other, without much success.

'I won't get there till ten tonight your time,' Jason told Stevie, 'and I probably won't know anything for another couple of hours after that. I'll go straight to the hospital from the airport and see her as soon as I can. But it'll be midnight for you by then.'

'Call me anyway. I'll stay up, and if I fall asleep, I'll keep my cell phone in my hand.' She gave him the number, and he took it, and promised to call her when he got to the hospital in Paris. After that, he told his secretary to cancel his appointments for that afternoon and the next day. He told her what he was doing, but warned her not to mention it to either of his children. The official version was that he had to go to an emergency meeting in Chicago. And five minutes later he left his office and hailed a cab. He was at his apartment on the Upper East Side twenty minutes later, and threw his clothes into a suitcase. It was two o'clock, and he had to leave the city at three for a six o'clock plane.

The next hour was agony as he waited to leave. And it was worse once he got to the airport. There was a surreal quality to all of it, he was going to see a woman in a coma in a Paris hospital, and praying it wouldn't be his ex-wife. They had been divorced for eighteen years, and he had known for the last fourteen that leaving her had been the biggest mistake of his life. He had left her for a twenty-one-year-old Russian model, who had turned out to be the biggest gold-digger on the planet. He had been madly in love with her at the time. Carole had been at the height of her career, doing two and three movies a year. She was always on location somewhere, or promoting a film. He was the whiz kid of Wall Street then, but his success was small potatoes compared to hers. She had won two Oscars in the two years before he left her, and it got to him. She'd been a good wife, but he realized later on that his ego had been too fragile to survive that kind of competition. He needed to feel like a big deal himself, and in the face of Carole's stardom, he never did. So he fell in love with Natalya, who appeared to worship him, and then took him to the cleaners, and left him for someone else.

The Russian model was the worst thing that had ever happened to them, and to him surely. She was staggeringly beautiful, and she'd gotten pregnant weeks after they started their affair. He'd left Carole for her, and married Natalya before the ink was dry on the divorce. She'd had another baby the following year, and then left him for a man with a lot more money than Jason had at the time. She'd had two husbands since, and was now living in Hong Kong, married to one of the most important financiers in the world. Jason hardly knew his two daughters. They were as beautiful as their mother, and virtually strangers to him, despite his visits to them twice a year. Natalya wouldn't let them come to the States to visit, and the New York courts had no jurisdiction over her whatsoever. She was a bitch on wheels, and screwed him over royally in the divorce, a year after Carole and the kids came back from Paris and moved to L.A. Although Carole had lived in New York with him while they were married, she had decided to go to Los Angeles. Her work was there, and it seemed like a fresh start after Paris. And after Natalya left, he had tried to go back to Carole. But it was too late. She wanted nothing to do with him by then. He'd been forty-one when he fell in love with Natalya, and having some kind of insane midlife crisis. And at forty-five, when he realized what a mistake he'd made, and what a mess he'd made of his life and Carole's, it was way too late. She told him it was over for her.

It had taken her several years to forgive him, and they didn't actually make friends again until after she married Sean. She was happy finally. And Jason had never married again. At fifty-nine, he was successful, and alone, and considered Carole one of his best friends. And never in his life would he forget the look on her face when he told her he was leaving her, eighteen years before. She looked as though he had shot her. He had relived that moment a thousand times since, and knew he'd never forgive himself. All he wanted now was to know that she was alive and well, and not lying in a hospital in Paris. As he boarded the plane that night, he knew he loved her more than ever. He actually prayed on the flight over, something he hadn't done since he was a boy. He was willing to make any deal he could with God, just so the woman in the Paris hospital wasn't Carole. And if it was, that she would survive.

Jason sat wide awake for the entire flight, thinking about her. Remembering when Anthony had been born, and then Chloe . . . the day he'd met her . . . how beautiful she had been at twenty-two, and was even now, twenty-eight years later. They had had ten wonderful years together, until he screwed it up with Natalya. He couldn't even imagine what that must have felt like to Carole. She'd been working on a major movie in Paris when he flew over and told her. It had been a flight like tonight, he'd had a mission then, to end their marriage so he could marry Natalya. And now he was praying for her life. He looked haggard and anxious as the plane landed in a driving rain at Charles de Gaulle Airport in Paris just before seven A.M. Paris time, the flight had come in a few minutes early. Jason had his passport in his hand as they landed. He couldn't stand the suspense any longer. All he wanted was to get to the hospital as fast as possible and see the unidentified bombing victim for himself.

4

Jason had brought nothing more to Paris than his briefcase and a small overnight bag. He had hoped to distract himself with work to do on the plane, but he had never touched his briefcase, and couldn't have concentrated on his papers. All he thought about that night was his ex-wife.

The plane touched down at 6:51 A.M. in Paris, local time, and parked far out on a distant runway. Passengers came down the stairs in the pouring rain to a waiting bus, and then lumbered and lurched toward the terminal, while Jason stood impatiently, desperate to get into town. With no luggage checked, he was in a cab at seven-thirty, and asked the driver in halting French to take him to the Pitié Salpêtrière hospital, where the unidentified woman was. He knew it was on the Boulevard de l'Hôpital, in the thirteenth arrondissement, and he had written it down so there would be no mistake. He handed the slip of paper to the driver, who nodded and said, 'Good. Understand,' in a heavy French accent, which was no better or worse than Jason's French.

The ride to the hospital took nearly an hour, as Jason fretted in the backseat, telling himself that the woman he was about to see probably wasn't Carole, and he'd wind up having breakfast at the Ritz, and run into her when she got back. He knew how independent she was now. She always had been, but she was even more so since Sean had died. He knew she traveled frequently to world conferences on women's rights, and had gone on several missions with groups from the UN. But he had no idea what she'd been doing in France. Whatever it was, he hoped it hadn't taken her anywhere near the tunnel at the time of the terrorist attack. With any luck at all, she had been somewhere else. But if so, what were her passport and handbag doing on her desk at the Ritz? Why had she gone out without them? If anything happened to her, no one would know who she was.

He knew how she loved her anonymity, and the ability to roam around freely without fans recognizing her. It was easier for her in Paris, but not much. Carole Barber was recognized everywhere in the world, which was the only thing that encouraged him to believe that the woman at the Pitié Salpêtrière hospital couldn't possibly be her. How could they not recognize that face? It was unthinkable unless something had rendered her unrecognizable. A thousand terrifying thoughts were running through his head, as the cab finally pulled up in front of the hospital. Jason paid the fare with a generous tip, and got out. He looked like exactly what he was, a distinguished American businessman. He was wearing a dark gray English suit, a navy blue cashmere topcoat, and an extremely expensive gold watch. He was still a handsome man at fifty-nine.

'*Merci*!' the cabdriver shouted at him from the window, giving him a thumbs-up for the good tip. '*Bonne chance!*' He wished him luck. The look on Jason Waterman's face told him he would need it. People didn't go from the airport straight to a hospital, particularly this one, unless something bad had happened. The driver could figure out that much. And Jason's eyes and worn face told him the rest. He looked like he needed a shave, a shower, and some rest. But not yet.

Jason strode into the hospital carrying his bag, hoping someone spoke enough English to help him out. The assistant manager at the Ritz had given him the name of the head of the trauma unit, and Jason stopped to speak to a young woman at the front desk, and showed her the slip of paper where he'd written her name. She answered in rapid French, and Jason let her know that he didn't understand, nor speak French. She pointed to the elevator behind her and held up three fingers as she said the words '*Troisième étage.*' Third floor. '*Réanimation,*' she added. It didn't sound good to him. It was the French term for ICU. Jason thanked her and walked to the elevator in long, quick strides. He wanted to get this over with. He was feeling extremely stressed and could feel his heart pound. There was no one in the elevator with him, and when he got out on three, he looked around, feeling lost. A sign pointed to '*Réanimation*.' He headed toward the sign, remembering that that was the word the girl had said downstairs, and he found himself at the front desk of a busy unit, with medical personnel scurrying everywhere, and lifeless-looking patients in cubicles all around the room. There were machines buzzing and whirring, beeps from monitors, people moaning, and a hospital smell that turned his stomach after the long flight.

'Does anyone here speak English?' he asked in a firm voice, while the woman he spoke to looked blank. '*Anglais. Parlez-vous anglais?*'

'Engleesh . . . one minute . . .' She spoke a mixture of English and French, and went to find someone for him. A doctor in a white coat appeared, a woman in hospital pajamas with a shower cap on and a stethoscope around her neck. She was about Jason's age, and her English was good, which was a relief. He was suddenly afraid that no one would understand what he said, and worse yet, he wouldn't understand them.

'May I help you?' she asked in a clear voice. He asked for the woman who was the head of the trauma unit, and the doctor at hand said she wasn't there, but offered her assistance instead. Jason explained why he had come, and forgot to add the *ex* before the word *wife*.

She looked him over carefully. He was well dressed, and looked like a respectable man. And he looked worried sick. Fearing that he must look more than a little crazed, he explained that he had just gotten off the flight from New York. But she seemed to understand. He explained that his wife had disappeared from her hotel, and he was afraid she might be their Jane Doe.

'How long ago?'

'I'm not sure. I was in New York. She arrived the day of the terrorist attack in the tunnel. No one has seen her since, and she hasn't gone back to the hotel.'

'That is almost two weeks,' she said, as though wondering why it had taken him so long to figure out that his wife had disappeared. It was too late to explain that they were divorced, since he had referred to her as his wife, and maybe it was better this way. He wasn't sure what kind of rights ex-husbands had in France as next of kin, probably none, like anywhere else.

'She was traveling, and this may not be her. I hope it's not. I flew over to see.' She seemed to approve of that and nodded at him, and then said something to the nurse at the desk, who pointed to a room with a closed door.

The doctor beckoned Jason to follow her, which he did. She opened the door to the room, and he couldn't see the patient in the bed. She was surrounded by machines, and there were two nurses standing next to her, blocking his view. He could hear the *whoosh* of the respirator and the *whir* of machines. There seemed to be a ton of apparatus in the room as the doctor led him in. He felt like an intruder suddenly, a medical voyeur. He was about to view someone who might not be anyone he knew. But he had to see her. He had to be sure she wasn't Carole. He owed this to her, and their kids, even if it seemed like a crazy thing to do. It did, even to him, like the far extremes of paranoia, or maybe just guilt. He walked behind the doctor, and saw a still figure lying there, with a respirator in her mouth, her nose taped shut, and her head tilted back. She was completely still, and her face was deathly pale. The bandage on her head looked huge, there was another on her face, and a cast on her arm, and at the angle he approached her, it was hard to see her face. He took another step forward to get a better look, and then caught his breath as tears filled his eyes. It was Carole.

His worst nightmare had just come true. He stepped up close to her, and touched the fingers sticking out of the cast, which were black and blue. Nothing moved. She was in another world, far from them, and looked as though she would never return. There were tears running down his cheeks as he stood and looked at her. The worst had happened. She was the unidentified victim from the tunnel bombing. The woman he had once loved and still did was fighting for her life in Paris, and had been there, alone, for almost two weeks, while none of them had any idea what had happened to her. Jason looked stricken as he turned to the doctor.

'It's her,' he whispered, as the nurses stared at him. It had been clear to all of them that he had identified her.

'I'm sorry,' the doctor said in a soft voice, and then gestured to him to follow her outside. 'It is your wife?' she asked, no longer needing confirmation. His tears spoke for themselves. He looked destroyed. 'We had no way to identify her,' the doctor explained. 'She had no papers, nothing on her, nothing with a name.'

'I know. She left her bag and passport at the hotel. She does that sometimes, goes out without her purse.' She always had. She stuffed a ten-dollar bill in her pocket and went out. She had done it years before when they lived in New York, although he'd always told her to carry ID. This time the worst had happened, and no one knew who she was, which still seemed hard for him to believe. 'She's an actress, a well-known movie star,' he said, although it didn't matter now. She was a woman with a major head injury in the

ICU, nothing more. The doctor looked intrigued by what he'd said.

'She is a movie star?' She looked stunned.

'Carole Barber,' he said, knowing the impact it would have. The doctor looked instantly shocked.

'Carole Barber? We did not know.' She was visibly impressed.

'It would be nice if the press doesn't find out. My children don't know. I don't want them to hear about it like that. I want to at least call them first.'

'Of course,' the doctor said, realizing what was about to happen to them. They would have cared for her no differently than they had, but now, when word got out that she was there, they would be besieged by the press. It was going to make life difficult for them. It had been a lot easier while she was just a Jane Doe, a victim of the attack. Having one of America's biggest movie stars in their *réanimation* unit was going to make life hell for everyone. 'It will be very hard to keep the press away, once they know,' she said, looking concerned. 'Perhaps we can use her married name.'

'Waterman,' he supplied. 'Carole Waterman.' Once upon a time that had been the truth. She had never taken Sean's name, which was Clarke. They could have used that too, and he realized that she might have preferred it. But what did it matter now? All that mattered was her life. 'Is she . . . is she . . . will she be all right?' He couldn't say the words, and ask if she was going to die. But it looked like a strong possibility. Carole looked terrible to him, and nearly dead.

'We don't know. Brain injuries are very hard to predict. She is doing better than she was, and the brain scans are good. The swelling is going down. But we cannot tell how damaged she will be until she wakes up. If she continues to do well, we will take her off the respirator soon. Then she must breathe for herself, and she must awaken from the coma. Until then, we cannot know how much damage there is, or the long-term effects. She will need re-education, but we are not there yet. We are a long way from it. She is still in danger. The risk of infection, complications, and her brain could swell again. She suffered a very serious blow to her head. She was very lucky not to be more badly burned, and her arm will heal. Her head is our greatest concern.' He couldn't even imagine telling the kids, but they had to know. Chloe had to come from London, and Anthony from New York. They had a right to see their mother, and he knew they'd want to be with her. And what if she died? He couldn't stand thinking about it, as he met the doctor's eyes again.

'Should she be anywhere else? Is there anything else that can be done?'

The doctor looked offended. 'We have done it all, even before we knew who she was. That means nothing to us. Now we must wait. Time will tell us what we need to know, if she survives.' She wanted to remind him that her survival was not a sure thing yet. It was only fair to him.

'Did she have surgery?'

The doctor shook her head again. 'No. We decided it was wiser not to traumatize her further, and the swelling came down on its own. We took a conservative approach, which I think was best for her.' Jason nodded, relieved. At least they hadn't cut into her brain. It gave him hope that she'd be herself again one day. It was all they could hope for now, and if not, they'd face that when the time came, as they would her death, if that happened. It was an overwhelming thought.

'What are you planning to do now?' he asked, wanting to take action. It wasn't his style to just sit around.

'Wait. There's nothing else we can do. We will know more in the coming days.' He nodded, looking around him at how grim the hospital was. He had heard of the American Hospital of Paris, and wondered if they could get her transferred there, but the assistant manager at the hotel had already told him that this was the best place for her to be, if it was indeed her. Their trauma unit was excellent, and she would get the best possible medical care for a case as serious as this apparently was.

'I'm going to go to the hotel and call my children, and then I'll come back this afternoon. If anything happens, you can reach me at the Ritz.' He gave her his international cell phone number as well, and they put it on Carole's chart with his name. She had a name now even if it wasn't really hers. Carole Waterman. She had a husband and children. But she also had a famous identity that was bound to leak out. The doctor said she would only tell the head of the trauma unit who Carole really was, but they both knew that it was only a matter of time before the press found out. They always did, with things like this. It was amazing no one had recognized her so far. But if someone talked, the press would arrive in swarms, and life would be hell for all of them.

'We'll do our best to keep it quiet,' she assured him.

'So will I. I'll be back this afternoon . . . and . . . thank you . . . for everything you've done so far.' They had kept her alive. That was something. He couldn't even imagine what it would have been like to see her in a Paris morgue and identify her body. It had come close to that, from everything the doctor said. She had been lucky after all. 'May I see her again?' he asked, and this time he went to the room alone. The nurses were still there, and stepped aside so he could approach her bed. He stood looking down at her, and this time touched her cheek. The tubes from the respirator covered her face, and he saw the bandage on her cheek and wondered how bad the damage was. The slight burn beside it was already healing, and her arm was covered in salve. 'I love you, Carole,' he whispered. 'You're going to be all right. I love you. Chloe and Anthony love you. You need to wake up soon.' There was no sign of life from the bed, and the nurses looked discreetly away. It was hard for them to watch, there was so much pain in his eyes. He bent to kiss her cheek then, and remembered the familiar softness of her face. Even all these years later, that hadn't changed. Her hair was fanned out behind her on the bed under the bandage. One of the nurses had brushed it for her, and commented on how beautiful it was, like pale yellow silk.

Seeing her brought back so many memories, all of them good. The bad ones were forgotten now, and had been for a long time. For him anyway. He and Carole never talked about the past when they spoke. They only referred to the kids, or their current lives. He had been very kind to her when Sean died, he felt sorry for her. It was a tough break for her. She had married a man five years younger than she was, and he had died a young man. Jason had come out for the funeral, and been very supportive to her and the kids. And now here she was, fighting for her own life, two years after Sean had died. Life was strange, and cruel at times. But she was still alive. She had a chance. It was the best news he could give their children. He dreaded telling them. 'I'll be back later,' he whispered to Carole as he kissed her again, and the respirator breathed rhythmically for her. 'I love you, Carole. You're going to get well,' he said with a decisive look, and then walked out of the room, fighting back tears. He had to be strong, for her, and for Anthony and Chloe. No matter how he felt.

He left the hospital and walked to the nearby Gare d'Austerlitz in the pouring rain. He was soaked by the time he found a cab, and gave the driver the address of the Ritz. He looked as grim as he felt, as though he'd aged a hundred years in one day. She didn't deserve what had happened to her. No one did. And Carole least of all. She was a good woman, a nice person, a great mother, and had been a good wife to two men. One had left her for a tart and the other one had died. And now she was fighting for her life after a terrorist attack. If he had dared, he would have been furious with God, but he didn't dare. He needed His help too much now, and as they drove toward the Place Vendôme in the first arrondissement, he begged God for His help telling the kids. He couldn't even imagine saying the words to them. And then he remembered another call he had to make. He took out his cell phone and dialed L.A. It was almost midnight for Stevie, but he had promised he'd call as soon as he knew.

Stevie answered on the first ring. She was wide awake and had been waiting for his call. It had taken too long, in her opinion, unless his plane had arrived late. She should have heard from him by then if it wasn't Carole. She had been sick with fear for the last hour, and her voice shook when she said hello.

'It's her,' he said, without even identifying himself. She knew.

'Oh my God . . . how bad is it?' Tears ran instantly down her cheeks.

'It's not good. She's on a respirator, but she's alive. She's in a coma from a head injury. They didn't operate, but she had a hell of a blow. She's still in danger, and they don't know yet how damaged she may be.' He gave it to her straight. He was planning to be gentler with his kids, but Stevie had a right to know the whole truth, and she wouldn't have settled for less.

'Shit. I'll get the first plane out.' But it was a ten-hour flight for her, at best, if the winds were good. And a nine-hour time difference against her. She wouldn't be there till the next day. 'Have you told the kids?'

'Not yet. I'm on my way to the hotel. There's nothing you can do. I don't know how much sense it makes for you to come.' She didn't need an assistant right now, and maybe never would again. But Stevie was her friend too. She had been a fixture in their family for years, and his children loved her too, as she loved them. 'There's nothing any of us can do,' he said with a tremor in his own voice again.

'I couldn't be anywhere else,' she told him simply.

'Neither could I.' He gave her the name of the hospital and told her he'd see her in Paris tomorrow. 'I'll get you a room at the Ritz.'

'I can stay in Carole's room,' Stevie said practically. There was no point paying for another room. 'Unless you are,' she said cautiously. She didn't want to intrude.

'I booked my own, and I'll get rooms for the kids. I'll try to get them near Carole's room, so we can be close together. We've got some tough times ahead, and so does she. This is going to be a long road, if she recovers. I can't even imagine what it's going to be like if she doesn't.' He was surprised to realize that he wanted her to live, even if she was severely brain damaged. He didn't care if she was a vegetable after all was said and done, he didn't want her to die, for himself or his kids. They loved her in whatever state she was, and he knew Stevie did too. 'I'll see you tomorrow. Have a good trip,' he said, sounding exhausted, and then hung up. Although it was three A.M. for her, he called his secretary at home after that, and told her not to tell his son, but to cancel all the appointments and meetings he had planned. 'I won't be back for a while.' He apologized for calling her in the middle of the night, but she said she didn't mind.

'It's Miss Barber then?' his secretary asked, sounding crushed. She was one of Carole's biggest fans, as a person and a star. Carole had always been lovely to her on the phone.

'Yes, it is,' he said, in a grim voice. 'I'll call Anthony in a few hours. Don't contact him till then. We're going to have a hell of a mess on our hands when the press find out. I just registered her at the hospital under my name, but that won't last. Sooner or later, word will get out, and you know what that's like.'

'I'm sorry, Mr. Waterman,' his secretary said as tears filled her eyes. People all over the world were going to be heartbroken for Carole, and praying for her. Maybe it would help. 'Let me know if there is anything I can do.'

'Thank you,' he said, and hung up as they reached the Ritz. He looked up the assistant manager he'd spoken to, at the front desk. He was wearing the formal uniform of the hotel, and met Jason with a sober face.

112

'I hope you have good news,' he said cautiously, but he could see that Jason didn't. It was written all over his face.

'No, I don't. It was her. We have to keep this as quiet as possible,' he said, slipping two hundred euros into the man's hand. It wasn't necessary, under the circumstances, but was appreciated anyway.

'I understand,' the assistant manager said. And then assured Jason that he would give him a three-bedroom suite across from Carole's. Jason told him Stevie would be arriving the next day, and would stay in Carole's rooms.

Jason followed the assistant manager upstairs. He didn't have the heart to see Carole's room, or the evidence of how alive she'd been so recently. Now she looked nearly dead to him. He walked into his suite behind the assistant manager and collapsed into a chair.

'Is there anything I can get you, sir?' Jason shook his head, and the young Englishman quietly left, as Jason stared miserably at the phone on the desk. He had a brief reprieve but knew that in a few hours, he would have to call

Anthony and Chloe. They had to know. She might not even live until they arrived. He had to call them as soon as possible. And he didn't want to call Chloe until Anthony woke up in New York. He waited until seven A.M. New York time. He had showered and paced the room until then. He couldn't eat.

At one P.M. Paris time, with lead feet, he walked to the desk, and called his son first. Anthony was up and about to leave for the office for a breakfast meeting. Jason caught him just in time.

'How's Chicago, Dad?' Anthony sounded young and vital and full of life. He was a great kid, and Jason loved having him work for him. He was hardworking, smart, and kind. He was a lot like Carole, only with his father's keen financial mind. He was going to be a great venture capitalist one day and was learning fast.

'I don't know how Chicago is,' Jason said honestly. 'I'm in Paris, and it's not so great.'

'What are you doing there?' Anthony sounded unsuspecting and surprised. He didn't even know his mother had gone away. She had made the decision to leave right after the last time she talked to him, so he had no idea. He'd been too busy to call her in the past eleven days, which was unusual for him. But he knew she'd understand. He was planning to call her that day.

'Anthony . . .' He didn't even know where to start, as he took a sharp breath. 'There's been an accident. Your mom is over here.'

He feared the worst instantly then. 'Is she okay?'

'No, she's not. There was a bombing in a tunnel here two weeks ago. I didn't know until a couple of hours ago that she was a victim of the attack. She's been unidentified until now. I came over last night to check it out. She disappeared from the Ritz the day it happened.'

'Oh God.' Anthony sounded as though a building had just fallen on him. 'How bad is it?'

'Pretty bad. She has a brain injury, and she's in a coma.'

'Is she going to be okay?' Anthony was fighting tears and felt about four years old as he asked.

'We hope so. She made it this far, but she's not out of the woods yet. She's on a respirator.' He didn't want their son to be shocked when he saw her. Seeing her on the respirator was overwhelming.

'Shit, Dad . . . how could this happen?' Jason could hear that his son was crying. They both were.

'Rotten luck. Wrong place at the wrong time. I was praying it wasn't her all the way over. I can't believe they didn't recognize her.'

'Is her face messed up?' If it wasn't, he couldn't imagine that anyone on earth hadn't recognized his mother.

'Not really. She has a cut and a small burn on one side of her face. Nothing a good plastic surgeon won't be able to fix up. Her head injury is the problem. We're just going to have to sit this out.'

'I'm coming over. Have you told Chloe?'

'I called you first. I'm going to call her now. There's a six o'clock flight out of Kennedy, if you can get a seat. It'll get you here tomorrow morning Paris time.'

'I'll be on it.' It was going to be an agonizing day for him, waiting to take the flight. 'I'll pack now and leave from the office. See you tomorrow, Dad . . . and Dad . . .' His voice broke again as he said the word. 'I love you . . . and tell Mom I love her too.' They were both crying openly by then.

'I already did. You can tell her yourself tomorrow. She needs us now. This is a tough fight for her . . . I love you too,' Jason said, and they both hung up. Neither of them could talk. The prospect of what might happen was too devastating to both of them.

His next call was to Chloe, which was infinitely worse. She burst into tears and got hysterical as soon as he told her. The good news was that she was only an hour away. When she finally stopped crying, she said she'd be on the next plane. All she wanted now was to see her mom.

At five o'clock that afternoon Jason picked his daughter up at the airport. She was sobbing and in his arms the moment she came through the gate, and they went back to the hospital together. Chloe stood clutching her father's arm as she looked at her mother and cried when she saw her.

It was upsetting for both of them, but at least they had each other. And at nine that night, after talking to the doctor again, they went back to the hotel. There was no change in Carole's condition, but she was holding on. That was something at least.

Chloe cried for hours when they got to the hotel. Jason put her to bed finally, and she fell asleep. He went to the minibar then and poured himself a Scotch. He sat drinking it quietly, thinking of Carole, and their children. It was the toughest thing they'd all been through, and all he kept hoping for was that Carole would survive.

He fell asleep on his bed, fully dressed, that night, and woke up at six o'clock the next morning. He showered, shaved, and dressed, and was sitting quietly in the living room of the suite, when Chloe woke up, and came out to find him with her eyes swollen. He could tell that she felt even worse than she looked. She still couldn't believe what had happened to her mom.

They met Anthony's plane at seven o'clock, got his bag, and went back to the hotel for breakfast. Anthony looked somber and exhausted, in blue jeans and a heavy sweater. He needed a shave, but didn't bother. They hung around the room until Stevie arrived at the Ritz at twelve-thirty.

Jason ordered a sandwich for her, and at one o'clock they left for the hospital together. Anthony fought valiantly, but broke down as soon as he saw her. Chloe stood crying quietly with Stevie's arm around her, and all four of them were crying when they left the room. The only comfort they had was hearing that Carole's condition had improved slightly during the night. They were going to take the respirator out that evening, and see how she managed, breathing on her own. It was encouraging, but even that presented a risk. If she failed to breathe without the respirator, they would intubate her again, but if that was the case, it didn't bode well for what lay ahead. Her brain had to be alive enough to tell her body to breathe, and that remained to be seen. Jason looked gray when the doctor mentioned it, and both children looked panicked. Stevie quietly said that she would be there when they took her off the respirator, and both children said they would too. Jason nodded and agreed. It was going to be a crucial moment for Carole, to see if she was able to breathe on her own.

They had dinner at the hotel, though none of them could eat. They were exhausted, jet-lagged, frightened, and overwhelmingly upset. Stevie sat with them, as they stared at their plates without touching the food that was on them, and then they went back to the hospital, for yet another ordeal in the nightmare that was Carole's fight for survival.

There was total silence in the car, as they drove back to La Pitié. They were each lost in their own thoughts and their private memories of Carole. The doctor had explained to them that the part of the brain stem that had been damaged controlled her ability to breathe. And whether or not she breathed on her own would tell them if her brain was repairing. It was going to be a terrifying moment for all of them when the tubes came out of her mouth and they turned off the respirator and waited to see what would happen.

Chloe stared out the window of the car, with

silent tears running down her cheeks, as her brother held her hand tightly.

'She's going to be okay,' he whispered to her softly, and she shook her head and turned away. Nothing was okay in their world anymore, and it was hard to believe it would ever be again. Their mother had been a vital force in their lives, and the hub of their existence. Whatever Chloe's differences had been with her, they no longer mattered. All she wanted now was her mommy. And Anthony felt the same. There was something about her being so reduced and in such danger that made them both feel like children. They felt vulnerable and frightened beyond belief. Neither of them could imagine a life without their mother. Nor could Jason.

'She'll do fine, guys,' their father tried to reassure them. He tried to exude a confidence he didn't feel.

'What if she doesn't?' Chloe whispered, as they approached the hospital and passed the now-familiar Austerlitz train station.

'Then they'll put her back on the respirator again until she's ready.' Chloe didn't have the heart to pursue her line of thinking any further. Not out loud at least, she knew the others were just as worried as she was. They were all dreading the moment when the doctor would turn the respirator off. Just thinking about it made Chloe want to scream.

They got out of the car at the hospital, and Stevie followed silently behind them. She had been through a similar experience once before, when her father had open heart surgery. The crucial moment had been unnerving, but he had survived. Carole's case seemed more delicate somehow, with the extent of her brain damage unknown, and what long-term effects it might have. She might never be able to breathe on her own. The group looked gray-faced and wide-eyed as they rode up in the brightly lit elevator to her floor, and filed soundlessly into her room, to wait for the doctor to arrive.

Carole looked about the same, her eyes were closed, and she was breathing rhythmically with the help of the machine. A few minutes later the doctor in charge walked in. They all knew why they were there. The procedure had been

122

explained to them earlier that day, and they watched in terror as a nurse took the sealing tape off Carole's nose. Until then, she could only breathe through the tube in her mouth. But now her nose was open, and after asking them if they were ready, the doctor gestured to the nurse to take the tube out of Carole's mouth, and with a single gesture he turned off the machine. There was a hideously long moment of silence as everyone stared at Carole. There was no sign of breathing, as the doctor took a step toward her, with a brief glance at the nurse, and then Carole began to breathe on her own. Chloe let out a sharp cry of relief and burst into tears, as tears rolled down Jason's cheeks and Anthony choked on a sob. Instinctively, Chloe buried herself in Stevie's arms. Stevie was laughing and crying all at once, as she held Chloe in a tight hug. And even the doctor smiled.

'That's very good news,' he said with a reassuring look. For an instant, he thought she wouldn't do it, and then just as they all began to panic, she did. 'Her brain is telling her lungs what to do. It's a very good sign.' They also knew that it was possible for her to stay in a coma forever, even with the ability to breathe on her own. But if she hadn't been able to, her chances of recovery would have been even slimmer than they were now. It was a first step back toward life.

The doctor said that they would be watching her closely through the night to be sure that she continued breathing without assistance, but there was no reason to think that her independent respiration would stop again. With every passing moment, her condition was more stable. There had been no sign of life or movement from the still form in the bed, but they could all see her chest rising and falling gently with each breath. If nothing else, there was still hope.

They all stood around her bed afterward for over an hour, enjoying the victory they'd shared that night. And then Jason finally suggested they go back to the hotel. They had all had enough stress for one day, and he could see that his children needed to rest. Watching the respirator being turned off had been traumatic for each of them. They walked out quietly, and Stevie was the last to leave the room. She stopped for a moment next to the bed and touched Carole's fingers. She was still deep in her coma, and her fingers were cold. Her face looked more familiar now without the breathing tube in her mouth and the tape on her nose. It was the face Stevie had seen so often, and that all her fans knew and loved. But it was more than that to Stevie, it was that of the woman she admired so much, and had been loyal to for so many years.

'That was good, Carole,' Stevie said softly, as she bent to kiss her cheek. 'Now be nice, make just a little more effort, and try to wake up. We miss you,' she said, as tears of relief rolled down her cheeks, and she left the room to join the others. All things considered, it had been a very good night, although a hard one.

5

The inevitable happened two days after they had all gathered in Paris. Someone, either at the hotel or the hospital, tipped off the press. Within hours there were dozens of photographers outside the hospital, and half a dozen of the most enterprising ones sneaked upstairs and were stopped at the door to her room. Stevie stepped into the hallway from Carole's room, and in language worthy of a sailor, she stopped them cold, and had them thrown out. But from then on, all hell broke loose.

The hospital moved Carole to another room, and posted a security guard outside. But it complicated things for all of them, and made things even harder for the family. Photographers lay in wait for them at the hotel, and stood outside the hospital. There were TV cameras in both places, and flashes in their faces whenever they went in or out. It was a familiar scene for all of them. Carole had always shielded her children from the public, but Carole Barber in a coma, as the victim of a terrorist attack, was world news. There was no hiding from the press this time. They just had to live with it, and make the best of it. The best news of all was that Carole was breathing on her own. She was still unconscious, but they had taken her off sedation, and the doctors were hoping she would show some sign of life soon. If not, it had long-term implications that none of them wanted to face yet. In the meantime, they were constantly hassled by the press. Carole was on the front page of newspapers all over the world, including *Le Monde, Le Figaro,* and the *Herald Tribune* in Paris.

'I always loved that picture of her,' Stevie said, trying to make light of it, as they all read the papers over breakfast the next day. They had been in Paris for three days.

'Yeah, me too,' Anthony said, eating his second pain au chocolat. His appetite had improved. They were getting used to going to the hospital together every day, talking to the doctors, and sitting with Carole for as long as they could. Afterward they came back to the hotel, and sat in the living room of their suite, waiting for news. Night visits were discouraged, and she was still in a deep sleep. And all the while, people around the world were reading about her, and praying for her. Fans had started gathering at the hospital, and holding up signs when the family arrived. It was touching to see.

As they left for the hospital that morning, a man in a Paris apartment on the rue du Bac poured his café au lait, put jam on a slice of toast, and sat down to read his morning newspaper as he did every day. He opened it as he always did, smoothed out the creases, and glanced at the front page. His hands shook as he stared at the photograph. It was a picture taken of Carole while she'd been making a movie in France years before. The man staring at it knew it instantly, he'd been with her on that day, watching the shoot. Tears sprang to his eyes as he read the article, and as soon as he finished reading, he got up and called the Pitié Salpêtrière. He was connected to the *réanimation* unit, and asked for news of her. They said her condition was stable, but that they were not authorized to give out detailed reports over the phone. He thought of calling the head of the hospital, and then decided to go to the Pitié himself.

He was a tall, distinguished-looking man. He had white hair, and the eyes behind his glasses were a brilliant blue. Although no longer young, it was easy to see that he had once been a handsome man, and still was. And he moved and spoke like someone who was accustomed to command. There was an aura of authority about him. His name was Matthieu de Billancourt, and he had once been the Minister of the Interior of France.

He had his overcoat on, and was out the door and in his car within twenty minutes of reading the article in the paper. He was shaken to the core by what he'd read. His memories of Carole were still crystal clear, as though he'd seen her yesterday, when in fact it had been fifteen years since he had last seen her, when she left Paris, and fourteen years since he had spoken to her. He had had no news of her since, except what he read of her in the press. He knew she had married again, to a Hollywood producer, and he had felt a pang even then, although he was happy for her. Eighteen years before, Carole Barber had been the love of his life.

Matthieu de Billancourt arrived at the hospital, and parked his car on the street. He strode into the lobby, and asked the woman at the desk for Carole's room. He was stopped instantly and told that no bulletins could be issued about her, and there were no visitors allowed to her room. He asked to see the head of the hospital, and handed the woman at the desk his card. She glanced at it, saw his name, and immediately disappeared.

Within three minutes the head of the hospital appeared. He stared at Matthieu as though to verify that the name on the business card was real. It was the card from Matthieu's family law firm, where he had been now for the last ten years, since he retired from government. He was sixty-eight years old, but had the look and step of a younger man.

'*Monsieur le ministre?*' the head of the hospital asked nervously, wringing his hands. He had no idea what had brought him here, but Matthieu's name and reputation had been legendary when he was Minister of the Interior, and one still saw his name in the press from time to time. He was frequently consulted, often quoted. He had been a man of power for thirty years. He had a look of unquestionable command. 'What may I do to help you, sir?' There was something almost frightening about the look in Matthieu's eyes. He looked worried and deeply disturbed.

'I am here to see an old friend,' he said in a somber voice. 'She was a friend of my wife's.' He didn't want to draw attention to his visit, although asking for the head of the hospital would inevitably attract some notice to him, but he could only hope the man would be discreet. Matthieu didn't want to wind up in the press, but at that point he would have risked almost

131

anything to see her again. He knew it might be his last chance. The reports in the paper said she was still critically ill, and in danger of losing her life after the terrorist attack. 'I was told she can't have visitors,' Matthieu explained, and the director of La Pitié Salpêtrière guessed instantly who the patient was. 'Our families were very close.' Matthieu looked desperate and grim, which didn't go unnoticed by the short, officious-looking man.

'I am certain we can make an exception for you, sir. Without question. Would you like me to accompany you upstairs to her room? We are speaking of Mrs. Waterman . . . Miss Barber . . . are we not?'

'We are. And yes, I would appreciate it if you would take me to her room.' Without another word, the director of the hospital led him to the elevator, which came almost immediately, filled with doctors, nurses, and visitors, who exited, and then Matthieu and the director stepped in. His guide pressed the button, and a moment later they were on her floor. Matthieu could feel his heart beating faster. He had no idea what he'd see when he entered her room, or who would be there. It seemed unlikely to him that her children would remember him, they had been very young at the time. He assumed that her current husband would be there with her. He was hoping they would be out, taking a break.

The director stopped at the nursing desk, and said a few hushed words to the head nurse. She nodded, glanced at Matthieu with interest, and pointed to a door farther down the hall, which was Carole's room. Matthieu followed him without a word, and in an agony of pain and concern for her, in the bleak hospital lighting, he looked his age. The director stopped at the door the nurse had indicated, and opened it, motioning Matthieu inside. He hesitated and then whispered.

'Is her family with her? I don't want to intrude if it's not a good time.' He had suddenly realized that he might walk into an awkward scene. For a moment, he had forgotten that she no longer belonged to him.

'Would you like me to announce you if they are with her?' the director asked, and Matthieu shook his head, and did not offer to explain. The director understood. 'I'll check.' He took a few steps into the room, as Matthieu waited outside and the door whooshed closed. He had been able to see nothing in the room. The director emerged a moment later. 'Her family is with her,' he confirmed. 'Would you like to wait in the waiting room?'

Matthieu looked relieved at the suggestion. 'Yes, I would. This must be very hard for them,' he said, as the director led him back down the hall again, to a small private waiting room, which was normally used for an overflow of visitors, or people in deep grief who needed privacy. It was perfect for Matthieu, who wanted to avoid prying eyes, and preferred to be alone, while he waited to see her. He had no idea how long her family would be with her, but he was prepared to stay all day, or even into the night. He had to see her now.

The director of the hospital motioned to a chair and invited Matthieu to sit down. 'Would you like something to drink, sir? A cup of coffee perhaps?'

'No, thank you,' Matthieu said, and extended his hand. 'I appreciate your help. I was shocked when I heard the news.'

'We all were,' the hospital director commented. 'She was here for two weeks before we knew who she was. A terrible thing.' He looked appropriately reserved.

'Will she be all right?' Matthieu asked, with a look of sorrow in his eyes.

'I believe it's too soon to tell. Head injuries are treacherous and difficult to predict. She's still in a coma, but breathing on her own, which is a good sign. But she's not out of danger yet.' Matthieu nodded. 'I'll come back and check on you later,' the director promised, 'and the nurses will bring you anything you like.' Matthieu thanked him again, and he left. The man who had once been the Minister of the Interior of France sat as sadly as any other visitor, thinking of someone he loved, lost in thought. Matthieu de Billancourt was still one of the most respected and once-powerful men in France, and he was as frightened as any other visitor to the *réanimation* floor. He was terrified for her, and himself. Just knowing she was there, in a room so nearby, made his heart stir again as it hadn't in years.

Jason, Stevie, Anthony, and Chloe had been with Carole for hours by then. They took turns sitting in a chair next to her, stroking her hand, or talking to her.

Chloe kissed her mother's blue fingers sticking out of the cast, begging her to come back. 'Come on, Mommy, please . . . we want you to wake up.' She sounded like a child, and then finally she just sat there and sobbed, until Stevie put an arm around her, got her a drink of water, and someone else took her place near Carole's bed.

Anthony was trying to be brave, but could never get past a few words before breaking down. And Jason stood behind them, looking distraught. They kept trying to talk to her, because there was always the remote possibility that she could hear them. And they were praying that might bring her back. Nothing else had so far. Her children and Jason were looking exhausted, jet-lagged and grief-stricken, and Stevie tried valiantly to keep their spirits buoyed, although she was in no better shape than they. But she was determined to do all she could to help, for Carole's sake and theirs. But at heart, she was as devastated as they. Carole was a beloved friend.

'Come on, Carole, you've got a book to write. This is no time to slack off,' she said as though her employer could hear her, when it was her turn in the chair, and Jason smiled. He liked Stevie. She was a woman of substance, and was being wonderful to all of them. He could see how deeply she cared about Carole. 'You know, this really is taking the concept of writer's block to extremes, don't you think? Have you thought about the book? I really think you should. The kids are here too. Chloe looks terrific, she has a new haircut, and a ton of new accessories. Wait till you get the bill!' she said, and the others laughed. 'That ought to wake her up,' Stevie commented to them. It was a long afternoon, and it was obvious that nothing had changed. They desperately wished it would. It was an agony watching her still form and deathly pale face.

'Maybe we should go back to the hotel,' Stevie finally suggested. Jason looked like he was about to faint. None of them had eaten since that morning, and barely then. He was gray, and Chloe was crying more and couldn't seem to stop. Anthony didn't look much better, and Stevie was feeling weak herself. 'I think we all need food. They'll call us if anything happens, and we can come back tonight,' she said practically, and Jason nodded. He wanted a drink, although he wasn't much of a drinker. But at least right now it was some form of relief.

'I don't want to go.' Chloe sat and sobbed.

'Come on, Clo.' Anthony put his arms around her and gave her a hug. 'Mom wouldn't want us to be like this. And we have to keep up our strength.' Earlier Stevie had suggested a swim at the hotel when they went back, and it sounded good to him. He needed exercise to deal with the intense tension they were under. Stevie was longing for a swim herself.

She finally got them rounded up and out the

door of the room, with a nod to the nurse. It was no mean feat to move them, since none of them really wanted to leave Carole, nor did she, but she knew they had to keep their spirits as buoyant as they could. There was no telling how long this would go on, and they couldn't afford to fall apart. They would be of no use to Carole if they did, Stevie was well aware of that. So she made it her responsibility to take care of them. It took forever to get them to the elevator. Chloe had forgotten her sweater, and Anthony his coat. They went back one by one, and then finally got into the elevator, promising each other that they would be back in a few hours. They hated leaving her alone.

From his seat in the private waiting room, Matthieu saw them leave. He didn't recognize anyone in the group, but knew who they were. He heard them speak to each other in American accents. There were two women and two men. And as soon as the elevator doors closed, he approached the head nurse again. Normally, all visitors were forbidden, but he was Matthieu de Billancourt, venerated former Minister of the

Interior, and the head of the hospital had told her to do whatever Matthieu wished. It was clear that the rules didn't apply to him, and he didn't expect them to. Without saying a word, the head nurse led him into Carole's room. She lay there like a sleeping princess, with IVs in her arm, as a nurse watched over her, and checked the monitors attached to her. Carole lay perfectly still and deathly pale, as he looked at her, and then gently touched her face. Everything he had once felt for her was in his eyes. The nurse stayed in the room, but discreetly turned away. She sensed that she was seeing something deeply private to both of them.

He stood for a long time, watching her, as though waiting for her to open her eyes, and then finally, his head bowed, with damp eyes, he left the room. She was as beautiful as he had remembered her, and appeared untouched by age. Even her hair was still the same. They had taken the bandage off her head, and Chloe had brushed her mother's hair before she left.

The former Minister of the Interior of France sat in his car for a long time, and then he buried his face in his hands and cried like a child, thinking of everything that had happened, all he had promised and never given her. His heart ached for what should have been, and hadn't. It was the only time in his life he had failed to keep his word. He had regretted it bitterly for all the years since, and yet even now, he knew there had been no other choice. She had known it too, which was why she had left. He didn't blame her for leaving him, and never had. He had too many other responsibilities at the time. He only wished he could speak to her about it now, as she lay in her deep sleep. She had taken his heart with her when she left, and owned it still. The thought of her dying now was almost more than he could bear. And all he knew, as he drove away, was that whatever happened, he had to see her again. In spite of the fifteen years since he'd last seen her, and everything that had happened to both of them since, he was still addicted to her. One look at her face had intoxicated him again.

6

Five days after the arrival of Carole's family in Paris, Jason asked for a meeting with all of her doctors to clarify her situation for them. She was still in a coma, and other than the fact that she was no longer on a respirator and was breathing for herself now, nothing had changed. She was no closer to consciousness than she had been in nearly three weeks. The possibility that she would never wake up again was terrifying all of them.

The doctors were kind, but blunt. If she didn't regain consciousness soon, she would be brain-damaged forever. Even now it was an ever greater possibility. Her chances for recovery were getting slimmer by the hour. Their concerns for her put words to Jason's worst fears. Nothing could be done medically to alter her situation. It was in the hands of God. People had woken up from comas after even longer, but with time her chances of recovering normal brain function were diminishing. The entire group was in tears when the doctors left the waiting room where they'd met. Chloe was sobbing, and Anthony was holding her, with tears running down his cheeks. Jason sat in tearful silence, and Stevie wiped her eyes and took a breath.

'Okay, guys. She's never been a quitter. We can't be either. You know how she is. Carole does things on her own schedule. She'll get there. We can't lose faith now. What about going some-where today? You need a break from all this.' The others looked at her like she was insane.

'Like where? Shopping?' Chloe looked out-raged, and the two men were dismayed. They had done nothing but go back and forth between the hospital and the hotel for days, and their misery was acute in either place. So was Stevie's, but she tried to rally the group.

'Anything. The movies. The Louvre. Lunch somewhere. Versailles. Notre-Dame. I vote for something fun. We're in Paris. Let's figure out what she'd want us to do. She wouldn't want you all sitting here like this, day after day.' Her suggestion was met with a total lack of enthusiasm at first.

'We can't just leave her here and forget about her,' Jason said, looking stern.

'I'll stay with her. You guys do something else for a couple of hours. And yes, Chloe, maybe shopping. What would your mom do?'

'Get her nails done and buy shoes,' Chloe said with an irreverent look and then giggled. 'And wax her legs.'

'Perfect,' Stevie agreed. 'I want you to buy at least three pairs of shoes today. Your mom never buys fewer than that. More is okay. I'll make a manicure appointment for you at the hotel. Manicure, pedicure, leg wax, the works. And a massage. A massage would do you gentlemen some good too. What about booking a squash court at the health club at the Ritz?' She knew they both loved to play.

'Isn't that weird?' Anthony asked, looking guilty, although he had to admit he'd been craving exercise all week. He felt like an animal in a cage just sitting there.

'No, it's not. And you can both take a swim after you play. Why don't you all have lunch at the pool, and go from there? The boys play squash, Chloe gets her nails done, then massages for everyone. I can book the massages in your rooms, if you prefer.' Jason shot her a grateful smile. In spite of himself, he liked the idea. 'What about you?'

'This is what I do,' she said easily. 'I sit around and wait a lot, and organize things.' She had done the same for Carole when Sean was sick, and she would be at his bedside for days, especially after chemo. 'A few hours off won't hurt anyone. It'll do you a lot of good. I'll stay with her.' They all felt guilty every time they left her alone at the hospital. What if she woke up while they were gone? Unfortunately, it didn't look like an imminent possibility. Stevie called the hotel, and booked the appointments for them, and literally ordered Chloe to stop at the

Faubourg Saint Honoré on her way to lunch. There were plenty of shoes there, and even stores for the men. And as if they were children, she shooed them out of the hospital twenty minutes later and sent them on their way. They were grateful to her when they went. And she went back to sit quietly in Carole's room. The nurse on duty nodded to her. They had no language in common, but were familiar to each other by now. The woman caring for Carole that day was about Stevie's age. She wished she could have talked to her, but approached the still form on the bed instead.

'Okay, kiddo. No shit. You've got to get your ass in gear now. The doctors are getting pissed. It's time to wake up. You need a manicure, your hair is a mess. The furniture in this place looks like shit. You need to go back to the Ritz. Besides, you have a book to write.' Thanksgiving was only days away. 'You *have* to wake up,' Stevie said with desperation in her voice. 'This isn't fair to the kids. Or to anyone. You're not a quitter, Carole. You've had plenty of sleep. *Wake up!*' It was the kind of thing she'd said to her in the dark days right after Sean had died, but Carole had bounced back quickly then, because she knew Sean wanted her to, but this time Stevie didn't evoke his name. Only the kids'. 'I'm getting sick of this,' she added as an afterthought. 'I'm sure you are too. I mean, how boring is this? This Sleeping Beauty routine is really getting old.'

There was no sound or movement from the bed, and Stevie wondered how much truth there was to people hearing loved ones talk to them when they were in comas. If there was any, she was banking on it. She sat and talked to her employer all afternoon, in a normal voice, about ordinary things, as though Carole could hear her. The nurse went about her business, but looked sorry for her. By then the nursing staff had lost hope, and the doctors were right behind them. Too much time had gone by now since the bombing. The possibility of her recovering was dwindling by the hour. Stevie was well aware of it, but refused to be daunted by it.

At six o'clock, after eight hours at her bedside, Stevie left her to go back to the hotel and check on the others. They had been gone all day, and she hoped it had done them good. 'Okay, I'm leaving now,' Stevie said, just as she did when she left work in L.A. 'No more of this shit tomorrow, Carole. Enough is enough. I gave you the day off today. But that's it. You've had all the time you're going to get. Tomorrow we go back to work. You wake up, you look around, you eat breakfast. We do some letters. You have a shitload of calls to make. Mike has been calling every day. I've run out of excuses about why you're not talking to him. You have to call him yourself.' She knew she sounded like a nutcase, but it actually felt better talking to her as though she were there some-where, listening to what Stevie said. And it was true, Carole's friend and agent, Mike Appelsohn, called every day. Ever since the press had broken the news, he'd been on the phone to them twice a day. He was devastated. He had known her since she was a kid. He had discovered her him-self in a drugstore in New Orleans. He had bought a tube of toothpaste from her, and changed her life forever. He was like a father to her. He had turned seventy that year, and was still going strong. And now this had happened. He had no children of his own, just her. He had begged to come to Paris, but Jason had asked him to wait, a few more days at least. This was hard enough as it was, without others joining them, however well intentioned. Stevie was grateful that they didn't mind her being there, but she was helpful for them. Like Carole, they would have been lost without her. It was just her way. Carole had other friends too, in Hollywood, but because of the amount of time they'd spent together, and the things they'd been through during the past fifteen years, Carole was closer to her assistant than to any of them.

'Okay, so you got it? Today was your last day of just sleeping your life away. No more lying around here on your ass, making like a diva. You're a working girl. And you have to wake up and write your damn book. I'm not going to do it for you. You'll have to write it yourself. Enough of this lazy-ass shit. Get a good night's sleep tonight, and tomorrow you wake up. That's it. Time's up. This vacation is *over*. We're over it. And if you ask me, as far as vacations go, it sucked.' The nurse would have laughed if she'd understood.

She smiled at Stevie as she left. She was going off duty herself in another hour, and home to her husband and three kids. All Stevie had was a boyfriend, and the comatose woman lying on the bed, whom she dearly loved. She felt totally drained when she left. She had been talking to Carole all day. She hadn't dared do that when the others were around, other than a few words of endearment here and there. She hadn't planned this, but once they were gone, she decided to try it. They had nothing to lose. It couldn't do any harm.

Stevie closed her eyes and laid her head back as the cab took her to the hotel. The now-familiar paparazzi were outside the Ritz, hoping to get shots of Carole's kids, and Harrison Ford and his family had just arrived from the States. Madonna was due the next day. For reasons of their own, they were spending Thanksgiving in Paris. So was Carole's family, and depressed about it, given the tragic reason they were there. Stevie had already spoken to the head caterer, to organize a real Thanksgiving dinner for them in a private dining room. It seemed like the least she could do. The marshmallows for the sweet potatoes were impossible to find here. She had had her boyfriend, Alan, FedEx them to her from the States. She was keeping him posted by phone every day, and like everyone else, he wished Carole well and said he was praying for her. He was a good guy, Stevie just couldn't imagine herself married to him, or anyone else. She was married to her job, and to Carole, more than ever now at her time of extreme need, and with so much at risk.

The others were in much better spirits that night, and at Stevie's urging, they had dinner downstairs at the Espadon, the hotel's main restaurant. It was bright and cheerful and busy, and the food was fabulous. Stevie didn't join them. She had a massage, ordered soup from room service, and went to bed. They all thanked her for the activities she'd planned for them that day. They felt almost human again. In a burst of nervous energy, Chloe had bought six pairs of shoes and a dress at Saint Laurent. Jason couldn't believe it, but he'd bought two pairs of John Lobbs at Hermès while he waited for her, and although Anthony hated shopping, he bought four shirts. Both men had bought some extra clothes, mostly sweaters and jeans to wear at the hospital, since they had brought so little with them. They felt refreshed after swimming and massages. And Jason had beat his son at squash, a rare occurrence, and major victory for him. In spite of the horrifying circumstances that had brought them to Paris, they had had a decent day, thanks to Stevie, and her positive outlook about everything. She was wiped out herself when she went to bed, and was sound asleep at nine o'clock.

The hospital called at six o'clock the next morning. Stevie's heart sank when she heard the phone ring. It was Jason. They had called him first. A call at that hour could mean only one thing. He was crying when Stevie answered.

'Oh my God . . .' Stevie said, still groggy, but she was instantly alert.

'She's awake,' he said, sobbing. 'She opened her eyes. She's not speaking, but her eyes are open and she nodded at the doctor.'

'Oh my God . . . oh my *God* . . .' It was all

Stevie could say. She had thought she was dead.

'I'm going over. Do you want to come? I thought I'd let the kids sleep. I don't want to get their hopes up, till we see how she is.'

'I'm coming. I'll be dressed in five minutes.' And then she laughed through her own tears. 'She must have heard me.' She knew her eight-hour monologue wasn't what had done it. God and time had finally done their work. But maybe her words hadn't hurt.

'What did you say to her?' he asked, wiping the tears of relief off his face. He had lost hope at the doctor's conference the day before. But now, she was awake. It was an answer to their prayers.

'I told her that we were sick of this shit, and to get off her dead ass and get back to work. Something like that.'

'Good job,' he said, laughing. 'We should have tried that before. You must have made her feel guilty.'

'I hope so.' This was going to be one incredible Thanksgiving gift for all of them.

'I'll knock on your door in five minutes,' Jason said, and hung up. When he did, she was wearing jeans and a sweater, and carrying the heavy coat she had brought. She was wearing the cowboy boots she often wore to work. She had found them in a thrift shop and loved them. She said they were her lucky boots. They sure were now. She had been wearing them the day before too.

They chatted excitedly on their way back to the hospital, and passed all the landmarks that were all too familiar to them now. They could hardly wait to see her, and Jason reminded Stevie that the doctor said she wasn't talking yet. That might take a while. But she was awake. Everything had turned around overnight. In the silent hospital, they raced to her room, where the security guard stood outside. He nodded to them both as they went in, and assumed their early-morning arrival wasn't a good sign. It was a cold sunny morning, and the most beautiful day of Stevie's entire life, and for Jason it was second only to the birth of his children. This time Carole had been born again. She was awake!

Carole was lying on the bed with her eyes open when they walked in, with the doctor in charge of her case standing at her side. She had just arrived.

They had called her first, and she came right in. She smiled at Stevie and Jason, and then down at her patient. Carole met the doctor's eyes as she spoke to her in heavily accented English, but didn't respond. She made no sound, and didn't smile. She just watched, but when told to, she squeezed the doctor's hand. The pressure was slight, and she shifted her eyes to her two visitors when she heard them, but didn't smile at them either. Her face was expressionless, like a mask. Stevie spoke to her as though she were the same person she always had been, and Jason leaned down to kiss her cheek. Carole didn't react to that either. And eventually, she closed her eyes and went back to sleep again. The doctor, Jason, and Stevie left the room to talk outside.

'She's not responsive,' Jason commented, looking worried. Stevie was thrilled, determined not to look a gift horse in the mouth. This was a start, and a hell of a lot better than where she'd been.

'This is only the beginning,' the doctor said to Jason. 'She may not recognize you yet. She may have lost a great deal of memory. Her cerebral cortex and hippocampus were affected, both of which store memories. We can't be sure what's left, or how easy it will be for her to access them again. With luck, her memory and normal brain function will come back to her. But it will take time. She has to remember everything now. How to move, how to speak, how to walk. Her brain had a tremendous shock. But we have a chance now. Now we begin.' She looked greatly encouraged. They had almost given up on her ever gaining consciousness again. This proved to all of them that miracles really did happen, when you least expected them. She smiled at Stevie then. 'The nurses tell me that you spoke to her all day yesterday. You never know what they hear, or what makes a difference.'

'I think it was just time,' Stevie said modestly. Long overdue in fact, from their perspective. It had been a nightmarish three weeks for Carole, and an agonizing week for them. But at least she'd been unaware of what was going on. They had had to face the terror of losing her, fully conscious. They had been the worst days of Stevie's life. It put a whole new spin on the meaning of life.

'We want to do some more CT scans and MRIs today, and I'll send a speech therapist in to see how she responds. It's possible that she just can't remember the words yet. We'll give her a little push to get her started. I want to find some-one who speaks English,' the doctor said. Stevie had told them she spoke French, but they wanted to re-educate her in her own language. Doing it in French would have been much harder.

'I can work with her if someone shows me how,' Stevie volunteered, and the doctor smiled at her again. This was an enormous victory for her.

'I think you did fine work with her yesterday.' The doctor was generous with her praise. Who knew what had awakened her?

Jason and Stevie went back to the hotel then to tell Anthony and Chloe. Their father woke them both, and they had the same reaction Stevie had when he called her. Raw terror was on their faces and in their eyes the moment they woke up.

'Mom?' Anthony said, looking panicked. He was twenty-six years old, and a man, but she was still his mommy.

'She's awake,' Jason said, crying again. 'She can't

157

talk yet, but she saw us. She's going to be okay, son.' Anthony burst into sobs. None of them knew how okay yet, but she was alive, and no longer in a coma. It was definitely a start, and a huge relief for them.

Chloe threw her arms around her father's neck and laughed and cried all at once, like a child, and then she jumped out of bed and did a little dance. And then ran over to give Stevie a hug.

They were all laughing and talking at breakfast, and at ten o'clock they went back to see her. She was awake again by then, and looked at them with interest as they walked into the room.

'Hi, Mom,' Chloe said easily as she walked over to the bed and took her hand, and then bent to kiss her mother's cheek. There was no visible response from Carole. If anything, she looked surprised. But even her facial expressions were limited now. The bandage had been off her cheek for several days, but the gash she'd gotten had left a nasty scar, which was the least of her problems. They were all used to it by now, although Stevie knew Carole would be upset when she saw it, but that wouldn't be for a while. And as Jason had said, a good plastic surgeon could deal with it when they got home.

Carole lay on her bed, watching them, and turned her head several times to follow them with her eyes. Anthony kissed her too, and her eyes were filled with questions, and then Jason came to stand beside her and held her hand. Stevie stood back against the wall, smiling at her, but Carole didn't seem to notice her. It was possible that she couldn't focus yet from a distance.

'You've made us very happy today,' Jason said to his ex-wife with a loving smile, as he kept her hand in his own. She looked at him blankly. It took her a long time but she finally formed a single word and said it to him.

'Tii . . . rr . . . ed . . . tired.'

'I know you're tired, sweetheart,' he said gently. 'You've been asleep for a long time.'

'I love you, Mom,' Chloe added, and Anthony echoed her words. Carole stared at them as though she didn't know what that meant, and then spoke again.

'Waa . . . ter.' She pointed to the glass with a

weak hand, and the nurse held it to her lips. It reminded Stevie suddenly of Anne Bancroft in *The Miracle Worker*. They were starting way back at the beginning. But at least they were headed in the right direction now. Carole said nothing directly to any of them, and said none of their names. She just watched them. They stayed with her till noon, and then they left her. Carole looked exhausted, and her voice, the two times she spoke, didn't sound like her own. Stevie suspected she was still hoarse from the respirator, which had been removed not long before. Her throat sounded sore, and her eyes looked huge in her face. She had lost a lot of weight, and had been thin before. But she was still beautiful, even now. More so than ever, however wan. She looked as though she could have been playing Mimi in *La Bohème*. She seemed like a tragic heroine as she lay there, but hopefully for all of them, the tragedy was over.

Jason met with the doctor again late that afternoon. Chloe had decided to go shopping again, this time to celebrate. Retail therapy, as Stevie called it. And Anthony was at the gym, working out. They felt a lot better, and less guilty about returning to normal activities and life. They had even eaten a huge lunch at Le Voltaire, which was Carole's favorite restaurant in Paris, as they knew well. Jason said it was a celebration lunch for her.

The doctor in charge said that Carole's MRI and CT scans looked good, as they had for a while. There was no visible damage to her brain, which seemed remarkable. The initial small tears in the nerves had already healed. But there was also no way to assess how much memory loss she'd sustained, or to predict how many of her normal brain functions would return. Only time would tell. She was still acknowledging people when they spoke to her, and had said a few more words that afternoon, most of which related to her physical state and nothing else. She had said 'cold' when the nurse opened the window, and 'ow' when they took blood from her arm, and again when they readjusted her IV. She was responsive to pain and sensation, but she looked blank when the doctor asked her questions that went beyond yes and no. When they asked her her name, she shook her head. They told her it was Carole, and she shrugged. It was of no apparent interest to her. And the nurse said that when they called her by name, she didn't respond. And since she didn't know her own name, it was unlikely that she remembered theirs. More important, the doctor was fairly certain that for the moment Carole had no recollection of who they were.

Jason refused to be discouraged by it, and when he reported it to Stevie later on, he said it was just a matter of time. He had a firm grip on hope again. Maybe too firm, Stevie thought. She had already acknowledged to herself the possibility that Carole might never be the same again. She was awake, but there was a long way to go before Carole would be herself, if she ever would be again. It was still a question with no answer.

There was a leak to the press at the hospital again that day, and the next morning, the press reported that Carole Barber was out of her coma. She had already been off the critical list for several days. She still remained a hot news item. And it was obvious to Stevie that someone at the hospital was getting paid for news about Carole. It wouldn't have been unusual, even in the States, but it seemed disgusting to her anyway. It came with the territory of being a star, but seemed like a high price to pay. There were allusions in the article to the fact that she might be permanently brain-damaged. But the photograph they ran with the story was gorgeous. It had been taken ten years before, in her prime, although she still looked damn good now, before the bombing anyway. And all things considered, she looked pretty good for a woman with a brain injury and who had survived a bomb at close range.

The police came to visit her, once they knew that she was awake. The doctor let them speak to her briefly but within minutes, it was evident to them that she had no memory of the bombing or anything else. They left with no further information from her.

Jason and the children continued to visit Carole, as did Stevie, and she continued to add words to her repertoire. *Book. Blanket. Thirsty. No!* She was very emphatic on that one, particularly when they came to take blood, and she pulled her arm away the last time and glared at the nurse and called her 'bad,' which made them all smile. They took her blood anyway, she burst into tears, looked surprised, and said 'cry.' Stevie talked to her as though she were normal, and sometimes Carole just sat and stared at her for hours, saying nothing. She could sit up now, but she still couldn't put words into a sentence, or say their names. It was clear by the day before Thanksgiving, three days after she'd awakened, that she had no idea whatsoever who they were. She recognized no one, not even her children. They were all upset by it, but Chloe was the most distressed.

'She doesn't even know me!' Chloe said with tears in her eyes when she left the hospital with her father to go back to the hotel.

'She will, sweetheart. Give her time.'

'What if she stays like that?' She voiced their worst fear. No one else had dared to say it.

'We'll take her to the best doctors in the world,' Jason reassured her, and he meant it.

Stevie was worried about it too. She continued to have conversations with Carole, while her friend and employer looked blank. She smiled once in a while at the things Stevie said, but there wasn't even a spark of memory for who Stevie was in her eyes. Smiling was new for her. And laughing was too. It frightened Carole the first time she did it, and she instantly burst into tears. It was like watching a baby. She had a lot of ground to cover, and hard work ahead. The speech therapist was working with her. They had found a British one who pushed Carole hard. She told Carole her name and asked her to repeat it many times. She hoped that the patterning would cause a spark, but thus far nothing did.

On Thanksgiving morning Stevie told her what day it was and what it meant in the States. She told her what they would have at the meal, and Carole looked intrigued. Stevie hoped it had jolted her memory, but it hadn't.

'Turkey. What's that?' She said it like she'd never heard the word before, and Stevie smiled.

'It's a bird we'll eat for lunch.'

'Sounds disgusting,' Carole said, making a face, and Stevie laughed.

'Sometimes it is. It's a tradition.'

'Feathers?' Carole asked with interest. It was down to basics. Birds had feathers. She remembered that much at least.

'No. Stuffing. Yum.' She described the stuffing to her, as Carole listened with interest.

'Hard,' she said then, as tears filled her eyes. 'To talk. Words. Can't find them.' She looked frustrated for the first time.

'I know. I'm sorry. They'll come back. Maybe we should start with dirty ones. Maybe that would be more fun. You know, like *shit, fuck, ass, asshole,* the good ones. Why worry about *turkey* and *stuffing*?'

'Bad words?' Stevie nodded, and they both laughed. 'Ass,' Carole said proudly. 'Fuck.' She clearly had no idea what it meant.

'Excellent,' Stevie said with a loving look. She loved this woman more than her own mother or sister. She truly was her best friend.

'Name?' Carole asked, looking sad again. '*Your* name,' she corrected. She was trying to stretch herself. The speech therapist wanted her to speak in sentences, and most of the time she couldn't. Not yet.

'Stevie. Stephanie Morrow. I work for you at home in L.A. And we're friends.' There were tears in her eyes as she said it, and then she added, 'I love you. A lot. I think you even love me too.'

'Nice,' Carole said. 'Stevie.' She tried out the word. 'You are my friend.' It was the longest sentence she'd formed so far.

'Yes, I am.'

Jason walked in then to give Carole a kiss before their Thanksgiving dinner at the hotel. The kids were at the Ritz getting dressed, and had gone swimming again that morning. Carole looked up at him and smiled.

'Ass. Fuck,' she said, and he looked startled, and then glanced at Stevie, wondering what had happened, and if Carole was losing it again. 'New words.' She smiled broadly.

'Oh. Great. That should be useful.' He laughed and sat down.

'Your name?' she asked. He had told her before, but she had forgotten.

'Jason.' For a moment he looked sad.

'Are you my friend?'

He hesitated for a moment before he answered,

167

and tried to sound normal and somewhat casual when he did. It was a heavy moment, and indicated again that she remembered nothing of her past. 'I was your husband. We were married. We have two children, Anthony and Chloe. They were here yesterday.' He sounded tired, but mostly sad.

'Children?' She looked blank, and then he realized why.

'They're big now. Grown-ups. They are our children, but they're twenty-two and twenty-six years old. They've been here to visit you. You saw them with me. Chloe lives in London, and Anthony lives in New York, and works with me. I live in New York too.' It was a lot of information for her all at once.

'Where do I live? With you?'

'No. You live in Los Angeles. We're not married anymore. We haven't been for a long time.'

'Why?' Her eyes dove deep into his as she asked. She needed to know everything now, in order to find out who she was. She was lost.

'That's a long story. Maybe we should talk

about that another time.' And neither of them wanted to tell her about Sean. It was too soon. She didn't even know she'd had him, she didn't need to know she had lost him two years before. 'We're divorced.'

'That's sad,' she said. She seemed to understand what *divorced* meant, which Stevie found intriguing. She got some concepts and words, and others seemed to be completely gone. It was odd what was left.

'Yes, it is,' Jason agreed. And then Jason told her about Thanksgiving too, and the meal they were going to have at the hotel.

'Sounds like too much food. Sick.' He nodded and laughed.

'Yeah, you're right, it is. But it's a nice holiday. It's a day to be thankful for good things that have happened, and the blessings we have. Like you sitting here talking to me right now,' he said with a tender look. 'I'm grateful for you this year. We all are, Carole,' he said as Stevie started to leave the room discreetly, but he told her she could stay. They had no secrets from each other these days.

'I am thankful for both of you,' she said, looking at the two of them. She wasn't sure who they were, but they were good to her, and she could sense their love for her flowing toward her. It was palpable in the room.

They chatted with her for a while, and a few more words came back to her, most of them related to the holiday. The words *mince pie* and *pumpkin pie* sprang out of nowhere, but she had no idea what they were. Stevie had only mentioned apple pie to her, because the hotel couldn't do the others. And then finally, Stevie and Jason got up to leave.

'We're going back to the hotel to have Thanksgiving dinner with Anthony and Chloe,' Jason explained with a gentle look at Carole as he held her hand. 'I wish you were coming with us.' She frowned when he mentioned the hotel, as though trying to pull something elusive out of her mental computer but it just wouldn't come.

'What hotel?'

'The Ritz. It's where you always stay in Paris. You love it. It's beautiful. They're making a turkey dinner for us in a private dining room.'

They had a lot to be grateful for this year.

'That sounds nice,' Carole said, looking sad. 'I can't remember anything, who I am, who you are, where I live . . . the hotel . . . I don't even remember Thanksgiving, or the turkey or pies.' There were tears of sorrow and frustration in her eyes, and seeing her that way tore at their hearts.

'You will,' Stevie said quietly. 'Give it time. It's a lot of information to try and get back all at once. Go slow,' she said with a loving smile. 'You'll get there. I promise.'

'Do you keep your promises?' she asked, looking Stevie in the eye. She knew what a promise was, even if she didn't remember the name of her hotel.

'Always,' Stevie said, holding up her hand in a solemn oath, and then ran two fingers in an X across her chest, as Carole broke into a smile and spoke in unison with her.

'Cross my heart! I remember that!' she said victoriously. And Stevie and Jason laughed.

'See! You remember the important stuff, like "Cross my heart." You'll find the rest,' Stevie said with a loving look.

'I hope so,' Carole said fervently, as Jason kissed her forehead and Stevie squeezed her hand. 'Have a nice dinner. Eat some turkey for me.'

'We'll bring you some tonight,' Jason promised. He and the children were planning to come back after the meal.

'Happy Thanksgiving,' Stevie said as she leaned down to kiss Carole's cheek. It was a little strange doing it because to Carole, Stevie was a stranger now, but she did it anyway, and Carole caught her hand in her own as she did.

'You're tall,' she said, and Stevie grinned.

'Yes, I am.' She was taller than Jason, in high heels, and he was over six feet. 'So are you, but not as tall as I am. Happy Thanksgiving, Carole. Welcome back to the world.'

'Fuck,' Carole said with a grin, and they both laughed. There was a spark of mischief in her eyes this time, and along with deep gratitude for the fact that Carole was awake and alive, she could only hope that Carole would once more be herself, and that the good times would come again. Jason had already left the room by then, as Stevie grinned at her.

'Fuck you,' Stevie said. 'That's a good one to know too. Very useful.'

Carole smiled broadly and looked into the eyes of the woman who was her friend and had been for fifteen years. 'Fuck you too,' she said clearly, and both women laughed, as Stevie blew her a kiss and left the room. It wasn't the Thanksgiving any of them had expected to have, but it was the best one of Stevie's life. And maybe Carole's too.

7

Matthieu came to see Carole on Thanksgiving afternoon, by sheer happenstance, while her family and Stevie were having their Thanksgiving meal at the hotel. He had been cautious about coming to visit her. He didn't want to run into them. He still felt awkward about that, whatever the circumstances now. And things had been so desperate at first, he didn't want to intrude on them in the midst of their shock and grief. But he had read in the newspaper that she was awake and doing better, so he had come again. He couldn't resist.

He walked slowly into the room and looked

at her, drinking her in. It was the first time he had seen her awake. And his heart leaped as he saw her. There wasn't even a flicker of recognition in her eyes. He wasn't sure at first if it was due to the distance of time, or the blow to her head. But after all they'd meant to each other, he couldn't imagine that she didn't remember him. He had thought of her every day. It was difficult to believe that, in her normal state, she wouldn't do the same, or at least recall his face.

She turned toward him with surprise and curiosity as he walked into the room, and didn't remember ever seeing him before. He was a tall, handsome white-haired man with piercing blue eyes and a serious face. He looked like a person of authority, and she wondered if he was a doctor.

'Hello, Carole.' He was the first to speak. He spoke to her in heavily accented English, unsure if she still remembered her French, which for now she didn't.

'Hello.' It was obvious that she didn't recognize him, and it nearly broke his heart, given all they'd felt for each other. She looked blank. 'I've probably changed a lot,' he said. 'It's been a long time. My name is Matthieu de Billancourt.' Nothing registered on her face, but she smiled pleasantly at him. Everyone was new to her now, even her ex-husband and kids, and now this man.

'Are you a doctor?' she asked clearly, and he shook his head. 'Are you my friend?' she said carefully, although realizing full well that if not, he wouldn't be there. But it was her way of asking him if she knew him. She had to rely on others for that information. But he was startled by the question. Just seeing her again, he was in love with her. For her, there was nothing left. He couldn't help wondering what she had still felt for him before the accident. But clearly, nothing now.

'Yes . . . yes . . . I am. A very good friend. We haven't seen each other for a long time.' He readily understood that her memory had not returned, and he was careful about the information he gave her. He didn't want to shock her. She still looked very frail, propped up in the big hospital bed. He didn't want to say too much because her nurse was in the room. He didn't know if she spoke English, but he was cautious just in case. And he couldn't tell secrets anyway to a woman who didn't remember ever seeing him before.

'We knew each other when you lived in Paris.' He had brought her flowers, and handed the large bouquet of roses to the nurse.

'I lived in Paris?' It was news to her. No one had mentioned that to her yet. There was so much she didn't know about herself it frustrated her constantly. He could see it in her eyes. 'When?' She knew she lived in Los Angeles now, and had lived in New York with Jason, but no one had mentioned Paris.

'You lived here for two and a half years. You left fifteen years ago.'

'Oh.' Carole nodded, and asked no more questions, she just watched him. There was something in his eyes that rattled her, it was like something she couldn't reach, but could see in the distance. Carole wasn't sure what it was, if it was good or bad. There was something about him that was very intense. She wasn't frightened by it, but she felt it, and couldn't identify the feeling by name.

'How do you feel?' he asked politely. It seemed safer to talk about the present than the past.

Carole thought about it for a long time, looking for the word, and then found it. The way he spoke to her, like an old friend, she had a sense that she knew this man well, but wasn't sure. It was a little like Jason, but different. 'Confused,' she said in answer to his question about how she felt. 'I don't know anything. Words. I can't find them. Or people. I have two children,' Carole said, still looking surprised. 'They're grown up now,' she explained, as though reminding herself. 'Anthony and Chloe.' She looked proud that she remembered their names. She was retaining all they told her. It was a lot to absorb.

'I know. I knew them. They were wonderful. And so were you.' She was still as beautiful as she had been. It was amazing to him how little time had touched her, although he noticed the scar on her cheek and didn't mention it. It looked very fresh to him. 'You will remember. Things will

178

come back to you.' She nodded, but looked unconvinced. There was still so much missing and she was well aware of it.

'Were we good friends?' she asked him, as though searching for something. Whatever it was, she couldn't access it. She couldn't find him in her head. Whatever he had been to her was gone, along with all the other details of her life. Her mind was a clean slate.

'Yes, we were.' They sat in silence then for a little while, and finally, he cautiously approached the bed and gently took her hand in his. She let him, not knowing what else to do. 'I'm very glad that you're getting better. I came to see you while you were still asleep. It's a great gift that you're awake.' She knew it was to the others too. 'I've missed you, Carole. I thought about you for all these years.' She wanted to ask him why, but didn't dare. It sounded too complicated for her. Something about the way he looked at her made her feel anxious. She couldn't identify the feeling, but it was very different from the way Jason looked at her, or her children. They seemed much more direct. There was something hidden

179

about this man, as though there was much he wasn't telling her but saying it with his eyes. It was hard for her to read.

'It's nice of you to visit,' she said politely, finding a phrase that seemed to come out all at once. It happened that way sometimes, and at other times she had to struggle for a single word.

'May I come to see you again?' She nodded, not sure what else to say. Social subtleties were confusing for her, and she still had no idea who he was. She had a sense that he'd been more than a friend, but he didn't say they'd been married. It was hard for her to guess who and what he'd been in her life.

'Thank you for the flowers. They are beautiful,' she said, searching his eyes for the answers he didn't put into words.

'So are you, my dear,' he said, still holding her hand. 'You always were, and still are. You look like a girl.'

She looked surprised then as she realized something she hadn't thought of before. 'I don't know how old I am. Do you?' It was easy for him to make the calculation, by adding fifteen years to the age she'd been when she left. He knew she had to be fifty, although she didn't look it, but he didn't know if he should say it to her.

'I don't think it matters. You're still very young. I'm an old man now. I'm sixty-eight.' His face showed his age, but his spirit didn't. He was infused with so much energy and strength that his looks belied his age.

'You look young,' she said kindly. 'If you aren't a doctor, what do you do?' she asked. He still looked like a doctor to her, minus the white coat. He was wearing a well-cut dark blue suit, and a dark gray topcoat over it. He was well dressed, with a white shirt and somber tie, and his mane of white hair was well cut and neat, his rimless glasses typically French.

'I'm an attorney.' He didn't tell her what he'd been before. It didn't matter anymore.

She nodded, watching him again, as he raised her hand to his lips and gently kissed her fingers. They were still bruised from her fall. 'I'll come to see you again. You must get well now.' And then he added, 'I think about you all the time.' She had no idea why. It was so frustrating to remember nothing of her past, not even how old she was or who she was. It gave everyone an advantage over her. They knew everything she didn't. And now this stranger who knew a piece of her past too.

'Thank you' was all she could think of to say to him, as he gently put her hand back on the bed. He smiled at her again, and a moment later, he left. The nurse in the room had recognized him, but she said nothing to Carole. It wasn't her place to comment on former ministers visiting her. She was a movie star, after all, and probably knew half the important people in the world. But it was obvious that Matthieu de Billancourt was enormously attached to her and knew her well. Even Carole could sense that.

The others came back that evening after their dinner. They were in good spirits, and Stevie had brought her a sample of everything that had been on their plates, and identified all of it to her. Carole tasted it with interest, said she didn't like the turkey, but thought the marshmallows were very good.

'You hate marshmallows, Mom,' Chloe informed her with a stunned look. 'You always say they're garbage and you wouldn't let us eat them when we were kids.'

'That's too bad. I like them,' she said with a shy smile, and then held her hand out to her youngest child. 'I'm sorry I don't know anything right now. I'll try to remember.' Chloe nodded as tears filled her eyes.

'That's okay, Mom. We'll fill you in. Most of it isn't important.'

'Yes, it is,' Carole said gently. 'I want to know everything. What you like, what you don't, what we like to do together, what we did when you were a little girl.'

'You were away a lot,' Chloe said softly, as her father shot her a warning look. It was way too early to talk about that.

'Why was I away a lot?' Carole looked blank again.

'You worked very hard,' Chloe said simply, as Anthony held his breath too. He had heard it for

183

years, and those conversations between his mother and sister never ended well. He hoped it wouldn't happen now too. He didn't want Chloe upsetting their mother at this point. She was far too fragile still, and it would be too unfair to accuse her of things she didn't know. Carole had no way to defend herself.

'Doing what? What did I do?' Carole glanced at Stevie as she asked, as though the young woman could fill her in. She had already sensed the bond between them, even if she knew no details, and remembered neither her face nor name.

'You're an actress,' Stevie explained to her. No one had said that to her yet. 'A very important actress. You're a big star.'

'I am?' Carole looked stunned. 'Do people know me?' The whole concept seemed foreign to her.

They all laughed, and Jason spoke first. 'Maybe we should keep you humble and not tell you. You're probably one of the most well-known movie stars in the world.'

'How weird.' It was the first time she had

remembered the word *weird,* and they all laughed.

'It's not weird at all,' Jason said. 'You're a very good actress, you've made a hell of a lot of movies, and won some very major awards. Two Oscars and a Golden Globe.' He wasn't sure she'd remember what those were now, and the look on her face said she didn't. But the word *movies* sparked a memory for her. She knew what they were. 'Everyone in the world knows who you are.'

'What's that like for you?' she turned and asked Chloe, and looked like her old self for a minute. Everyone in the room held their breath as she waited for Chloe's answer.

'Not so good,' Chloe whispered. 'It was hard when we were little.' Carole looked sad for her as she said it.

'Don't be silly,' Anthony interrupted, trying to lighten the mood. 'It was great having a movie star for a mom. Everyone envied us, we got to go to cool places, and you were gorgeous. You still are.' He smiled at his mother. He had always hated the friction between them, and Chloe's resentment as they grew up, although it was better in recent years.

'Maybe it was cool for you,' Chloe snapped at him. 'It wasn't for me.' She turned back toward her mother then, as Carole looked at her with compassion and squeezed her hand.

'I'm sorry,' Carole said simply. 'It doesn't sound like fun to me either. I would want my mom around all the time if I was a kid.' And then suddenly she looked at Jason. She had just remembered another important question. It was terrible not knowing anything. 'Do I have a mother?' He shook his head, relieved to have changed the subject for a moment. Carole had just returned from the dead after weeks of terror for them, he didn't want Chloe upsetting her, or worse, starting a fight with her, and they all knew she was capable of it. There were a lot of old issues there, between mother and daughter, less so between mother and son. Anthony had never resented his mother's work, and had always expected less of her than Chloe did. He had been far more independent, even as a child.

'Your mother died when you were two,' he

explained. 'Your father died when you were eighteen.' She was an orphan then. She remembered the word instantly.

'Where did I grow up?' she asked with interest.

'In Mississippi. On a farm.' She remembered none of it. 'You were discovered and went to Hollywood at eighteen. You were living in New Orleans, when they found you.' She nodded, and turned her attention back to Chloe. She was more concerned with her now than with her own history. That was new. It was as though she had come back as someone different, subtly different, but perhaps forever changed. It was too soon to know. She was starting with a clean slate, and had to rely on them to fill her in. Chloe had done that with her usual honesty and bluntness. It had worried all of them at first, but Stevie suddenly thought it might be for the best. Carole was responding well. She wanted to know everything about herself, and them, both good and bad. She needed to fill in the blanks, there were so many of them.

'I'm sorry I was away a lot. You'll have to tell me about it. I want to hear all about it, and what it was like for you. It's a little late, you're all grown up. But maybe we can change some things. How is it for you now?'

'It's okay,' Chloe said honestly. 'I live in London. You come to visit me. I go home for Christmas and Thanksgiving. I don't like L.A. anymore. I like London a lot better.'

'Where did you go to college?' Carole inquired.

'Stanford.'

Carole looked blank. It didn't ring a bell.

'It's a great school,' Jason volunteered, and Carole nodded, and then smiled at her daughter.

'I wouldn't expect anything less of you.' This time Chloe smiled.

They chatted about easier subjects after that, and eventually they went back to the hotel. Carole looked tired when they left. Stevie was the last to leave the room, and whispered to her friend, as she lingered for a minute.

'You did great with Chloe.'

'You're going to have to tell me some things. I don't know anything.'

'We'll talk,' Stevie promised, and then noticed

the roses on a table in a corner of the room. There were at least two dozen of them, red, long stem. 'Who are those from?'

'I don't know. A French man who came to see me. I forget his name. He said we were old friends.'

'I'm surprised security let him in. They're not supposed to.' Only family members were supposed to visit her, but no French security guard was going to turn away a former minister of France. 'Anyone can say they're an old friend. If they're not careful, you'll be overrun by fans.' They had stopped hundreds of bouquets downstairs. Stevie and Jason had had them distributed to all the other patients. They would have filled several rooms. 'You didn't recognize him?' It was a foolish question, but she thought she'd ask anyway, just in case she did. You never knew. Sooner or later some memories from the past would surface. Stevie was expecting that to happen any day, and was hoping it would.

'Of course not,' Carole said simply. 'If I don't remember my own children, why would I recognize him?'

'Just asking. I'll tell the guard to be more careful.' She had already noticed a few things she didn't like about their security, and complained about it. When the guard on duty went on a break, no one replaced him, and anyone could have walked in. Apparently someone had. They wanted better security for Carole than that. 'Nice flowers anyway.'

'He was nice. He didn't stay long. He says he knew my children too.'

'Anyone can say that.' They needed to protect her, from gawkers, paparazzi, and fans, or worse. She was who she was, after all. And the hospital had never dealt with a star of her magnitude before. She and Jason had discussed hiring a private guard for her, but the hospital had insisted they could handle it. Stevie was going to remind them to tighten things up. The last thing they wanted was a photographer getting in and taking a picture of her. The now unfamiliar intrusion would have been upsetting to Carole although before she had dealt with it nearly every day. 'I'll see you tomorrow. Happy Thanksgiving, Carole,' Stevie said with a warm smile.

'Fuck you,' Carole said happily, and they both laughed. She was getting better by the hour. For a minute she almost sounded like her old self.

8

Jason, Chloe, and Anthony went to the Louvre, and then did some shopping again the next day. They came back for a late lunch at the hotel, in the bar downstairs. And then Jason and Anthony went back to their rooms to call their office and do some work. They were both falling behind on deals they were working on. But the circumstances were extraordinary, and their clients understood. Several of Jason's partners were standing in for them with various accounts. And they planned to catch up when they got back.

Chloe went for a swim and massage while her brother and father worked. She had taken a leave from her own job, and they'd been nice about it. They told her to stay in Paris with her mother as long as she needed to. She even had time, that afternoon, and was finally in the mood to call a boy she had recently met in London. They chatted for half an hour, and Chloe liked him. She told him about her mother's accident, and he was kind and sympathetic. He promised to call her soon, and said he wanted to see her when she got back to London. He'd been meaning to call her, and was delighted she'd called him. His name was Jake.

The others being busy gave Stevie a chance to spend time alone with Carole. The doctors had told her to tell Carole everything she could about her life. They were hoping that hearing the details would jog her memory and bring back the rest. Stevie was willing to do that, but didn't want to upset Carole by reminding her of unhappy things, and she'd had her fair share of them.

Stevie brought a sandwich with her, and sat down across from Carole to chat. She had nothing particular in mind, and Carole had been asking a lot of questions, like about her parents the day before. She was starting from scratch.

Stevie was halfway through her sandwich when Carole asked her about her divorce. But in that case, Stevie had to admit she didn't know much.

'I didn't work for you then. I know he was married to someone else after you, a Russian supermodel, I think. He got divorced from her about a year after you got back from France. I was with you, but I was new, and you didn't tell me much. I think he came out to see you a couple of times, and I suspected that he asked you to come back to him. It was just a feeling I had, you never told me. And you never went back to him. You were pretty mad at him in those days. It took a couple of years to settle down. Before that, you were always fighting with him on the phone, about the kids. For the last ten years, you've been good friends.' Carole could see that now, and nodded as she listened, groping back in her mind for some recollection of her marriage to Jason, and found nothing. Her memory was blank.

'Did I leave him, or did he leave me?'

'I don't know that either. You're going to have to ask him some of this stuff. I know you lived in New York while you were with him. You were married to him for ten years. And then you went to France. You made a major movie there. You were already getting divorced by then, I think. And you stayed on in Paris for two years after the movie, with your kids. You bought a house, and sold it a year after you moved to L.A. It was a beautiful little house.'

'How do you know?' Carole looked puzzled. 'Did you work for me in Paris?' She was confused again. There was so much to sort out and put in chronological order.

'No, I went over to close it for you. You came over for a couple of days, told me what you wanted to keep and send back to L.A., and I took care of the rest. The place was small, but gorgeous. Eighteenth century, I think, with *boiseries* and parquet floors, big French windows looking out over a garden, and fireplaces all over the place. I was kind of sorry you didn't keep it.'

'Why didn't I?' Carole asked, frowning as she

listened to her. She wanted to remember all these things, but didn't.

'You said it was too far away. And you were working a lot then. You didn't have time to run off to Paris between movies. You do now, but you didn't then. And I don't think you wanted to come back here.' Stevie didn't volunteer the rest. 'You were trying to spend more time with your kids between films, especially Chloe. Anthony was always more independent.' Stevie had known him since he was eleven, and even then he had been content to spend time with friends and on his own, and visiting his father in New York during his vacations. Chloe had wanted more of her mother, and there had never been enough of Carole to suit her. She had been a very needy child, in Stevie's opinion, and still was, although less so now. These days, Chloe had her own life, and was less demanding of her mother's time. But she still liked being the center of attention when she was with her mother.

'Was she right about what she said yesterday?' Carole looked genuinely worried. What she really wanted to know was if she was a good person or not. It was scary not to know.

'Not all of it,' Stevie said fairly. 'Some maybe. You must have worked hard when she was small. You were twenty-eight when she was born, and at the height of your career. I didn't know you then. I came along seven years later. But she was already angry at you. I think you took the kids on location to most of your movies, when you could, with a tutor, unless they were in crazy places, like Kenya. But if it was civilized, you took them, even when I was first working for you. Eventually Anthony didn't want to go, and when they got to high school, you couldn't take them out of school. But before that they went most of the time, and their schools bitched like crazy. But so did Chloe, when you didn't.' More than that, as Chloe got older, Stevie often suspected that she wanted to *be* her mom, which was a bigger problem. But Stevie didn't say that to Carole. 'I'm sure it's not easy to be the child of a celebrity, but I've always been impressed by how hard you tried, and how much time you spend with them, even now. You never travel anywhere without going through London and

New York, to see them. I'm not sure Chloe realizes how unusual that is, or how much effort it takes on your part. She doesn't give you a lot of credit, at least not for time you spent with her during her childhood. And from all I know you were very good about it. I guess she just wanted more.'

'Why?'

'Some people are just like that,' Stevie said wisely. 'She's still young, she can work it out, if she wants to. She's basically a nice kid. It just upsets me when she's hard on you. I don't think it's fair to you. She's still a baby in a lot of ways. She needs to grow up.' And then Stevie smiled at her. 'And besides, you've spoiled her. You give her everything she wants. I know. I pay the bills.'

'Shame on me,' Carole said benignly. She was speaking well now. She had found the words, just not the history that went with them. 'Why do you suppose I do that?'

'Guilt. Generosity. You love your kids. You've done well and want to share it with them. Chloe takes advantage of it sometimes, trying to make you feel guilty, although some of the time I think she genuinely feels she got cheated as a child. I think what she wanted was a mother who was a regular suburban housewife who picked her up and dropped her off all day, and had nothing else to do. You picked her up at school every day, when you were in town, but you did more than just make movies. You had a very busy life.'

'Like what?' Listening to Stevie was like listening to her talk about someone else. Carole had no sense that this was about her. The woman Stevie was describing was a stranger.

'You've been involved in women's rights causes for years. You've traveled to underdeveloped countries, spoken to the Senate, gone to the UN, gave speeches. You put your money where your mouth is, when you believe in something, which I think is a great thing. I've always admired you for it.'

'And Chloe? Does she admire me for it too?' Carole said sadly. It didn't sound like it from what Stevie said.

'No. I think if anything, it pisses her off, if it takes time or money away from her. Maybe she's too young to care about those things. And admittedly, you traveled a fair amount for that too, between films.'

'Maybe I should have stayed home more,' Carole said, wondering if the damage between them was reparable at this point. She hoped it was. It sounded as though she had some things to make up to her daughter, even if she was a little spoiled.

'That wouldn't have been you,' Stevie said simply. 'You always have a million irons in the fire.'

'And now?'

'Not so many. You've slowed down in the last few years.' Stevie was cautious about what she said, because of Sean. She wasn't sure if Stevie was ready to hear about that, and deal with the feelings that might come with it, particularly if she remembered.

'Have I? Why? Why have I slowed down?' Carole looked troubled, trying to jog her mind.

'Tired, maybe. You're pickier about the movies you do. You haven't done one in three years. You've turned down a lot of parts. You want to do parts that have meaning to you, not just something showy and commercial. You're writing a book, or trying to.' Stevie smiled. 'That's why you came to Paris. You thought it might give you deeper insight to come back here.' And instead it had damn near cost her her life. Stevie would regret forever that Carole had taken this trip. She still felt traumatized herself from nearly losing this woman she loved and admired so much. 'I think you'll start doing more movies again after you finish the book. It's a novel, but I think there must be a lot of you in it. Maybe that's why you were blocked.'

'Are those the only reasons why I slowed down?' Carole looked at her with the innocent eyes of a child, and Stevie paused for a long minute, not sure what to say to her, and decided to tell the truth.

'No, they're not. There was another reason.' Stevie sighed. She hated to tell her, but someone would sooner or later, better it was her. 'You were married, to a wonderful man. A really, really nice guy.'

'Don't tell me I got divorced again,' Carole

said, looking unhappy. Two divorces seemed too much to her. Even one was sad.

'You didn't,' Stevie reassured her, if you could call it that. Being widowed and losing a man she loved was so much worse. 'You were married for eight years. His name was Sean. Sean Clarke. You married him when you were forty and he was thirty-five. He was a very successful producer, although you never worked on a movie together. He was an incredibly kind man, and I think you were both very happy. Your kids loved him. He didn't have any kids of his own, nor with you. Anyway, he got sick three years ago. Very sick. Liver cancer. He was in treatment for a year, and he was very philosophical about it. Very peaceful. He accepted what happened to him in a very dignified way.' Stevie took a breath as she went on. 'He died, Carole. In your arms. A year after he got sick. That was two years ago. It's been a big adjustment. You've done a lot of writing, some traveling, spent time with the kids. You've turned a number of parts down, although you've said you'll go back to work after you write the book. And I believe you will, write the book, and go back to movies. This trip was part of that. I think you've grown a lot since he died. I think you're stronger now.' Or at least she had been until the bomb. It was amazing she had come through it, and who knew what the fallout from that would be, when all was said and done. It was too soon to know. As Stevie looked at her, there were tears rolling down Carole's cheeks. Stevie reached over and touched her hand. 'I'm sorry. I didn't want to tell you all that. He was a lovely man.'

'I'm glad you told me. It's so sad. I lost a husband I must have loved, and whom I don't even remember now. This is like losing everything you ever cared about or owned. I've lost all the people in my life, and the history we had. I don't even remember his face or his name, or my marriage to Jason. I don't even remember when my babies were born.' It felt like a tragedy to her, even more than the actual impact of the bomb. Her doctors had explained all that to her. It sounded so unreal. But so did everything else. Like someone else's life, and not hers.

'You haven't lost anyone except for Sean.

Everyone else is still here. And you had wonderful times with him you'll remember again one day. The others are all here, in one form or another. Your children, Jason, your work. The history is there too, even if you can't remember it yet. The bond you have to them is still there. The people who love you aren't going anywhere.'

'I don't even know who I was to them, who I am . . . or who they were to me,' Carole said miserably, and blew her nose on the tissue the nurse handed her. 'I feel like a ship went down with everything I owned.'

'It didn't go down. It's out there in the fog somewhere. When the fog clears, you'll find all your stuff, and everyone on the ship. Most of it is just baggage anyway. Maybe you're better off.'

'And what about you?' Carole asked, looking at her. 'What am I to you? Am I a good employer? Do I treat you well? Do you like your job? And what kind of life do you have?' She wanted to know who Stevie was as a person, not just in relation to herself. She really cared. Even without her memory, Carole was still the fine woman she had always been, and whom Stevie loved.

'I love my job, and you. Maybe too much. I'd rather work for you than do anything in the world. I love your kids, the work we do together, the causes you speak out for. I like who you are as a human being, which is why I love you so much. You're really a good person, Carole. And a good mom too. Don't let Chloe try to convince you otherwise.' Stevie was upset about that. Chloe had contributed more than her fair share to any problems they had had. She was hard on her mother, and sometimes bitter about the past. Stevie thought she should let it go and that she hadn't been fair to bring it up.

'I'm not so sure Chloe got such a great deal from me,' Carole said quietly, 'but I'm glad you think I'm a good person, it's awful not to know. Not to have any idea who you are, or what you've done to people. For all I know, I'm a total shit, and you're being kind to me. I hate not remembering any of it, or who meant what to me in my life. It's scary to think about.' It truly frightened her. It was like flying in the dark. She had no idea when she might hit a wall, just as she had when the bomb went off. 'What about your own life?' she asked Stevie then. 'Are you married?'

'No. I live with someone,' Stevie said, and paused before she added more.

'Do you love him?' Carole was curious about her. She wanted to know everything, about all of them. She needed to know who they were, and discover who she was.

'Sometimes,' Stevie said honestly. 'Not always. I'm not sure what I feel for him, which is why I've never married him. Besides, I'm married to my job. His name is Alan, he's a journalist. He travels a lot, which works for me. What we have is convenient and comfortable. I'm not sure I'd call it love. And when I think about marrying him, it makes me want to run like hell. I've never thought marriage was such a great thing, particularly if I don't want kids.'

'Why don't you? Do you know?'

'I have you,' Stevie teased, and then grew serious again. 'I think it's always been a missing piece in my chemistry. I've never felt a need to be a mother. I'm happy the way I am. I have a cat, a dog, a job I love, and a guy I sleep with some of the time. Maybe for me, that's enough. I like to keep things simple.'

'Is it enough for him?' Carole was curious about her, and the life she described. It sounded limited to Carole. Stevie was obviously afraid of something, and Carole couldn't figure out what.

'Probably not in the long run. He says he wants kids. But he can't have them with me,' Stevie said simply. 'He's turning forty, and he thinks we should get married. That may do us in. I don't want children. I never did. I made that decision a long time ago. I had a shit childhood myself, and I promised myself I wouldn't do that to someone else. I'm happy being a grown-up, without encumbrances, or someone to bitch at me later on about everything I did wrong. Look at you with Chloe. For what it's worth, I think you've been a great mom to her, and she's pissed off anyway. I never wanted that in my life. I'd rather spend time with my dog. And if I lose Alan because of it, it wasn't meant to be anyway. I told him right from the beginning I didn't want kids, that was fine with him. Now maybe his biological clock is ticking. Mine isn't. I don't have one. I threw mine away years ago. In fact, I was so sure of it, I had my tubes tied when I was in college, and I'm not going to have that undone. I don't want to adopt. I love my life just the way it is.' She sounded absolutely certain of what she was saying, as Carole looked intently at her, trying to sort out what was fear and what was truth. There was a lot of both.

'What happens when something happens to me? I'm older than you are. What if I die? Or when I die, not if. I could have died anytime in the last three weeks. What then? If I'm the most important thing in your life, what happens to you when I go? That's a scary place for you to be in.' It was true, whether Stevie wanted to face it or not.

'It's scary for everyone. What happens when a husband dies? Or a kid? Or your husband leaves you and you wind up alone? We all have to face that sooner or later. Maybe I'll die before you do. Or maybe you'll get mad and fire me one day, if I fuck something up. There are no guarantees in life unless we all jump off a bridge together when we're ninety years old. You take your chances in life. You have to be honest and know what you want. I'm true to myself.

'I was honest with Alan. If he doesn't like that, then he can go. I never lied to him and said I wanted kids. I told him in the beginning that I didn't want to get married and my job meant everything to me. Nothing's changed for me. If he can't live with that, or doesn't like me for it, then he has to go out and find what he wants. It's all any of us can do. Sometimes the pieces only fit for a while.

'That must have happened with you and Jason, or you'd still be married to him. Most things don't last forever. I'm willing to accept that in the scheme of things, and give it my best shot. It's all I can do. And yeah, sometimes Alan plays second fiddle to you, and to my job. Sometimes I play second fiddle to his. It works for me. But maybe not for him. If not, we're history, and it was nice for a while. I'm not looking for Prince Charming or the perfect love story. I just want something practical and real that works for me. For both of us. He's not my prisoner, and I don't want to be his. Marriage feels like that to me.' It was as honest as she'd ever been. Stevie never lied to anyone, and didn't kid herself either. She was practical about everything, her life, her job, her men. It made her solid, real, and nice to be around. Carole could see that. Stevie was totally genuine in every way, and honest to her core.

'Did I feel that way?' Carole asked, looking puzzled again.

'I think you've always been true to yourself too, from what I know. I think you could have taken Jason back, when he came back to you after Paris, and for whatever reason, you didn't. I think you're more willing to compromise than I am, which is why marriage works for you. But I've never known you to sacrifice your values or your principles, or who you are, for anything or anyone. When you believe in something, you see it through till the end. I love that about you. You're willing to stand up for what you believe in, no matter how many times you get knocked down. That's a great trait in a person. Who you are as a human being is what matters most.'

'It's important to me to know I've been a good

mother,' Carole said softly. Even without her memory, Carole knew that it was a big piece of who she was.

'You are,' Stevie said with a reassuring look.

'Maybe. I feel like I have a lot to make up to Chloe for. I'm willing to accept that. Maybe I couldn't see that before.' Now that she was starting over, Carole was willing to take a closer look and do things better this time. It was a great gift to have that opportunity, and she wanted to live up to that gift now. At least Anthony seemed satisfied with what he'd gotten from her, or maybe he was just more polite about it. Maybe boys didn't need as much from their moms. But Chloe obviously did, and at least Carole could try to bridge the gap between them. She was longing to try.

They talked until dark that night, about pieces of her life that Stevie knew and remembered, her children, her two husbands, and Carole asked her if there had been a man in Paris while she lived there. Stevie said vaguely that she thought there was. 'Whatever happened, it didn't end well. You didn't talk about it much. And when we closed the house, you couldn't wait to leave Paris. You looked stricken the whole time we were there. You didn't see anyone, and the minute you finished giving me instructions, you checked out of the hotel and went back to L.A. Whoever he was, I think you were scared of seeing him again. You weren't involved with anyone seriously for the first five years I worked with you, until you fell in love with Sean. I always had the feeling that you'd been badly burned before. I didn't know if it was Jason or someone else, and I didn't know you well enough to ask.' Now Carole wished she had. There was no other way for her to know.

'And now I have no way to find out,' Carole said sadly. 'If there was someone in Paris, he's lost forever in my memory. Maybe it doesn't matter anymore.'

'You were pretty young. You were thirty-five when you came back. And forty when you got involved with Sean. The others I saw you with before him were just window dressing, people you went out with. You were all about your kids, work, and causes then. We spent a year in New

York, while you did a play on Broadway. It was fun.'

'I wish I could remember at least some of it,' Carole said, looking frustrated. She couldn't access any of it yet.

'You will,' Stevie said confidently, and then laughed. 'Believe me, there's plenty I'd love to forget about my life. My childhood, for instance. What a mess that was. Both my parents were alcoholics. My sister got pregnant at fifteen and wound up in a home for wayward girls. She gave the baby away, had two more she gave away, had a nervous breakdown, and wound up in an institution by the time she was twenty-one. She committed suicide at twenty-three. My family was a nightmare. I barely got out alive. I guess that's why marriage and families don't sound so great to me. Just a lot of heartbreak, headaches, and grief.'

'Not always,' Carole said gently. 'I'm sorry. That sounds rough.'

'It was,' Stevie said with a sigh. 'I've spent a fortune in therapy to get over it. I think I have, but I'd rather keep my life simple. I'm happy living vicariously through you. It's pretty thrilling working for you.'

'I can't imagine why. It doesn't sound like it to me. I guess the movie stuff must have been exciting. But divorces, dying husbands, heart-breaks in Paris. That doesn't sound like a lot of fun to me. More like real life.'

'That's true. None of us escape it. Even if you're famous, you still have to put up with the same shit we all do, or maybe more. You handle your fame amazingly well. You're incredibly discreet.'

'That's something at least. Thank God for that. Am I religious?' she asked, curious about that.

'Not very. A little bit around the time Sean was dying and just afterward. Otherwise you don't go to church much. You grew up Catholic, but I think you're spiritual more than formally religious. You live it, you're a good person. You don't have to go to church for that.' She had become the mirror for Carole, to show her who she had been and who she was.

'I think I'd like to go to church when I get out

of the hospital. I have a lot to say thank you for.'

'So do I,' Stevie said, smiling at her. She said goodnight to her then, and went back to the hotel, thinking about all they'd said that day. Carole was exhausted by it, and sound asleep in her room before Stevie got back to the hotel. It took an incredible amount of energy, trying to rebuild a life that had vanished into thin air.

9

On the Saturday after Thanksgiving, the family came to visit Carole briefly, but she was still tired from the day before. Her long conversation with Stevie, asking her a million questions about her life, her history, herself, had left her drained. They could all see that she needed rest, and they only stayed for a short time. She was asleep again before they left the room, and Stevie felt guilty she hadn't cut it short the previous afternoon, but there was so much Carole wanted to know.

Chloe and Anthony planned to go to Deauville on Sunday for the day, and convinced

Stevie to go with them. It sounded like fun to her, and Jason had mentioned to her that he wanted some time alone with Carole. She was feeling better again after resting the day before. And she was happy to have Jason to herself. There was much she wanted to know from him too, so many details of the life they had once shared.

He arrived in her room, kissed her cheek, and sat down. They talked about their children at first, and what good people they were. He said Chloe seemed excited about her first job. And that Anthony was working hard for him in New York, which was hardly surprising.

'He's always been a terrific kid,' Jason said proudly. 'Responsible, kind. He was a great student. He played varsity basketball in college. He sailed right through adolescence. He was always crazy about you.' Jason smiled tenderly at her. 'He thinks you walk on water. He used to go to every one of your movies about three or four times. He went to one of them ten times, and took all his friends. We showed your latest picture at his birthday party every year. That's what he wanted. I don't think he's ever had a minute of resentment in his life. He just takes things as they come, and if something bad happens, he makes the best of it. It's a fantastic trait to have. He's got a great attitude about life and always comes out on top. In a funny way, I think your being busy was good for him. It made him resourceful, and very independent. I can't say the same for Chloe. I think your career was hard for her when she was little. Chloe is always hungry, and wants more than she's got. For Chloe, the glass is never even half full. For Anthony, it's overflowing. It's funny how different children of the same parents can be.'

'Was I gone most of the time?' Carole asked, looking worried.

'No. But you were gone a lot. You took Chloe with you on location many times. More than I thought you should. You would pull her out of school and take a tutor. But even that didn't help. Chloe is just very needy. She always was.'

'Maybe she has a right to be,' Carole said fairly. 'I don't see how I could make all those movies, and still be a good mother.' The thought of that appeared to genuinely upset her. Jason tried to reassure her.

'You managed. Pretty damn well, in fact. I think you're a terrific mother, not just a good one.'

'Not if my daughter, our daughter,' she corrected with a smile, 'is unhappy.'

'She's not unhappy. She just needs a lot of attention. Meeting her needs is a full-time project, if you let it. No one can stop everything they're doing and focus all their attention on a child. When we were married, I'd have wanted some of that myself. Yes, you were busy when they were small, but you paid a lot of attention to both of them, especially between films. There were a couple of rough years, right around the time you won your Oscars, when you were making movies back to back. But even then you took them with you. You made an epic in France, and had them with you the whole time. Carole, if you'd been a doctor or a lawyer, it would have been worse. I know women who have normal jobs, some of them on Wall Street for instance, who never spend time with their kids. You always did. I think Chloe just wanted a full-time mom, who never worked, stayed home baking cookies with her on weekends, and did nothing else but drive car pool. And how boring would that be?'

'Maybe not so boring,' Carole said sadly, 'if it was what she needed. Why didn't I give up acting when we got married?' It sounded sensible to her now, but Jason laughed and shook his head.

'I don't think you understand yet how big a star you are. Your career was skyrocketing when I met you, and it just got hotter. You're way up there, Carole. It would have been a shame for you to give up a career like that. It's an incredible accomplishment to achieve what you have, and you even manage to support causes that are important to you, and the world, and put your name to good use. And you still managed to be a good mother. I think that's why Anthony is so proud of you. We all are. I think Chloe would have felt she got short shrift no matter what. It's just the way she is. Maybe it's how she gets what she wants, or needs. Believe me, neither of your children was ever neglected or unloved. Far from it.'

'I just wish Chloe felt better about it. She looks so sad when she talks about her childhood.' It made Carole feel guilty even though she didn't know what she'd done, or hadn't.

'She goes to a therapist,' he said quietly. 'She has for the past year. She'll get over all that. Maybe this accident will finally make her realize how lucky she is to have you. You're a four-star mother.' And even now, with no memory, she was worried about her children, and grateful for his reassurance. As she listened to him, she was wondering if Chloe would like it if she went to London for a few weeks, once she was better. It might show her that her mother truly cared about her, and wanted to spend time with her.

She couldn't recapture the past or rewrite history, but she could at least try to do things better in the future. It was clear that Chloe felt she had been cheated as a child. And maybe this was Carole's chance to make it up to her, and give her what she felt she'd never had. She was willing to do that. She had nothing more important on her agenda. The book she'd been trying to write, if she could ever get back to it, could wait. Her priorities were different, since the bomb. It had been one hell of a wake-up call, and a last chance to do things right. She wanted to seize that opportunity while there was still time.

They talked about a variety of subjects for a while, and then she looked at him quietly as he sat in the chair where Stevie had sat the day before, telling her about her life. She wanted to know his part too.

'What happened to us?' Carole asked, looking sad. Their story obviously hadn't had a happy ending, if they got divorced.

'Wow . . . that's a big question . . .' He wasn't sure she was ready to hear it all, but she said she was. She needed to know who they had been, what had happened to them, and why they had gotten divorced, as well as what had happened since. She knew about Sean now, from Stevie, but she knew very little about her life with Jason, except that they had been married for ten years, lived in New York, and had two kids. The rest was a mystery to her. Stevie knew none of the details, and Carole wouldn't have dared to ask her kids, who were probably too young at the time to know what had happened anyway.

'I'm not sure, to be honest with you,' he answered finally. 'I tried to figure it out for years. I guess the easiest answer is that I had a midlife crisis, and you had a major career. Both of those elements collided and blew us up. But it was more complicated than that. It was great at the beginning. You were already a star when I married you. You were twenty-two and I was thirty-one. I'd been lucky on Wall Street for about five years by then, and I wanted to back a movie. There was no great financial benefit to it, it just sounded like fun. I was a kid myself, and I wanted to meet pretty girls. Nothing much deeper to it than that. I met Mike Appelsohn at a meeting in New York, he was a big producer then, and had been acting as your agent since he discovered you. He still does.' He filled her in. 'He invited me to L.A., he was putting together a deal. So I went, put my name on the dotted line to finance a film, and I met you.

'You were the most beautiful girl I'd ever seen in my life, and on top of it, you were nice. You were sweet and young and innocent. And still very southern then. You had been in Hollywood for four years, and you were still this adorable, innocent kid, and already a big star. It was like all that stardom and fame hadn't touched you. You were the same decent, warm, honest person you must have been growing up on your dad's farm in Mississippi. You still had a southern accent then. I loved that too. And then Mike had you get rid of it. I always missed it. It was part of the sweetness I loved about you. You really were just a kid. I fell head over heels in love with you, and so did you, with me.

'I flew out a dozen times while you were making the movie, just to see you. We wound up all over the tabloids and the trades. Wall Street Whiz Kid Courts Hollywood's Hottest Star. You were the real deal. You were about as glamorous as it gets.' He smiled at her then. 'You still are,' he said generously. 'I just wasn't used to it then. I don't think I ever got used to it. I used to wake up in the morning and pinch myself, unable to believe I was married to Carole Barber. How much better could it get?

'We got married six months after we met, when you finished the film. At first you said you were too young to get married, and you probably were. I talked you into it, and you were honest. You said you weren't ready to give up your career. You wanted to make movies. You were having a ball, and so was I being with you. I've never had so much fun in my life as we did then.

'Mike flew us to Vegas one weekend in his plane, and we got married. He was our witness, along with some girlfriend of yours at the time. She was your roommate, and I can't for the life of me remember her name. She was the bridesmaid. And you were the most gorgeous bride I've ever seen. You borrowed a dress from Wardrobe from some 1930s movie. You looked like a queen.

'We went to Mexico for our honeymoon. We spent two weeks in Acapulco, and then you went back to work. You were doing about three movies a year then. That's a hell of a lot. The studios had you cranking them out one after the other, with big stars, big names, major producers, and turning down scripts as fast as they came in.

You were an industry unto yourself. I've never seen anything like it. You were the hottest star in the world, and I was married to you. We were in the press constantly. That's heady stuff for two young kids, and I guess it gets old eventually. But it didn't for you. You loved every minute, and who could blame you? You were the darling of the world, the most desirable woman on the planet . . . and belonged to me.

'You were on location most of the time, and between pictures, we lived in New York together. We got a great apartment on Park Avenue. And whenever I could, I'd fly out to see you on location. We actually saw a lot of each other. We talked about having babies, but there was no time. There was always another film to do. And then Anthony came along. He was kind of a surprise, and we'd been married for two years by then. You took about six months off, as soon as it started to show, and went back to work when he was three weeks old. You were doing a movie in England, you took him with you, with a nanny. You were over there for five months, and I came over every couple of weeks. It was a crazy way to live, but your career was too hot to put a damper on, and you were too young to want to quit. I totally understood. You actually took a few months off when you were pregnant with Chloe. Anthony was three years old. You took him to the park, like all the other moms. I loved it. Being married to you was like playing house, with a movie star. The most beautiful woman in the world was mine.' He still had stars in his eyes when he said it, as Carole watched him from her bed, wondering why she hadn't slowed down. He didn't seem to question that as much as she did. Her career didn't seem as important now, to her anyway. But it had been then. He made that clear.

'Anyway, a year after Chloe was born, when Anthony was five, you got pregnant again. A real accident this time, and we were both upset. I was building my business and working like crazy, you were working like a dog on movie sets all over the world. Anthony and Chloe seemed enough then, but we went ahead with it. But you lost the baby. You were devastated, and I actually was too. I'd gotten used to the idea by then of a third child.

You'd been on a set in Africa doing your own stunt work, which seemed crazy, and had a miscarriage. They made you go back to work four weeks later. You had a miserable contract, and two pictures backed up behind it. It was a constant merry-go-round. Two years later you won your first Oscar, and the pressure only got worse. I think something happened then, not to you, but to me.

'You were still young. You were thirty when you got the Oscar. I was turning forty, and I never admitted it to myself then, but I think I was pissed off having a wife who was more successful than I was. You were making a god-damn fortune, everyone in the world knew you. And I think I was tired of dealing with the press, the gossip, everyone looking at you every time we walked into a room. It was never about me, always about you. That gets old, or it's hard on a guy's ego. Maybe I wanted to be a star too, what do I know? I just wanted a normal life, a wife, two kids, a house in Connecticut, maybe Maine in the summer. Instead I was flying all over the world to see you, you either had our kids with you, or I had them, and you were miserable without them. We started fighting a lot. I wanted you to quit, but I didn't have the balls to tell you, so I took it out on you. I hardly saw you, and when we did, we were fighting. And then you won another Oscar two years later, and I think that did it. That was the end. I felt hopeless after that. I knew you were never going to quit, not for a long time anyway. You signed on to do a picture for eight months in Paris, and I was pissed out of my mind. I should have told you, but I didn't. I don't think you knew what was going on with me. You were too busy to think about it, and I never told you how upset I was. You were making movies, trying to keep our kids with you on the set, and flying around to see me whenever you had a couple of days off to do it. Your heart was in the right place. There just weren't enough days in the year to do everything you wanted to do, your career, our kids, and me. Maybe you'd have quit then if I'd asked you. Who knows? But I didn't ask.' He looked at her then with regret for not having asked her to quit. It had taken Jason years to acquire the insights he had now, and he was sharing them all with Carole.

He went on with a somber look as Carole watched him, intent and silent. She didn't want to interrupt him. 'I started drinking and going to parties then, and I'll admit, I got out of line at times. I wound up in the tabloids more than once, and you never complained about it. You asked me what was going on a couple of times, and I said I was just playing, which was true. You tried to come home more often, but once you started the movie in Paris, you were stuck there, you were shooting six days a week. Anthony was eight, so you put him in school there, Chloe was four, she was in kindergarten part-time and the rest of the time you had her on the set with you, with the nanny. And I started acting like a bachelor at home. Like a fool actually.' He looked genuinely embarrassed as he looked at his ex-wife and she smiled at him.

'It sounds like we were both young and foolish,' she said generously. 'It must have been miserable being married to someone who was gone most of the time, and worked so much.'

He nodded, grateful for what she said. 'It was hard. The more I think about it, the more I know I should have asked you to quit, or at least slow down. But with two Oscars under your belt, you were zooming. I didn't feel I had the right to screw up your career, so I screwed up our marriage instead, and just so you know, I'll always regret it. I've never told you that before, but it's how I feel.'

Carole was listening quietly and nodded. She appreciated his honesty. She remembered none of it, but she was grateful for his honesty, even about himself. He seemed like a genuinely kind man. It was fascinating as their story unfolded. As always now, it sounded like someone else's life and sparked no visual memory in her head. As she listened she kept wondering why she herself hadn't had the brains to quit and save their marriage, but listening to it was like hearing about an avalanche that couldn't have been stopped. The early warning signs had been there, but apparently her career had been too powerful then. It was a force unto itself, with a life of its own. She could see now how their problems had

231

happened, and so could he. It was a shame they hadn't done something about it then, but neither of them had. She had been oblivious, wrapped up in the excitement of her career, and he had been resentful and concealed it from her, eaten up inside, and eventually took it out on her. It had taken years for him to acknowledge that, even to himself. It was classic, and tragic to hear it. She was sorry that she hadn't been wiser then. But she'd been young, if that was an adequate excuse.

'You left for Paris with the kids. You landed a great role playing Marie Antoinette. It was one of those major epics. And a week after you left, I went to a party, given by Hugh Hefner. I've never seen such beautiful girls in my life, almost as beautiful as you.' He smiled ruefully at her, and she smiled back. It was sad to listen to. The end was predictable. No surprises here. She knew how the movie had turned out, and they didn't live happily ever after, or he wouldn't be telling her this story.

'They weren't women like you. You were always decent, kind, and sincere, and good to me. You worked constantly, and you were gone a lot, but you were a good woman, Carole. You always have been. These girls were a different breed. Cheap gold-diggers, pros some of them, wannabe starlets, models, tramps. I was married to the real thing. These girls were showy fakes, and they worked the crowd like magic. I met a Russian supermodel named Natalya. She was making a big splash in New York then. Everyone knew her. She had come out of nowhere, from Moscow, via Paris, and she was after the big bucks, in every way. Mine and everyone else's. I think she'd been the mistress of some playboy in Paris, I forget now. In any case, she's had plenty of guys like that since then. She's currently married to her fourth husband, in Hong Kong. I think he's Brazilian, and an arms dealer or something, but he has a shitload of money. He pretends to be a banker, but I think he's in much rougher trade than that. Anyway, she blew my socks off. To be honest, I drank too much, did a little coke someone handed me, and wound up in bed with her. We weren't at Hefner's place by then. We were on someone's yacht in the

Hudson River. It was a racy crowd. I was forty-one, she was twenty-one. You were thirty-two, and working in Paris, trying to be a good mom, even if you were an absentee wife. I don't think you ever cheated on me. I don't think it crossed your mind, and you didn't have time. You had a lily-white reputation in Hollywood, but I can't say the same for me.

'I wound up all over the tabloids with her. I think she saw to that. We had a torrid affair, which you politely ignored, which was gracious beyond belief. And she got pregnant two weeks after I met her. She refused to have an abortion, and wanted to get married. She told me she loved me, and wanted to give up everything for me, her career, modeling, her country, her life, and stay home and raise our kids. Music to my ears. I was ready for a full-time wife by then, and you weren't ready to do that, or likely to, from what I could see. Who knew? I never asked you. I just lost my mind over her.

'She was having my baby. I wanted more kids, and having Chloe had been too hard on you. Besides, given your schedule, it would have been crazy for us to have more kids. It was hard enough dragging two kids all over the world, even I couldn't see you doing it with three or four, and Anthony was getting older. And I wanted my kids at home with me. Don't ask me how, but she convinced me that marriage was the best solution, for her. We were going to be a cozy little couple with a bunch of babies. I bought a house in Greenwich, and called a lawyer. I think I lost my mind. Classic midlife crisis. Wall Street financier goes nuts, and destroys his life, and fucks over his wife. I flew to Paris and told you I was divorcing you. I never saw anyone cry like that in my life. For about five minutes, I wondered what I was doing. I spent the night with you, and almost came to my senses. Our kids were adorable and I didn't want to make them or you unhappy. And then she called me. She was like a witch, weaving a spell, and it worked.

'I went back to New York, and filed the divorce. You asked for nothing except child support. You were making plenty of money on your own, and you had too much pride to take anything from me. I told you Natalya was pregnant, and I think it damn near killed you. I was the cruelest sonofabitch I've ever known. I think I was getting even for every minute of your success, or every second you didn't spend with me. Six months later I was married to her, and you were still in Paris. You wouldn't speak to me, understandably. I came over a couple of times to see the kids, and you had them delivered to me at the Ritz by the nanny. It was total blackout from you. In fact, you didn't speak to me directly for two years, only through lawyers, secretaries, and nannies. You had a lot of all three. The bad joke was that two and a half years later, when you moved to L.A., you slowed down your career to a dull roar. You were still making movies, but fewer, and spending time with the kids. I could have lived with that, a lot better than your earlier pace. I never knew you'd do that. But I didn't have the balls to wait it out or ask you.

'Natalya had the baby two days after I married her, and another one a year later. She gave up her modeling career for those two years, and then told me she was bored to death. She left me and went back to modeling. She left the kids with me for a while, and then took them. She met some fabulously rich playboy, divorced me, and married him, and took me to the cleaners in the process. Don't ask me why, but I didn't bother to get a prenup. So she cashed in her chips and moved on. I didn't even see those kids for five years. She wouldn't let me. They were out of our jurisdiction, and she was floating all over Europe and South America, collecting husbands. It was basically high-end prostitution, and she's terrific at it. And meanwhile, I had destroyed you and our marriage.

'When you moved back to L.A., I kind of waited for the dust to settle, and eventually I came out to see you, allegedly to see the kids, but I came to see you. You had calmed down, and I told you what had happened. I was honest with you, and told you the truth as I saw it. I don't think I had the insight then that I have now, that I was jealous of your career and your stardom. I asked you to give it a shot with me again. I said it was for the kids' sake, but it was for mine. I still loved you. I still do,' he said simply. 'I always have.

'I went totally nuts with that Russian girl. But you no longer wanted me when I asked you. I don't blame you. It doesn't get much worse than that. You were polite, gracious, and you very nicely told me to get fucked, in so many words. You said it was over for you, and I had destroyed all the feelings you'd had for me, that you had truly loved me, and you were sorry that your career had upset me so much, and you were gone so often. You said you would have slowed down if I asked you, although I'm not entirely sure that's true, in the early years anyway. You had a good head of steam up, and it would have been hard to let that go, at that point.

'So I went back to New York, and you stayed in L.A. Eventually, we got to be friends. The kids grew up. And we did too. You married Sean about four years after I came out to see you, and I was happy for you. He really was a good guy, and great to our kids. I was sad for you when he died. You deserved a man like that, a really good one, not a shit like I'd been to you. And then he died. I felt awful for you. And now here we are, we're friends. I'll be turning sixty next year. I've been smart enough never to marry again since Natalya. She lives in Hong Kong, and I see the girls twice a year. They treat me like a stranger, which I am. She's still beautiful, after a lot of surgery. Shit, she's only thirty-nine years old. The girls are seventeen and eighteen and very exotic looking. The child support I still pay for them could finance a small nation, but they have a pretty racy lifestyle. They're both modeling now. And Chloe and Anthony have never met them, which is probably just as well.

'So here we are. I'm sort of part brother, part friend, an ex-husband who still loves you, and I think you have a good life on your own. I've never had the feeling you regretted not coming back to me and giving me another chance, particularly once you met Sean. You don't need me, Carole. You have your own money, which I invested pretty well for you a long time ago, and you still ask me for advice now. We love each other in an odd way. I'll always be there for you, if you need me. And I suspect you'd do the same for me. It'll never be more than that now, but I have some incredible memories with you. I'll never forget them. I'm sad for you that you don't have that now, because we had some wonderful times. I hope you'll remember them again one day. I cherish every moment we spent together, and I'll never stop regretting the pain I put you through. I paid in spades for it, which I deserved.'

He had made a full confession to her, and listening to him, Carole was deeply touched. 'I hope you forgive me one day. I think you already had. Long ago. There's no bitterness in our friendship now, no sharp edges. It all wore smooth over time, in part because of who you are. You have an enormous heart, you were a good wife to me, and you're a terrific mother to our kids. I'm grateful to you for that.' He fell silent then, and watched her, as she looked at him with deep compassion.

'You've been through a lot,' she said kindly. 'Thank you for sharing all that with me. I'm sorry I wasn't smart enough to be the wife you needed me to be. We do such stupid things in our youth.' She felt very old after listening to him. The story had taken two hours to tell. She was tired, but she had a lot to think about. Nothing he had said had jarred her memory, but she had the strong impression he had tried to be fair, to both of them. The only one who had been lambasted in the tale was the Russian super-model, but it sounded as though she deserved it. He had picked himself a major lemon, and he knew it. She was a dangerous young woman. Carole never had been, and had always tried to be loving and honest with him. He had made that clear to her. She had little to reproach herself for except working too hard and being away too often.

'I'm grateful you're still alive, Carole,' he said gently to her before he left, and she could tell he meant it. 'It would have broken my heart, and our kids', if that bomb had killed you. I hope you get your memory back. But even if you don't, we all love you.'

'I know,' she said softly. She'd had proof of that from all of them, even him, though they were no longer married. 'I love you too,' she said softly. He bent to kiss her cheek and then was gone.

He added something to her life, not just memories and information about the past, but a tender friendship that had a flavor all its own.

10

After the Thanksgiving weekend, Jason and Anthony announced that they needed to go back to New York. And Chloe felt she had to get back to her job. Jake had also called her several times. There was nothing anyone could do for Carole, and they all knew she was out of danger. The rest of her recovery process was liable to be slow, and was a matter of time.

The children were coming to Los Angeles for Christmas, and she was expected to be out of the hospital and able to fly home by then, in another month. Carole invited Jason to join them for the holidays, and he accepted gratefully. It was an odd arrangement, but they felt like a family again, in some form. He was taking the kids to St. Bart's over New Year's after all, and invited her to come along, but she couldn't travel after she got back to L.A. The doctors didn't recommend it. She was still too fragile, and it was confusing for her. She wasn't walking yet, and with no memory, everything she did was harder work. She wanted to stay home once she got there. But she didn't want to deprive her children of the trip with their father. They had all been through so much since Carole's accident. She knew the vacation would be good for them.

Jason spent an hour alone with Carole on his last night in Paris, and said he knew it was too soon to talk about it, but he wondered if, once she recovered, she would be open to trying things with him again. She hesitated, still remembering none of their history, and she knew she had feelings of deep affection for him. She was grateful for the time he had just spent in Paris, and could see the good man he was. But she felt nothing more for him, and doubted that she would in time. She didn't want to lead him on, or encourage him to hope for something she couldn't give him. She had to concentrate on getting well now, becoming whole again, and she wanted to spend time with her children. She was in no condition to think about a man. And it sounded like their history was too complicated. They had come to a good place before her accident, and she didn't want to spoil or risk that again.

There were tears in her eyes when she answered him. 'I'm not even sure I know why yet, but I have the feeling that we'd both be smarter to leave things as they are. I don't know much about my life yet, but I know I love you. And I'm sure it was devastating when we broke up. But something has kept us apart since then, even if I don't remember what. I married someone else, and everyone tells me I was happy with him. You must have had other people in your life too, I'm sure we both did. And I can feel the strength we share, and the power of loving you and being loved by you as a friend. We have our children to bind us together forever. I wouldn't want to mess any of that up, or hurt you.

245

'I must have fallen short somehow, or disappointed you, for you to go off with someone else. I treasure the love we have now, as parents of the same children and as friends. I don't want to lose that for anything in the world, or do anything to jeopardize it. Something tells me that trying to revive our marriage would be very high-risk, and maybe disastrous for both of us. If it's okay with you' – she smiled tenderly at him – 'I'd like to keep things like this. It seems like we have a winning formula now, without adding anything to it. If I manage not to get blown to bits again, I'll be here for you forever. I hope that's enough for you, Jason. To me, what we have seems like an incredible gift. I don't want to screw that up.' She just didn't have romantic feelings for him, no matter how handsome and kind he was, or how much in love with her. She didn't feel that for him in the present tense, although she was sure she had years before. But no longer. She was certain of it.

'I was afraid you'd say something like that,' he said sadly. 'And maybe you're right. I asked you the same question after Natalya and I got divorced, once you moved back to L.A. You gave me pretty much the same answer, although I think you were still angry at me then. You had every right to be. I was a sonofabitch when I left you, and I deserved everything I got, in spades. The follies of youth . . . or in my case, middle age. I don't have any right to what I just asked you, I just had to give it another shot. And I'll be here for you too, forever. You can count on me, Carole. I hope you know that.'

'I just did,' she said, with tears brimming in her eyes. He had been incredible ever since her accident. 'I love you, Jason, in the very, very best way.'

'Me too,' he said, and they kissed chastely across her bed. In the end, keeping things the way they were felt right to her. And even to him. He had seen a flicker of hope for an instant, or wished he did, and wanted to ask her. If there was a chance, he didn't want to miss it. And if not, he loved her anyway. He always had. He was sad to be leaving Paris. Despite the circumstances, he had enjoyed spending time with her. And he knew he would miss her again when he left. But they'd be spending Christmas together at least, in L.A. with their kids.

Stevie was planning to stay in Paris with Carole until she flew back to L.A., no matter how long it took. She had spoken to Alan several times, and he was understanding about her staying in Paris. For once, it made sense to him that she was there with Carole. He was supportive of the stress she was going through, and didn't complain. Stevie loved him for it. There were times when Alan really was a good guy, no matter how different their needs and goals were, or their views about marriage.

Anthony came to see his mother at the hospital before he left for New York, spent an hour with her, and told her, as Jason had, how grateful he was that she'd survived. Chloe had said the same thing to her, when she came to say goodbye to her mother an hour before, on her way to the airport. They were all so deeply relieved that she was alive.

'Try to stay out of trouble, at least for a little while, until I get home. No more crazy trips like this on your own. At least take Stevie with you next time.' Anthony wasn't sure it would have changed anything, if she'd been in the wrong place at the wrong time. But the thought that he had almost lost his mother in a bomb blast in Paris still made him shudder. 'Thanks for inviting Dad to spend Christmas with us. That was nice of you.' He knew that otherwise his father would have been alone. There hadn't been an important woman in his life for quite some time. And it was the first holiday the four of them would be spending together in eighteen years. The last one they had shared as a foursome was a dim memory for him, and he wasn't sure it would happen again after this year, so it meant a lot to him, and to his father as well.

'I'll behave,' Carole promised, looking proudly at her son. Even though she no longer remembered the details of his childhood, it was easy to see he was a fine young man, just as his father had said. And his love for his mother shone brightly in his eyes, as did hers for him.

They both cried when they hugged for the last time, even though she knew she'd be seeing him again soon. She cried easily now, and everything seemed more emotional to her. She had so much to learn and absorb. It was truly like being reborn.

As Anthony was about to leave her room, after they hugged, a man walked in. It was the tall, erect Frenchman who had visited her before and brought her flowers. She could never remember his name, and what remained of her French eluded her completely. She could understand what the doctors and nurses said around her, but she couldn't answer them in French. It was hard enough speaking English again, and remembering all her words. She was speaking well now, but speaking French was still beyond her.

Anthony seemed to freeze where he stood, and the Frenchman looked at Anthony with a small smile and a nod. She could see that her son recognized him, as Anthony's whole body appeared to stiffen and the look in his eyes was one of ice. Clearly, he was not happy to see this man. The Frenchman had said he was a friend of the family and knew her children, so she wasn't surprised that they recognized each other. But she was upset to see that Anthony looked shocked.

'Hello, Anthony,' Matthieu said quietly. 'It's been a long time.'

'What are you doing here?' Anthony said unpleasantly. He hadn't seen him since he was a child. He glanced at his mother protectively, as Carole watched them, trying to understand.

'I came to see your mother. I've been here several times.' There was a distinct chill between the two men, and Carole had no idea why.

'Does she remember you?' Anthony asked coldly.

'No, she doesn't,' Matthieu answered for her. But Anthony remembered him only too well, and how much he had made his mother cry. He had forgotten it until now. He hadn't seen him in fifteen years, but he remembered as if it had been yesterday how devastated she had been when she told him and Chloe they were leaving Paris. She had cried as though her heart would break, and he had never forgotten it.

Anthony had liked Matthieu before that, a lot in fact. He had played soccer with him, but he hated him when he watched his mother cry, and she told him why. It was Matthieu who had made her cry. And he remembered now that there had been tears before that. For many months. He had been happy to go back to the States, but not to see his mother so distraught when they left. As he recalled, she had been sad for a long time, even once they were back in L.A. He knew she had sold the house eventually and said they were never going back. It didn't matter to Anthony by then, although he had made good friends there. But he knew it mattered to his mother, and if she had had her memory, it might matter to her even now. It worried Anthony considerably to see Matthieu in her room.

Matthieu had an air about him that said he had the right to do anything he wanted. He hesitated at nothing, expected people to listen to him, and do as he wished. Anthony remembered not liking that about him when he was a child. Matthieu had sent him to his room once for being rude to his mother, and Anthony had shouted at her that he wasn't his dad. Matthieu had apologized to him later, but Anthony could still sense his air of authority as he stood in the room, as though he belonged there. He didn't, and it was obvious to her son that Carole still had no idea who he was.

'I'll only stay a few minutes,' Matthieu said politely, as Anthony came to hug his mother again and looked fiercely protective of her. He wanted Matthieu out of her room, and life, forever.

'I'll see you soon, Mom,' he promised. 'Take care. I'll call you from New York.' He said the last words glancing at Matthieu, and hated to leave him in the room with her. There wasn't much he could do to her, she didn't remember him, and there was a nurse with her at all times. But Anthony didn't like it anyway. He had left her life years before, after causing her immense pain. There was no reason for him to come back, at least in her son's eyes. And she was so vulnerable now. It tore at her son's heart.

Carole looked at Matthieu, after her son left the room, with a question in her eyes. 'He remembered you,' she said, watching him. There was no mistaking the fact that her son disliked this man. 'Why doesn't he like you?' She had to rely on others to supply the things she should have known herself, and more important, she had to rely on them to tell the truth, as Jason had. She admired him for that, and knew it had been hard. Matthieu looked far more guarded and less inclined to expose himself to her. She had the feeling that he was being cautious when he came to visit her. She had also seen the nurses react. It was obvious they knew this man, and more than ever, she wondered who he was. She wanted to ask Anthony about him when he called.

'He was a little boy when I last saw him,' Matthieu said with a sigh as he sat down. 'He saw the world with a child's eyes then. He was always very protective of you. He was a wonderful boy.' She knew that much herself. 'I made you unhappy, Carole.' There was no point denying it to her. The boy would tell her, although he didn't know the whole story. Only he and Carole did, and he was not yet ready to tell her. He didn't want to love her again, and was afraid he would. 'Our lives were very complicated. We met while you were making a movie in Paris, right after your husband left you. And we fell in love.' He said it with eyes filled with longing and regret. He loved her still. She could see it in his eyes. It was different from what she saw in Jason's eyes. The Frenchman was more intense, and grim in some ways. He almost frightened her, but not quite. Jason had a warmth and gentleness Matthieu didn't. He affected her strangely. She couldn't decide if she was afraid of him, trusted him, or even liked him. There was an air of mystery to him, and smoldering passion. Whatever had existed between them years before, the embers had not yet gone out for him, and it stirred something in her as well. She couldn't remember him. But she felt something for him and couldn't identify what it was, if it was fear, or love. She still had no idea who he was, and unlike the nurses, she did not recognize his name. He was just a man who said that they had been in love. And like the others, she remembered him not at all. She had no sense of who he was, neither good nor bad. All she had were the unidentifiable feelings he aroused in her, which made her feel uncomfortable, but she had no idea why. None at all. Everything she had ever known or felt for him was beyond her reach.

'What happened after we fell in love?' Carole asked him as Stevie walked into the room, and seemed surprised to see him. Carole introduced them, and then with a questioning look Stevie walked out again, to wait in the hall. She told Carole she'd be nearby. It was comforting to Carole to know that she was. Although she knew he couldn't hurt her, she felt almost naked being alone in the room with him. His eyes never lost their grip on hers.

'Many things happened. You were the love of my life. I want to talk to you about it, but not now.'

'Why not?' His secretiveness worried her. He was holding back, which seemed ominous to her.

'Because there is too much to tell in a short time. I was hoping that you'd remember once you were conscious again, but I can see that you don't. I'd like to come another day, and talk to you about it.' And then he startled her by what he said next. 'We lived together for two years.'

'We did?' She was stunned. 'Were we married?' He smiled and shook his head. She was finding husbands everywhere. Jason. Sean. Now this man, who said he had lived with her. Not just an admirer, but a man she had obviously been committed to. No one had told her about him. Perhaps they didn't know. But clearly, Anthony did, and his reaction was not good, which said a lot to her. This had not been a happy story, and since they were not together, obviously had not ended well.

'No, we were not. I wanted to marry you, and you wanted to marry me. We couldn't. I had family complications, and a difficult job. It wasn't the right time.' Timing was everything. It had been the case with Jason too. It was all Matthieu wanted to say for now. He stood up then, and promised to come back. She wasn't sure she wanted him to. Perhaps this was a story she would rather not know. The room seemed filled with sadness and regret as he spoke, and then he smiled. He had eyes that dug down deep into her, and she remembered something about him, but she had no idea what. She didn't want him to come back, but didn't have the courage to say it. If he did, she was going to keep Stevie with her, to protect her. She felt as though she needed someone to shield her from him. He frightened her. There was something incredibly powerful about him.

He stooped to kiss her hand as she watched. He was formal in his manner, very proper, and yet at the same time very bold. He was in the room of a woman who didn't remember him, and yet he told her that they had loved each other, lived together, and wanted to get married. And when he watched her, she could sense the desire he still felt for her.

Stevie came back into the room as soon as he left.

'Who is that man?' she asked, looking uncomfortable, and Carole said she didn't know. 'Maybe he's the mysterious Frenchman who broke your heart that you never talked to me about,' Stevie said with interest, and Carole laughed.

'God, they're really coming out of the woodwork, aren't they? Husbands, boyfriends, French mystery men. He said we lived together and wanted to get married, and I don't remember him any better than anyone else. Maybe in this case, it's nice having a clean slate. He seems a little odd to me.'

'He's just French. They're all a little strange,' Stevie said unkindly, 'and so damn intense. That's not my style.'

'I don't think it's mine either. But maybe it was then.'

'Maybe that's who you lived in the little house with, the one you sold when I first came to work.'

'Maybe so. Anthony looked furious to see him. And he admitted he made me very unhappy,' Carole said with a pensive look.

'At least he's honest about that.'

'I wish I remembered some of it,' Carole said, looking ill at ease.

'Has any of it come back?'

'No. Absolutely nothing. The stories are fascinating, but it's like listening to someone else's life. From what I can gather, I worked way too hard and was never at home with my husband. I lost him to a twenty-one-year-old supermodel who dumped him after he dumped me. Apparently, right after that, I fell in love with this

Frenchman, who made me miserable and whom my son hated. And then I married a lovely man who died way too young, and now here I am.' There was a spark of humor in her eyes as she said it, and Stevie smiled.

'Sounds like an interesting life. I wonder if there was anyone else?' She sounded almost hopeful, and Carole looked horrified.

'I hope not! This is already way too much for me. I'm worn out thinking about these three. And my kids.' She was still worried about Chloe and what she felt her daughter hadn't gotten and still needed from her. That was her first priority for now. Jason was no longer an issue although she loved him, Sean was gone, and whoever the Frenchman was, she had no interest in him, other than curiosity about what he'd meant to her. But she somehow suspected she was better off not knowing. It didn't sound good to her. She didn't want painful memories to add to the rest. The story Jason had told her of their life was enough. She could well imagine that she had been devastated at the time. And then the Frenchman had made her unhappy too. It must have been an awful time in her life, it was easy to figure that much out. Thank God for Sean. The reviews on him seemed to be unanimously good. And she'd lost him too. It didn't sound to her as though she'd been lucky with the men in her life, only her kids.

Stevie got her out of bed then, with the help of the nurse. They wanted her to practice walking.

She was amazed at how hard it was. It was as though her legs had forgotten how to do their job. She felt like a toddler as she stumbled and fell, and had to learn how to pick herself up. And then finally her motor memory seemed to kick in and she walked unsteadily down the halls with Stevie and a nurse on either side. Learning to walk again was hard work too. It all was. She was exhausted every day by nightfall and asleep before Stevie left the room.

Anthony did as he had promised and called her from New York as soon as he arrived. He was still furious about Matthieu.

'He has no business visiting you, Mom. He broke your heart. That's why we left France.'

'What did he do?' Carole asked, but Anthony's memories were those of a child.

'He was mean to you and made you cry.' It sounded so simple, she smiled.

'He can't hurt me now,' she reassured her son.

'I'll kill him if he does.' He no longer remembered the details himself, but the residual feelings were still strong. 'Tell him to get lost.'

'I promise, if he's mean to me, I'll have him thrown out.' But she wanted to know more.

Two days after Jason and Anthony left, Mike Appelsohn said he was coming to Paris to see her. He had been calling every day and talking to Stevie. She told him Carole was strong enough to see him, although she was coming back to L.A. in a few weeks and he could see her there. He said he didn't want to wait, and took a plane from L.A. He was in Paris the next day, after weeks of being worried sick about her. She was like a daughter to him and had been since they met, when she was eighteen.

Mike Appelsohn was a handsome, portly man with lively eyes and a booming laugh. He had a great sense of humor, and had been producing movies for fifty years. He had found Carole in New Orleans thirty-two years before, and convinced her to come to Hollywood for a screen test. The rest was Hollywood history. The screen test had been perfect, and she shot to stardom like a rocket, thanks to him. He got her into her first movies and watched over her like a mother hen. He had been there when she met Jason, and introduced them, although he hadn't realized the impact it would have. And he was the godfather of her first child. Her children loved him and thought of him as a grandfather. And he had acted as her agent since he launched her career. She had discussed every movie she'd ever made with him, before signing the contracts, and had never done a single project without his approval and wise advice. When he heard about the accident, and the condition she'd been in, he was devastated. He wanted to see her now with his own eyes. Stevie warned him that Carole had no memory yet. She wasn't going to recognize him, or remember their history together, but once she knew how important she'd been to him, and he to her, Stevie was sure she'd be happy to see him.

'She still remembers nothing?' he asked, sounding upset on the phone. 'Will her memory come back?' He had been worried sick about her since Stevie's call when she got to Paris. She had wanted to warn him before he read of Carole's accident in the press. He had cried when Stevie called.

'We hope so. Nothing's jogged it yet, but we're all trying,' and so was Carole. She tried for hours sometimes to remember the things people had told her about since she'd come out of the coma. She couldn't access any of it yet. Jason had had his secretary send photographs and a baby album from his house. The photographs were beautiful, but Carole stared at them without even a spark of recognition for the memories they should have evoked and didn't. But the doctors were still hopeful, and the doctor in charge of her case, a neurologist, still said it could take a long time, and there were areas of her memory that might never return. Both the blow to her head, the trauma, and the coma afterward had taken a toll. How great a toll, and how long-lasting or permanent the damage, still remained to be seen. It was frustrating for Carole most of all.

But in spite of Stevie's warnings, Mike Appelsohn wasn't prepared for her complete lack of recognition when he walked into her room. He had expected something to be there at least, a memory of his face, of some part of their involvement with each other over the years. There was nothing, and she looked blank when he walked in. Fortunately, Stevie was in the room too. She saw the look of devastation on his face as Carole stared at him. Stevie told her who he was, and had warned her that he was coming. Despite every effort not to, Mike burst into tears as he gave her a hug. He was a big, warm bear of a man.

'Thank God' was all he could say at first, and then finally calmed down as he loosened his hug and released Carole from his arms.

'You're Mike?' Carole asked softly, as though they were meeting for the first time. 'Stevie told me so much about you. You've been wonderful to me.' She sounded grateful, although she knew it secondhand.

'I love you, kid. I always have. You were the sweetest girl I've ever met.' He had to fight back tears as he looked at her, and she smiled at him. 'You were an absolute knockout at eighteen,' he said proudly. 'You still are.'

'Stevie says you discovered me. It makes me sound like a country, or a flower, or a rare bird.'

'You are a rare bird, and a flower,' he said, dropping into the room's only comfortable chair, while Stevie stood nearby. Carole had asked her assistant to stay with her. Even now, with no previous memory of what Stevie did for her, Carole had come to rely on her. She felt safe and protected by the tall, dark-haired young woman.

'I love you, Carole,' he said, even though she didn't remember him. 'You're an incredible talent. We've made some great movies together over the years. And we will again, after you get all this behind you.' He was still deeply respected and active in the business, and had been for half a century, as long as Carole had been alive. 'I can't wait to get you back in L.A. I've lined up the best doctors for you at Cedars-Sinai.' Her doctors in Paris were going to recommend doctors for her at home, but Mike liked to feel useful and be in control. 'So where do we start?' he asked expectantly of Carole. He wanted to do whatever he could to help her. He knew much about her early life in Hollywood, and before. More than anyone else. Stevie had explained that to her before he arrived.

'How did I meet you?' Carole wanted to hear the story.

'You sold me a tube of toothpaste at a corner drugstore, in New Orleans, and you were the most beautiful girl I'd ever seen,' he said kindly. He had made no mention of the scar on her cheek. She had seen it by then, now that she was walking. She had been to the bathroom and looked in the mirror. It shocked her at first, and then she decided it didn't matter. She was alive, and it was a small price to pay for her survival. It was her memory she wanted back, not her flawless beauty.

'I invited you to come to L.A. for a screen test, and you told me later, you thought I was a pimp. Nice, huh?' He was a big jolly man, and at the memory of it, he roared with laughter. He had told the story a million times. 'First time anyone ever thought I was a pimp.' Carole laughed with him. She had also recovered all of her vocabulary by then, and understood the word. 'You'd come to New Orleans from Mississippi,' he went on. 'From your dad's farm. He had just died a few months before, and you sold it. You were living off the money, and you wouldn't even let me pay for your ticket. You said you didn't want to be "beholden" to me. You had a hell of a drawl then. I loved it. But it didn't work for movies.' Carole nodded. Jason had told her the same thing. She had still had a touch of it when he married her, her Mississippi drawl, but it was long gone now, and had been for years. 'You came to L.A., and your screen test was terrific.'

'What happened to me before that?' He had known her longer than anyone, and she thought he might know something about her childhood. Jason had been sketchy about that, and didn't know all the details.

'I'm not sure,' he said honestly. 'You talked a lot about your dad, when you were a kid. It sounds like he was good to you, and you loved growing up on the farm. You lived in some tiny town outside Biloxi.' When he said the word, something clicked for her. She had no idea why, but a word came to mind and she said it.

'Norton.' She stared at him in amazement, and so did Stevie, as the word fell out of her mouth.

'That was it. Norton.' He looked delighted. 'You had pigs and cows and chickens, and—' She interrupted him.

'A llama.' She herself looked stunned as she said the word. It was the first thing she had remembered on her own.

Mike turned around to glance at Stevie, who was watching Carole intently, and Carole was nodding. Her eyes looked into Mike's. He was opening a door for her that no one else could.

'I had a llama. My father gave her to me for my birthday. He said I looked just like her, because I had big eyes, long eyelashes, and a long neck. He always told me I was funny-looking.' She was speaking almost as though she could hear him. 'My dad's name was Conway.' Mike nodded, afraid to interrupt her. Something important was happening, and all three of them knew it. These were the first memories she'd had. She had to go back to the very beginning. 'My mom died when I was little. I never knew her. There was a picture of her on the piano, with me on her lap. She was really pretty. Her name was Jane. I look like her.' As she said it, tears filled Carole's eyes. 'And I had a grandma named Ruth, who made me cookies and died when I was ten.'

'I didn't know that,' Mike said softly. The memory of her was sharp in Carole's mind.

'She was pretty too. My dad died right before graduation. His truck turned over in a ditch.' She remembered everything now. 'They said I had to sell the farm, and I . . .' She looked blank, then suddenly stared at them. 'And then I don't know what happened.'

'You sold it and went to New Orleans, and I found you.' He filled in for her, but she wanted it from her own mind, not his. And she could go no further. That was all that was there right now. No matter how much she wanted to remember more, she just couldn't. But she had remembered a lot in a short time. She could still see her mother's photo and Grandma Ruth's face.

They chatted about other things then for a little while, and Mike reached over and took her hand in his. He didn't say it, but it killed him to see her so hampered. He just prayed her memory would come back, and she'd go back to being the bright, busy, intelligent, talented woman she'd once been. It was frightening to think that she might not, that she might be forever limited, with no memory of anything beyond last week. She was having some problems with short-term memory too. There was no way she could ever act again if she stayed like this. It would be the end of an important career, and a lovely woman. The others had been concerned about the same thing, and in her own way, so was Carole. She was fighting for every scrap of memory she could get. Her visit with Mike had been a major victory of sorts. It was the most she had remembered so far. Until now nothing had opened those doors, and remarkably he had. She wanted to remember more.

She and Stevie talked about her going back to Los Angeles, and her house. Carole had no memory of what it looked like. Stevie described it to her, and already had several times. She talked about her garden, and then looked at Stevie strangely and said, 'I think I had a garden in Paris.'

'Yes, you did,' Stevie said softly. 'Do you remember that house?'

'No.' Carole shook her head. 'I remember my father's barn, where I milked the cows.' Bits and pieces were coming back, like a jigsaw puzzle. But most of it didn't fit. Stevie wondered now if Carole remembered the Paris garden, would she eventually remember Matthieu? It was hard to guess. She almost hoped not, if he had made her so unhappy. She remembered how upset Carole had been when they closed that house.

'How long are you staying in Paris?' Stevie asked Mike.

'Just till tomorrow. I wanted to see my little girl here, but I've got to get back.' It was a long way to come, for a man his age, for one night. He would have gone around the world for her in a

272

flash, and had wanted to ever since Stevie called. Jason had asked him to wait, so he had, but he'd been desperate to come.

'I'm glad you came,' Carole said, smiling at him. 'I haven't remembered anything till now.'

'You will when you get back to L.A.,' Mike said with a confidence he didn't feel. He was genuinely frightened for her. He had been told what to expect, but this was worse somehow. Looking into her eyes and knowing that she remembered nothing of her life or career, or the people who loved her, made him want to cry. 'If I were stuck here, I'd have memory lapses too.' Like Sean, Mike had never liked Paris. The only thing he liked there was the food. He found the French hard to deal with in business, disorganized, and unreliable at best. What made the city bearable for him was the Ritz, which he said was the best hotel in the world. Other than that, he was happier in the States. And he wanted to get Carole back there too, to doctors he knew. He had already lined up some of the city's best. As a self-declared, devoted hypochondriac, he was on the board of two hospitals and a medical school.

He hated to leave her that night to go back to the hotel, but he could see that she was tired. He had been with her all afternoon, and he was exhausted too. He had tried to jog her memory further with stories of her early Hollywood days, but nothing more had come back. Just bits and pieces of her childhood in Mississippi. But nothing past eighteen, when she left the farm. It was a start.

Talking to people at length was still wearing for her, and trying to push her memory exhausted her. She was ready to go to sleep, as Mike got ready to leave. He stood next to her bed for a long moment before he left, and smoothed the long blond hair with his hand. 'I love you, baby.' He had always called her that, ever since she was a kid. 'Now you get better and come home as soon as you can. I'll be waiting for you in L.A.' He had to fight back tears again as he gave her a hug, and then left the room. He had a driver downstairs, waiting to take him to the hotel.

Stevie stayed until Carole fell asleep, and then she left too. Mike called her in her room when she got back, and he was upset. 'Jesus,' he said. 'She doesn't remember a damn thing.'

'The llama, her hometown, her grandmother, her mom's photo, and her father's barn were the first glimmer of hope we've had. I think you did her a lot of good.' Stevie was grateful and sincere.

'I hope we get past that soon.' Mike wanted her to be her old self, and back in her career. He didn't want it to end like this, with Carole brain-damaged and impaired.

'I hope so too,' Stevie agreed, and he told her he had given a brief interview outside the hospital. An American journalist had recognized him and asked how Carole was doing, and if he had come to see her. He said that he had, and she was doing fine. He had told the reporter that her memory was coming back, in fact she remembered almost everything. He didn't want the word staying out there that she had lost her mind. He thought it was important for her career to paint a rosy picture of her progress. Stevie wasn't sure he was right, but it couldn't do any harm. Carole wasn't talking to reporters herself, so there was no way for them to know the truth, and her doctors weren't allowed to talk to them. Mike really cared about Carole, but he always had her career in mind.

A brief report of his conversation with them turned up on the AP wires the next day, and ran in papers around the world. Movie star Carole Barber was recovering in Paris, her memory had returned, in a quote from Mike Appelsohn, producer and agent. He said she was coming back to L.A. soon, to resume her career. The article didn't mention that she hadn't done a movie in three years. It just said that her memory had returned, which was all that mattered to him. As he always had, Mike Appelsohn was looking out for her, and had her best interests in mind.

11

For the next several days after Mike's visit, Carole was feeling awful. She had caught a terrible cold. She was still prey to ordinary human miseries, just like everyone else, in addition to the neurological damage she was trying to overcome, and learning to walk with ease again. Her doctor had two physical therapists working with her and a speech therapist who came every day. The walking was going better, but the cold had her feeling miserable. And Stevie caught the cold too. Not wanting to get Carole even sicker, she stayed in bed at the Ritz. The hotel doctor came to check her, and gave her antibiotics in case she got worse. She had a nasty sinus infection and a vicious cough. She called Carole who sounded nearly as bad.

There was a new nurse on duty who left Carole alone during lunch. Carole was lonely without Stevie to talk to, and for the first time since she'd been there she turned on the TV, and watched the news on CNN. It was something to do. She couldn't concentrate well enough yet to read a book. Reading was still hard for her. And writing was worse. Her handwriting had suffered too. Stevie had long since realized that she wouldn't be writing her book anytime soon, although she hadn't said as much to Carole. There was no way she could write it now anyway. She no longer remembered the plot, and her computer was at the hotel. She had more basic problems to deal with. But for now Carole was enjoying watching TV, as she lay alone in her room. The new nurse hadn't been much company anyway, and was pretty dour.

With the sound from the TV, Carole didn't hear the door of the room open, and was startled to see someone standing near the foot of her bed.

When she turned her head, he was there, watching her. He was a young boy, in jeans, and looked about sixteen years old. He was dark skinned, and had big almond-shaped eyes. He looked malnourished and scared, as his eyes met her. She had no idea what he was doing in her room, and his eyes never left hers. She assumed the security guard outside her door had let him in. He was probably a delivery boy come to deliver flowers, but she saw no evidence of a bouquet. She tried to speak to him in halting French, but he didn't understand. She tried English then. She wasn't sure what nationality he was.

'Can I help you? Are you looking for someone?' Maybe he was lost, or a fan. They had had a few of those, looking for her, although the guard was supposed to keep them out.

'You are a movie star?' he asked, in an unfamiliar accent. He looked Spanish or Portuguese. And she couldn't remember Spanish at all. He could have been Italian too, or Sicilian. He was dark.

'Yes, I am.' She smiled at him. He seemed very young. He had a loose jacket on over a dark blue

279

sweater. The jacket looked like it belonged to someone else, twice his size, and he was wearing running shoes with holes, like the ones Anthony wore. Her son said they were his lucky shoes, and he had brought them to Paris. This boy looked like he owned nothing better. 'What are you doing here?' she asked him kindly, wondering if he wanted an autograph. She had signed a few since she'd been there, although badly. Her current signature bore no resemblance to her normal one. The bomb had done that too. Writing by hand was still hard for her.

'I am looking for you,' he said simply, as their eyes met. She knew she had never seen him before, and yet there was something about his eyes that she remembered. She could see a car in her mind's eye, and his face in the window, staring at her. And then she knew. She had seen him in the tunnel, in the car next to hers, before the bombs went off. He had jumped out and run away, and then everything exploded into fire and seconds later went black for her.

At the same time she saw the vision in her head, she saw him take a knife out of his jacket.

280

It had a long, ugly curved blade and a bone handle, and was an evil weapon. She stared at him, as he took a single step toward her, and she leaped out of bed on the other side.

'What are you doing?' She was terrified, as she stood in her hospital gown.

'You remember me, don't you? The newspaper said your memory came back.' He looked almost as terrified as she did, as he wiped the blade on his jeans.

'I don't remember you at all,' she said in a shaking voice, praying her legs would hold her up. She was within inches of an emergency button on the back wall that was for a code blue. If she could get to it, they might save her. If not, he was going to slit her throat. That she knew as an absolute certainty. The boy had murder in his eyes. 'You're an actress and a sinful woman. You're a whore,' he shouted in the silent room, as Carole backed away from him and he lunged.

Without warning, he slid across the bed, swinging the knife at her, and in the same instant she hit the black button as hard as she could. She could hear an alarm go off in the hall, as the boy reached out and tried to grab her hair, calling her a whore again. She threw her lunch tray at him, which caught him off balance, and at the same instant four nurses and two doctors charged into the room, expecting to find a code blue, and saw the boy with the knife instead. He was swinging wildly at them, still trying to reach Carole, hoping to kill her before he could be stopped. But the two doctors grabbed his arms and pinned him down, as one of the nurses ran to get help. There was a security guard in the room within seconds, who literally tore the boy from their hands, threw the knife into a corner, pinned him down, and put handcuffs on him, as Carole slid slowly to the floor, shaking from head to foot.

She remembered all of it now, the taxi, the car next to it, the laughing men in the front seat, honking at the car up ahead, and the boy in the backseat staring at her, meeting her eyes and then running away, back out of the tunnel ... the explosions ... the fire ... flying through the air ... and then the endless blackness that had claimed her . . . it was all crystal clear. He had come back to kill her after he had seen Mike's quote in the paper that her memory had returned. He was going to slit her throat so she couldn't identify him. The only thing she didn't know was how he had gotten past the guard outside.

Her doctor was in the room within minutes, to examine her, and help her into bed. She was enormously relieved to find her unharmed, although traumatized, and shaking in terror. The boy with the knife had already been taken away by the police.

'Are you all right?' the doctor asked her, deeply concerned.

'I think so . . . I don't know . . .' Carole said, still trembling. 'I remembered . . . I remembered everything when I saw him . . . in the tunnel. He was in the car next to my cab. He ran away, but he saw me first.' Carole was shaking violently and her teeth were chattering, as the doctor asked a nurse for warm blankets from the heater, which arrived promptly.

'What else do you remember?' the doctor asked.

'I don't know.' Carole looked like she was in shock, as the doctor put a blanket over her, and pressed her for details.

'Do you remember your bedroom in Los Angeles? What color is it?'

'Yellow, I think.' She could almost see it in her mind, but not quite. There was still mist around it.

'Do you have a garden?'

'Yes.'

'What does it look like?'

'There's a fountain . . . and a pond . . . roses I planted . . . they're red.'

'Do you have a dog?'

'No. She died. A long time ago.'

'Do you remember what you did before the bombing?' The doctor was pushing her hard, taking full advantage of the doors that had opened in her mind, blown open by the boy who had come to kill her with the ugly knife.

'No,' she said in answer to the question, and then she remembered. 'Yes . . . I went to see my old house . . . near the rue Jacob.' She remembered the address distinctly, walking there, and then taking a cab back to the hotel, and getting stuck in traffic in the tunnel.

'What does it look like?'

'I don't know, I can't remember,' Carole said in a small voice, as another voice in the room answered for her.

'It was a small house in a courtyard, with a garden, and beautiful windows. It had a mansard roof, and *oeil de boeuf* windows on the top floor.' It was Matthieu, standing near her bed, looking fierce. She looked up at him in tears, not wanting to see him, and yet relieved at the same time. She was confused, and he looked past her at the doctor on the other side of the bed.

'What happened here?' he asked in a booming voice. 'Where was the guard?'

'There was a misunderstanding. He went out to lunch and so did the nurse. His relief never came.' The doctor looked distressed in the face of Matthieu's fury, which was justified.

'And he left her alone?' he snapped at her.

'I'm sorry, *monsieur le Ministre,* it won't happen again.' Her voice was ice-cold. As impressive as he was, Matthieu de Billancourt didn't frighten her. She was only worried about her patient, and the horror that could have happened to her at the young Arab's hands.

'That boy came to kill her. He was one of the terrorists who bombed the tunnel. He must have seen that stupid article in the paper yesterday about her memory coming back. I want two guards on her door now, day and night.' He had no authority in the hospital whatsoever, but even the doctor knew that what he was saying made sense. 'And if you can't defend her properly, send her back to the hotel.'

'I'll take care of it,' the doctor reassured him, and almost before she could say the words, the head of the hospital walked in. Matthieu had summoned him immediately, as soon as he saw the boy being led out in handcuffs and the police told him what had happened. Matthieu had run up the stairs to Carole's room. He had been coming to visit her. And he had raised hell when he discovered what the boy had almost done. If she hadn't been able to reach the bell, she would have been dead.

The head of the hospital asked Carole if she

was all right, in broken English, and he bustled out again a minute later to bang some heads. The last thing they needed was an American movie star being murdered in their hospital. It would make for some very bad press.

The doctor left again then, with a warm smile at Carole, and a cool glance at Matthieu. She didn't like being told what to do by laymen, whether retired ministers or not, although in this case she knew he was right. Carole had very nearly been killed. It was a miracle that the boy hadn't succeeded in his mission. If he had found her asleep, he would have. A dozen ugly scenarios came to mind.

Matthieu sat down in the chair next to her bed and patted her hand, and then he looked at her with a gentle expression that had nothing to do with the way he had spoken to the hospital personnel. He had been outraged at how badly they had protected her. She could so easily have been killed. He thanked God she hadn't.

'I was planning to come to see you today,' he said softly. 'Would you like me to leave? You don't look well.'

She shook her head in answer.

'I have a cold,' she said, looking into his eyes. She felt a jolt of recognition gazing into them. They were eyes she had once loved. She didn't remember the details of what had happened between them, and she wasn't sure she wanted to, but she remembered both tenderness and pain, and a feeling of intense passion. She was still shaking from the shock of the incident that had just occurred. She had been terrified. But something about him made her feel protected and safe. He was a powerful man, in many ways.

'Would you like a cup of tea, Carole?' She nodded yes. There was a thermos of hot water in the room, and a box of the teabags she liked. Stevie had brought them from the hotel and left them for her. He made it just the way she liked it, not too strong and not too weak. He handed the mug to her, and she took it, sitting up on one elbow. They were alone in the room. The nurse had stayed outside, knowing who was in the room. If nothing else, she was in good hands, and she was in no medical danger now. The nurse was there for her comfort, not due to any dire need. 'Do you mind if I have a cup too?' She shook her head, and he went to make himself a mug of the same tea. She remembered then that he was the one who had first given it to her. They had always drunk that tea together.

'I've been thinking a lot about you,' he said to her after a sip of the vanilla tea. Carole hadn't said a word. She was too frightened by what had just happened.

'I've been thinking about you too,' she admitted. 'I don't know why, but I have. I've been trying to remember, but I just can't.' Some things had come back to her, but nothing about him. No details. She only remembered his eyes and that she had loved him. That was all. She still didn't know who he was, or why everyone jumped to attention when he approached. More importantly, she didn't remember living with him, or what their life together had been like, except for the tea, just now. She had the feeling that he had made tea for her before. Many times. At breakfast, at a kitchen table where sunlight poured into the room.

'Do you remember how we met?' She shook her head. She felt a little better after the tea. She put the empty mug on the table and lay down again. He was sitting very near her, but she didn't mind. She felt safe next to him. She didn't want to be alone. 'We met while you were making the movie about Marie Antoinette. There was a reception at the Quai d'Orsay, given by the Minister of Culture. He was an old friend of mine, and he insisted that I come. I didn't want to. I had something else to do that night, but he made such a fuss about it that I went. And you were there. You looked staggeringly beautiful. You had just come off the set, and you were still in costume. I'll never forget it. Marie Antoinette never looked anything like that.' Carole smiled at the memory. She vaguely remembered it now, the costume, and a spectacular painted ceiling at the Quai d'Orsay. She didn't remember him.

'It was spring. You had to go back to the set afterward and return the costume. I took you there, and after you changed, we went for a walk along the Seine. We sat by the river, on the dock, and talked for a long time. I felt as though the sky had fallen in on me, and you said you did too.' He smiled at the memory, and their eyes met again.

'It was a *coup de foudre*,' she said in a whisper. They had been his words after that first night . . . *coup de foudre* . . . bolt of lightning . . . love at first sight. She remembered his words, but not what had happened next.

'We talked for many hours. We stayed awake until you had to be back at the set at five that morning. It was the most exciting night of my life. You told me about your husband leaving you for another woman. She was very young, as I recall. Russian, I think. She was having his baby. You were devastated, we talked about it for hours. I think you truly loved him.' She nodded. She had gotten the same impression from Jason. It was strange, having to rely on all these people to tell her how she had felt. She had no recollection of it herself. Not with Jason. But she was beginning to recall some things about Matthieu, not so much events as feelings. She could remember loving him, and the excitement of that first night.

She vaguely remembered going back to the set, without having slept. But she didn't know how he had looked at the time. In fact, he had changed very little, except for the white hair. It had been dark then, almost black. He had been fifty when they met, and one of the most powerful men in France. Most people had been afraid of him. She never had been. He had never frightened her. He had loved her too much for that. All he had wanted to do was protect her, as he did now. He didn't want anyone to harm her. She could feel that now, as he sat close to her, talking about the past.

'I invited you to dinner the next night, and we went to some silly place from my student days. We had a good time, and talked all night again. We never stopped. I was never able to express myself to anyone like that in my life. I told you everything, all my feelings and secrets and dreams and wishes, and some things I shouldn't have, about my work. You never broke my trust. Never. I trusted you completely, right from the beginning, and I was right.

'We saw each other every day until you

finished the film five months later. You were going back to New York, or Los Angeles, you weren't sure where to go, and I asked you to stay in Paris. We were deeply in love by then, and you agreed. We found the house together. The one near the rue Jacob. We went to auctions together, we furnished it. I built a treehouse for Anthony in the garden. He loved it. He took all his meals there that summer. We went to the South of France when they went to see their father. We went everywhere together. I was with you every night. That summer, we spent two weeks on a sailboat in the South of France. I don't think I've ever been that happy in my life, before or since. They were the best days of my life.' Carole nodded as she listened. She couldn't remember the events, only the feelings. She had the sense that it was a magical time. Thinking about it made her feel warm, but there had been something else too, something that was wrong. There had been a problem of some kind. Her eyes searched his and then she remembered, and said it out loud.

'You were married,' she said sadly.

'Yes, I was. My marriage had been over for years, our children were grown. My wife and I were strangers to each other, we had led separate lives for ten years before you came along. I was going to leave her even before I met you. I promised you I would, and I meant it. I wanted to do it quietly, without embarrassment for any of us. I talked to my wife about it, and she asked me not to, not right away. She was afraid of the humiliation and scandal for her, with my leaving her for a famous movie star. It was painful for her, and it was liable to become an international cause célèbre in the press, so I agreed to wait six months. You were very understanding about it. It didn't seem to matter. We were happy, and I lived with you in our little house. I loved your children, and I think they liked me, in the beginning at least. You were so young then, Carole. You were thirty-two when we met, and I was fifty. I could have been your father, but I felt like a boy again when I was with you.'

'I remember the boat,' she said softly, 'in the South of France. We went to Saint Tropez, and the old port in Antibes. I think I was very, very happy with you,' she said dreamily.

'We both were,' he added sadly, remembering all that had happened after that.

'Something happened. You had to leave.'

'Yes, I did.' He was amazed that she remembered. He had almost forgotten it himself, although it had been an enormous drama at the time. They had radioed him on the boat. He had had to leave her at the airport in Nice, and had left on a military plane himself.

'Why did you leave? Someone was shot, I think.' She was frowning, trying to remember as she stared at him. 'Who was shot?' She had to know.

'The president of France. It was an assassination attempt, which failed. During the Bastille Day parade on the Champs Elysées. I should have been there, but I was with you instead.'

'You were in government . . . something very high up and very secret. What were you? . . . Was it secret police?' She was squinting at him from her bed.

'That was one of my duties. I was the Minister

of the Interior,' he said quietly, and she nodded. It came back to her now. There was so much she didn't recall about her own life, but she remembered that. They had sailed the boat into the harbor, and left for the airport in a cab. He had left her minutes later, and she had watched him take off in the military plane, and gone back to Paris on her own. He had been apologetic about leaving her that way, and there had been soldiers around him with machine guns. She wasn't frightened by it, but it seemed strange.

'There was something else like that . . . another time . . . someone was hurt, and you left me somewhere, on a trip . . . we were skiing, and you left by helicopter.' She could still see it rising in the air, blowing snow everywhere.

'The president had a heart attack, and I left to be with him.'

'That was at the end, wasn't it?' She looked sad.

He nodded, silent at first, remembering it too. It was the incident that had brought him to his senses and reminded him that he couldn't leave his job, and he belonged to France. They owned him, no matter how much he loved her, and wanted to leave everything for her. He couldn't in the end. They had had a little more time after that, but not much. And his wife had been making a lot of trouble then too. It had been an impossible time, for both of them. 'Yes, it was nearly the end. There were two years between those two events, and a lot of wonderful times.'

'That's all I remember,' she said, watching him, wondering what the two years had been like. She had a sense that they had been exciting, because he was, but hard at times, which he was too. As he had just told her, he had had a complicated life. Politics, and the drama that went with it, had been his life's blood. But for a time, so had she. She had been the heart that kept him alive.

'We spent Christmas in Gstaad together the first year, with the children. And then you started another movie in England, and I came over to see you every weekend. When you came back, I wanted to go to the lawyer to get divorced, and my wife begged me not to again. She said she couldn't face it. We'd been married for twenty-nine years, and I felt I owed her something, some respect at least, since I no longer loved her. She knew that, she knew how much I loved you, and she didn't hold it against me. She was very compassionate about it. I was planning to leave my job in the government that year, it would have been the perfect time to end it with her, and then I got named for another term. You and I had been together for a year by then, the happiest year of my life. You agreed to give it another six months. And I had every intention of getting divorced. Arlette promised not to stop it, but then there were scandals in the government involving other people, and I knew it was the wrong time. I promised that if you gave me another year, I would resign and come to the States with you.'

'You would never have done it. And you'd have been miserable in Los Angeles.'

'I felt I owed my country something . . . and my wife . . . I couldn't just walk away from either of them, without fulfilling my duty, but I had every intention of leaving and coming with you, and then . . .' He stopped for a moment, and Carole remembered what had happened. 'Something terrible happened . . .'

'Your daughter died . . . in a car accident . . . I remember . . . it was awful . . .' Their eyes met and held, and she reached out and touched his hand.

'She was nineteen. It happened in the mountains. She went skiing with friends. You were wonderful to me. But I couldn't leave Arlette then. It would have been inhuman.' Carole remembered his saying that to her.

'You always told me you would leave her. Right from the beginning. You said your marriage to her was over, but it wasn't. You always felt you owed something more to her. She always wanted another six months, and you gave it to her. You always protected her, and not me. I remember it now. I was always waiting for you to divorce her. You lived with me, but you were married to her. And to France. You always had to give one more year to France, and six more months to your wife, and suddenly it was two years later.'

She looked at him then, stunned at what she had just remembered. 'And I was pregnant.' He nodded, with a look of anguish. 'I begged you to divorce her then, didn't I?' He nodded again, looking humbled. 'I had a morals clause in my contracts then, and if anyone had found out I was living with a married man, and having his baby, my career would have been over. I would have been blackballed, or out of work at least. I risked that for you,' she said sadly. They had both known the risks going in. His country would have forgiven his having a mistress and cheating on his wife, it had been perfectly acceptable in France. Her country, or her industry at least, wouldn't have forgiven her an affair with a married man, and being his mistress, involved in a public scandal with a high government official. Let alone an illegitimate baby. The morals clause in her contracts had been rigid. Overnight she would have become a pariah. She had risked it because he had insisted that he would get divorced, but he had never even gone to see an attorney. His wife had begged him not to, so he never did. He just kept buying time with Carole. Always more.

'What happened to the baby?' she asked in a strangled voice, looking up at him. Some things were still lost for her, although there was so much about it that was coming back now.

'You lost it. A boy. You were almost six months pregnant. You fell off the ladder, decorating the tree at Christmas. I tried to catch you, but you fell right past me. You were in the hospital for three days, but we lost him. Chloe never knew you were pregnant, but Anthony did. We explained it to him. He asked me if we were going to get married, and I said we would. And then my daughter died and Arlette had a nervous breakdown and begged me not to. She threatened suicide, and you had lost the baby by then, so our getting married wasn't as pressing. I begged you to understand. I was going to resign in the spring, and by then I thought Arlette could survive it. I needed more time, or at least that was what I said.' He looked at Carole then with mournful eyes. 'In the end, I think you did the right thing.' It killed him to say it. 'I don't think I'd ever have left her. I meant to. I believed I would, but in fact I just couldn't. That, or my job. I didn't retire for another six years after you left Paris. And I'm not sure I could ever have left Arlette. There would have always been something, some reason why she wouldn't let me leave her. I don't even think she loved me, not as you did, or as I loved you. She just didn't want to lose me to another woman. If you'd been French, you would have put up with it. But you weren't. It all sounded like lies to you, and some of them were. I just didn't have the courage to tell you I couldn't do it. I lied to myself more than I did to you. When I told you I'd divorce her, I meant it. I hated you for leaving me. I thought you were being cruel to me. But you were right to do it. I would have broken your heart in the end, even more than I did. The last six months were a nightmare. Constant fights, constant crying. You were devastated after you lost the baby. So was I.'

'What finally did it? What made me leave?' Her voice was a whisper.

'Another day, another lie, another delay. You just got up one morning and started packing. You waited till the end of the school year. I'd done nothing about the divorce, and they were

302

asking me to do another term in the ministry. I tried to explain it to you, and you wouldn't listen. You left a week later. I took you to the airport, and neither of us could stop crying. You told me to call you, if I got divorced. I called, but I never got divorced, and I stayed on in the government. They needed me. And she did too, in her own way. She didn't love me, but we were used to each other. She felt I owed it to her to stay with her.

'I called you several times when you were back in L.A., and then you stopped taking my calls. I heard you had sold the house. I went there to look at it one day. It nearly broke my heart when I remembered how happy we'd been there.'

'I went to see it that day, before the bomb exploded in the tunnel. I was on my way back to the hotel when it happened,' she said, and he nodded. It had been a place of refuge for both of them, a haven, the love nest they had shared and where they had conceived their baby. She couldn't help wondering what would have happened if she'd had his child, if he would have finally divorced his wife. Probably not. He was French. Frenchmen had mistresses and illegitimate children. They had done it for centuries, and nothing much had changed. It was still acceptable, but not to Carole. She was a farm girl from Mississippi, no matter how famous she was, and she didn't want to live with another woman's husband. She had told him that right from the beginning. 'We never should have started,' she said, looking at him from where she lay with her head on the pillow.

'We had no choice,' Matthieu said simply. 'We were too much in love with each other not to.'

'I don't believe that,' she said firmly. 'I think people always have choices. We did. We made the wrong ones, and we paid a high price for them. I'm not sure, but I don't think I ever forgot you. I didn't get over you for a long time, until I met my last husband.' She remembered that clearly now.

'I read that you got married, about ten years ago,' he said, and she nodded. 'I was happy for you' – and then he smiled ruefully – 'and very jealous. He's a lucky man.'

'No, he isn't. He died two years ago of cancer.

Everyone says he was a wonderful person.'

'That's why Jason was here. I wondered why.'

'He would have come anyway. He's a good man too.'

'You didn't think that eighteen years ago,' Matthieu said, looking irritated. He wasn't sure she would have said the same about him, even today, that he was a good man. In her eyes, he hadn't been. She had said so at the time. She said he had lied to her and misled her, and was a dishonest, dishonorable person. It had cut him to the quick at the time. No one had ever accused him of that in his life, but she was right.

'I think he's a good person now,' Carole said about Jason. 'We all pay for our sins in the end. The Russian girl left him by the time I left Paris.'

'Did he try to come back to you?' Matthieu was curious about it.

'Apparently, he did. He says I didn't want him. I was probably still in love with you at the time.'

'Do you regret it?'

'Yes, I do,' she said honestly. 'I wasted two and a half years of my life with you, and probably another five getting over you. That's a long time to give to a man who wouldn't leave his wife.' And then she thought about it and wondered what had happened. 'Where is she now?'

'She died a year ago, after a long illness. She was very sick for the last three years of her life. I'm glad I was with her. I owed her that. We were married forty-six years in the end. It wasn't the marriage I would have wanted, or the one I thought I'd get when I married her at twenty-one, but it was the one we had. We were friends. She was very elegant about you. I don't think she forgave me, but she understood. She knew how in love with you I was. I never felt that way about her. She was a very cold person. But she was a decent, honest woman.' So he had stayed, just as she'd always thought he would. And even he had said she'd done the right thing by leaving. She had the answers now, the ones she'd come to Paris for. That it had been too late for her with Jason, by the time he came back. She no longer loved him, and she couldn't have stopped him from marrying the Russian supermodel. She had no choice there, and by the time she did, she didn't want him. She didn't even want him now. It was too late. And all she would ever have been to Matthieu was his mistress. He would never have left his wife until she died. Carole felt she understood that when she left Paris, which was why she had. But it was only now that she knew it was the right decision. He had confirmed it to her, which was a gift of sorts, long after the fact.

A lot of it had come back now, some of the events, and too many of the feelings. She could almost taste her disappointment and despair when she had finally given up and left him. He had very nearly destroyed her, and her career. He had even disappointed her children. Whatever his intentions had been in the beginning, or his love for her, he hadn't been honorable with her. At least what Jason had done, no matter how awful it had been for her, had been upfront and honest. He had divorced her and married the other woman. Matthieu never had.

'What are you doing now? Are you still in government?' she asked.

'I was until ten years ago, when I retired and went back to my family law firm. I practice with two of my brothers.'

'And you were the most powerful man in France. You controlled everything then, and you loved it.'

'Yes, I did.' He was honest about that at least, and he had been honest about the rest of it now too. It proved her right finally, but hearing it even now was painful. She remembered too well how much she had loved him, and how badly he had hurt her. 'Power is like a drug to men. It's hard to give up. I was addicted to it. But I was even more addicted to you. It nearly killed me when you left me. But I still couldn't divorce her, or give up my job.'

'I never wanted you to give up your job. That wasn't the issue. But I did want you to divorce her.'

'I couldn't.' He hung his head as he said it, and then looked her in the eye again. 'I didn't have the courage.' It was an enormous admission, and Carole didn't answer for a minute.

'That's why I left you.'

His voice was a whisper. 'You were right.' She nodded.

They sat together in silence for a long time,

and then as he looked at her, her eyes closed, and she drifted off to sleep. For the first time in a long time, she was at peace. He sat there, watching her, and then he finally stood up, and left the room on silent feet.

12

Carole awoke again that night, feeling better after a long sleep. She remembered then that Matthieu had visited her, what he'd said, and she lay in bed, thinking about him for a long time. Despite her spotty memory, he had exorcized a lot of ghosts for her. She appreciated that he'd been honest with her, finally, and told her that she'd been right to leave. It was a gift of freedom to hear that from him. She had always wondered what would have happened if she'd stayed – if she should have waited longer. He had confirmed to her now that it wouldn't have made a difference.

There was a nurse in the room with her when she woke up, and two guards outside her door, thanks to the fuss Matthieu had made. She had called Jason and her children to tell them about the attack. She assured them she was fine, and had been lucky once again. Jason had offered to come back to Paris, but she assured them the police had the matter well in hand. She was still shaken, but told them she was safe. All of them were horrified that she had been the victim of a terrorist incident on the heels of the first one. And Anthony warned her about Matthieu again. He was threatening to come and protect her himself, but she told him all was well.

She lay in bed thinking about all of it in the middle of the night. The terrorist, Matthieu, and the pieces of their history he'd shared. It all left her feeling anxious and unnerved.

She called Stevie then at the hotel, feeling foolish for bothering her, but desperate for a familiar voice, despite the late hour. Stevie had been asleep.

'How's your cold?' Carole asked her. She felt better herself although she was still sick, and shaken by the events of the day. It seemed more frightening now in retrospect.

'Better, I think, but not great,' Stevie said. 'What are you doing up at this hour?' Carole told her then what had happened, when the boy with the knife had gotten into her room. '*What?* Are you kidding? Where the fuck was the security guy?' Stevie was horrified, as Carole's family had been. It was beyond belief, and would be on the news the next day.

'Out to lunch. They said his relief never came.' Carole heaved a long sigh and lay in her bed, thinking how lucky she had been. 'It scared me to death.' She still shook when she thought about it. She was glad Matthieu had arrived right afterward.

'I'm coming over there right now. They can put a cot in your room. I'm not leaving you alone again.'

'Don't be silly. You're sick. I'm okay. They won't let something like that happen again. Matthieu was here, and he raised hell. He must still have some clout. The head of the hospital was up here bowing and scraping in about five minutes. And the police were around for hours. They won't let anything happen now. It just scared me to death.'

'No wonder.' It was hard to believe she had been the victim of two incidents.

The police had said they would come to take a detailed report from her the next day. They hadn't wanted to upset her further by pressing her right after it happened. And her assailant was in custody, so she was safe.

'I remembered him from the tunnel,' Carole said, still sounding shaken, so Stevie changed the subject to distract her, and asked about Matthieu.

'Did the mystery man shed any further light on your affair?' Stevie was still curious about him.

'Yes. I remembered a lot of it myself. I remembered the boy with the knife too,' she said, going back to the attack. 'He was in the cab next to me in the tunnel, and he ran away. The suicide bombers must have told him he was going to die. Apparently, he wasn't ready for the seventy-seven virgins he was going to get in Heaven.'

'No, he would rather have killed you. Christ, I can't wait till we get home.'

'Me too,' Carole said with a sigh. 'This has

been one hell of a trip. I think I got my answers though. If I ever get my memory back, and can learn how to use a computer again, I think I'm ready to write the book. I'll have to add something about all this. It's too good not to use.'

'You think maybe you could do a cookbook next time, or a children's book? I don't like the research you've been doing for this book.'

But the answers she'd gotten about Jason and Matthieu were what she had needed for herself. She knew that now. And better yet, she had heard it from them, instead of guessing and figuring it out on her own.

'What are you hearing from Alan?' Carole asked as they chatted and she started to unwind. It was nice to have someone to talk to late at night. She missed that with Sean. She was starting to remember now, just little bits. Stevie telling her things about him had brought some of it back.

'He says he misses me,' Stevie answered her. 'He's antsy for me to come home. He says he's pining for my cooking. He must have lost his memory too. What's to miss? Chinese takeout, or deli food? I haven't cooked a decent meal for him in four years.'

'I don't blame him. I missed you today too.'

'I'll be there tomorrow. And I'm sleeping there tomorrow night.'

'No one's coming after me,' Carole said reassuringly. 'All the other guys blew themselves up.' And they damn near blew her up too. 'There's no one left.'

'I don't care. I'd rather be there with you.'

'I'd rather be at the Ritz,' Carole laughed, 'than at the Pitié Salpêtrière. Hands down. You've got much better room service there.'

'Never mind,' Stevie said firmly. 'I'm moving in. And fuck them if they don't like it. If they can't even keep a security guard on your door through lunchtime, you need a watchdog over there.'

'I think Matthieu took care of that. They looked scared to death of him. And there are about a million guards in the hall tonight.'

'He scares me too,' Stevie said honestly. 'He looks like a tough guy.'

'He is.' Carole remembered that about him.

'But he wasn't with me. He was married. He just wouldn't leave his wife. We talked about it today. We lived together for two and a half years. He wouldn't divorce her, so I left.'

'I got into one of those once. They're hard to win. Most people don't. I never did it again. Alan may be an asshole at times, but at least he's mine.'

'Yeah, I guess it took me a while with Matthieu to figure that out. He told me he was leaving her when we met, that his marriage was over, and had been for ten years.'

'They always say bullshit like that. The only one who doesn't know about it is their wife. They never leave.'

'He stayed married to her till last year. He said I was right to go.'

'Apparently. And he divorced her now?' Stevie sounded surprised. At his age, no one got divorced. Especially in France.

'No, she died. He stayed with her till the bitter end. Forty-six years. Of a supposedly loveless marriage. What's the point in that?'

'Habit. Laziness. Chickenshit. God knows why people stay.'

'His daughter died when I was living with him. And then his wife threatened suicide. There was an endless string of excuses, some of them even valid, though most of them not, until I finally gave up. He was married to her, and to France.'

'Sounds like you didn't have a chance.'

'No, I didn't. He says that now too. He sure didn't say it then.' She didn't tell Stevie about the baby she'd lost, but she was going to talk to Anthony about it sometime, in case he remembered it. He had never said anything to her, but it had been obvious, in the hospital when they met, how much he had hated Matthieu in the end. Even her children had felt betrayed. It had left a lasting impression on her son, whatever the details.

'You looked miserable when we came back to pack up the house.'

'I was.'

'You seem to be remembering a lot of stuff,' Stevie commented. Carole had come far in the past few days. The boy with the knife had jogged her memory too.

'I am. Little by little, stuff is coming back. Feelings more than events.'

'That's a start.' Mike Appelsohn had helped her too, except for his interview with the press, which had set the boy with the knife after her. 'I hope they send you back to the hotel soon.' Stevie was deeply worried about the potential risk to her from remaining terrorists. But now, so were the police.

'So do I.'

They said goodnight then and hung up, and Carole lay in bed for a long time, thinking how lucky she was, how blessed to have her children, how miraculous her survival had been, and how fortunate she was to have Stevie as a friend. She tried not to let herself think of Matthieu, or the boy who had come to kill her with the terrifying knife. She lay in bed with her eyes closed, taking deep breaths. But no matter what she did, in her head she kept seeing the boy with the knife, and then her mind would race to the safety and protection of Matthieu. It was as though all these years later, he was still a place of refuge and peace, and would keep her safe from harm. She didn't want to believe that, but somewhere locked away in the memory of her heart, she still did. She could almost feel his arms around her as she drifted off to sleep at last.

13

The police came to take a report from Carole the next day. The boy they'd taken into custody was from Syria, and he was seventeen years old. He was a member of a fundamentalist group that had been responsible for three recent terrorist attacks, two in France and one in Spain. Other than that they knew very little about him, and Carole was the only person who could link him to the bombing in the tunnel. Although much of her memory was still fuzzy about it, as well as details of her own life, she distinctly remembered seeing him in the car next to her, as her cab had sat stuck in traffic underground. It had all come back to her when she saw his face in her room at the Pitié Salpêtrière. His eyes had riveted her as he lunged at her with the long, curved blade.

The police questioned her for nearly three hours, and showed her photographs of a dozen men. She recognized none of them, only the young man who had entered her room and tried to kill her. One of the photographs vaguely reminded her of the driver of the car next to her, but she hadn't paid as much attention to him as the boy in the backseat, and she couldn't be as sure. She had no doubt whatsoever about the boy who had attacked her, she remembered clearly his mournful face as he stared at her from the backseat. His attack had brought it all clearly into her mind again. The images were very sharp.

Other memories were returning too. Often they were out of sequence and made no sense to her. She could see her father's barn in her mind's eye, and she remembered milking the cows as though it were yesterday. She could hear her father's laughter, but no amount of concentration could help her recall his face. The meeting with Mike Appelsohn in New Orleans when he discovered her was a blank to her, but she recalled the screen test now, and working on her first movie. She had woken up thinking of it that day, but meeting Jason and her early days with him had vanished into thin air. She remembered their wedding day and the apartment in New York where they'd lived after they were married, and she had a vague memory of Anthony's birth, but nothing of Chloe's, the movies she'd made, or the Oscars she won, and she still had very little memory of Sean.

Everything was disjointed and out of sequence, like clips from a movie that had landed on the cutting-room floor. Faces would come to mind, or names, often unrelated, and then whole scenes would appear and be crystal clear. It was like a crazy patchwork quilt of her life, which she tried constantly to sort out and organize, and put into sequence again, and just as she thought she had it right and knew what she was remembering, she would remember another detail, face, name, or event, and the whole story changed again. It was like a kaleidoscope, constantly shifting, changing, the colors and shapes altered and moving. It was exhausting trying to absorb it all and make sense of it. For hours at a time now, she had total recall, and then for many more, her mind seemed to shut down, as though it had had enough of the sifting and sorting process that occupied her every waking hour. She was trying to force herself to remember it all, and asked a thousand questions as things came to mind, trying to make the focus more acute in the lens of her mind's eye. It was a full-time job, and the hardest one she'd ever done.

Stevie was well aware of how exhausting it was for her, and sat in silence in her room when she could see that Carole was trying to run things through her head. Eventually, Carole would say something, but for long hours she would lie on her bed, seemingly staring into space, thinking about it all. Some of it still made no sense, like photographs of people in an album with no labels to indicate who they had been, or why they were there. About some things she remembered too much. About others far too little. And all of it was jumbled in her head. Sometimes it took hours to identify a scene, face, or name, and it was a real victory for her when she did. She felt triumphant every time, and then would lie silent and drained of energy for a long time.

The police had been impressed by what she did remember. Initially, they had been told she had no memory at all. And many of the other victims they'd spoken to recalled even less than she did. They hadn't been paying attention when they'd been sitting in the tunnel, talking to other passengers, playing with the radio, or the shock of the event and their resulting injuries had wiped all recollection from their minds. The police and a special intelligence unit had been interviewing people for weeks. And until then they had been told that Carole would be unable to contribute anything to their search. Suddenly that had changed, and they were grateful for her help. They were providing additional security for her at the hospital. There were now two members of a SWAT team, the CRS, standing outside her door in combat boots and dark blue overalls. There was no mistaking who they were, or why they were there. The machine guns they carried said it all. The CRS was the most feared unit in Paris, brought in to break up riots, during threats, or after terrorism erupted somewhere. The fact that they had been called in confirmed the seriousness of the event that had brought her to the Pitié Salpêtrière.

There was no solid reason to believe that other members of the group would attempt an attack on her again. As far as they knew, all the perpetrators had died in the suicide bombing in the tunnel, with the exception of the one boy who had fled. Carole distinctly remembered him running backward to the entry of the tunnel just before the first bomb exploded. Her memory was more vague about the subsequent ones, because by then she herself had been blown out of the cab and was free-falling toward the tunnel floor. But the police still had a reasonable concern that she was a highly visible victim of the event. Eliminating her would be a plus for the terrorists, as well as an additional victory, in killing a well-known person to bring attention to their cause. In either case, the police and special intelligence units had no desire whatsoever to have Carole die on French turf. They wanted to do everything possible to keep her alive, at least until she left France. And since she was an American, they had contacted the FBI as well. They had promised to provide surveillance of her home in Bel-Air for the next several months, particularly once she was home. It was both frightening and reassuring at the same time.

The possibility of further danger to her was far from encouraging. She had already paid a high enough price for her presence in the tunnel during the suicide bombing. All she wanted to do now was get her memory back, leave the hospital, and get on with her life once she got home. She was still hoping to write her novel. And everything about her life, present and past, seemed more precious to her now, especially her children.

Matthieu showed up halfway through the interview with the police. He said nothing, slipped into the room quietly, and stood silently observing. He had nodded at Carole, and looked serious and concerned as he listened. He had made several phone calls to the intelligence unit that was handling it, and another to the head of the CRS. The current Minister of the Interior had received a call from him the day before. Matthieu wanted both the investigation and her protection handled without slip-up or flaw. He had left no question in anyone's mind that the matter was of the utmost importance to him. He had no need to explain why. Carole Barber was an important visitor to France, and to the Minister of the Interior he admitted that she had been a close personal friend for many years. The minister did not ask him in what guise.

Matthieu stood watching her face as they questioned her, and was surprised to hear how much she did remember, as were they. She was able to recall many details that had eluded her entirely before. This time she didn't mind Matthieu being there. It was comforting to have someone familiar close at hand, and he no longer frightened her. She thought her initial fear of him when he visited her came from the fact that she sensed that he had been important to her, but she had no idea why. Now she knew, and oddly, she remembered more details about their life together than she did about other people and events.

The high points of her time with him were sharply etched in her mind, emerging from the seas that had covered them, and she remembered a million small details as well, important moments, sunny days, torrid nights, tender moments, and the agony she had felt over his not leaving his wife, the arguments they'd had over it. His explanations and excuses stood out in her mind, even their sailboat trip in the South of France. She remembered almost every conversation they'd had while they drifted lazily near Saint Tropez, and his inconsolable sorrow when his daughter had died a year later. Their joint grief and disappointment when she miscarried. The memories of him overwhelmed her, and seemed to drown out all else. She could remember the pain he had caused her as though it were yesterday, and the day she had left France. She had given up all hope of a life with him by then. Knowing all that, it was odd being in a room with him now. Not frightening, but unsettling.

He had an austere, unhappy look about him, which was what had seemed ominous to her at first, but now that she recalled their history, his somber air was familiar to her. He didn't look like a happy man, and seemed tormented by his own memories of the time they'd shared. He had wanted to apologize to her for years, and now fate had given him that chance.

Carole looked exhausted when the police and officials left her room. Matthieu sat down next to her, and without inquiring first, he handed her a mug of tea. She looked gratefully at him and smiled. She was almost too tired to lift it to her lips. He saw her hand shake and held the cup for her. The nurse was still outside the room, chatting with the two CRS guards. The protests of the hospital about their machine guns had been overridden. Carole's protection was paramount and took precedence over hospital rules. The machine guns stayed. Carole had seen them herself when she took a walk down the corridor with her nurse, before the interrogation unit arrived to debrief her. She had been shocked to see their weapons, and yet reassured at the same time. Like Matthieu's presence next to her, it seemed both a curse and a blessing.

'Are you all right?' he asked quietly, and she nodded, as she sipped the tea he held for her. She was shaking all over.

It had been an upsetting morning, but less so than the day before, when the boy with the knife entered her room. It was an event and a sensation she knew she would never forget. She had been certain she was going to die, even more than when she was flying through the tunnel. This was far more personal, and specifically meant to harm her, like a missile aimed straight at her. When she thought of it, she was still frightened. Looking at Matthieu calmed her. He seemed very gentle as he sat there. There was a kind side to him she had not forgotten. It was in full evidence as he sat beside her bed, and his love for her shone in his eyes. She wasn't sure if it was the memory of it for him, or a fire that had never gone out, and she had no desire to ask him. Some doors were best left closed forever. What lay behind that door was too painful for both of them, or at least that was what she thought. He had given her no insights into the present, only the past, which was enough for her.

'I'm okay,' she breathed with a sigh, as she laid her head back on the pillow and met his eyes. 'That was hard,' she said, referring to the investigation, and he nodded.

'You did very well.' He had been proud of her. Carole had stayed calm, clear, and made every effort to pull every detail from her shattered memory bank. She had been impressive, which did not surprise him. She had always been a remarkable woman. She had also been extraordinary to him when his daughter died, and at a million other times, and never failed him in any way, as he had her. He knew it all too well, and had played it over countless times in his mind in the years since. He had been haunted by her face, her voice, her touch, for fifteen years, and now he was sitting next to her. It was almost too strange to believe.

'Did you talk to them first?' Carole was curious. The police had been kind and respectful to her, while pressing her relentlessly for every possible detail. But the way they had handled her seemed unusually gentle and respectful, and she suspected that he was responsible for it.

'I called the Minister of the Interior last night.' Ultimately, he was in charge of the investigation, and responsible for how it was handled, and its eventual success. It was the same job Matthieu had had when they met.

'Thank you,' she said, looking at him gratefully. They could have run roughshod over her, which was more their standard style, but they hadn't. They had worn kid gloves in how they handled it, thanks to him. 'Do you miss your old job?' It seemed natural to her that he would. He had had so much power, the most powerful man in France. It would be hard for anyone to give that up, particularly a man. He had thrived on it when she knew him, and was very hands-on in how he handled it, which was why he could never have left. He felt as though the well-being of his country was in his care at all times. The country that he loved. *Ma patrie*,' as he had so often said to her, burning with his passion for both his homeland and its people. It was unlikely that had changed, even if he had retired.

'Sometimes,' he said honestly. 'Responsibility of that kind is hard to give up. It's like love, it doesn't stop, even if it changes address. But times are different now. It's a harder job today, it's not as clean. Terrorism has changed many things, in all countries. No leader has an easy time of it now. It was simpler when I was in government. You knew who the bad guys were. Now they have no face, and you don't see them until after the damage is done, like what happened to you. It is harder to protect the country and the people. Everyone is more disillusioned, and some are very bitter. It's difficult to be a hero. People are angry at everyone, not only their enemies, but their leaders.' He said it with a sigh. 'I don't envy men in government today, but yes, I miss it.' He gave her one of his rare smiles. 'What man wouldn't? It was a lot of fun.'

'I remember how much you loved it,' she said with a misty smile in response. 'You worked crazy hours, and got calls all night long.' It was the way he wanted it. He wanted to know every detail of what was happening at all times. It had been an obsession with him.

And that morning he had stood in the room, hovering over the investigation, as though he were still in charge. Sometimes he forgot that he no longer was. And he was still deeply respected by the public and the men who had taken over his job. He took frequent stands on political issues, and was often quoted in the papers. They had called him several days before about his views on the tunnel attack and how the matter was being handled. He had been diplomatic, which was not always the case with him. When he was upset by something, or critical of the government, he did not mince words, and never had.

'France has always been my first love,' he responded. 'Until you,' he added softly. But she wasn't sure that was true, or had ever been. As she saw it, she had been third in line, after his country and his marriage.

'Why did you retire?' Carole asked him quietly, and reached over for her tea again. This time she held the mug herself. She was feeling better and calmer again. The questioning had rattled her, but she was finally settling down. He could see it too.

'I thought it was time. I served my country for a long time. I had done my job. My term was over, the government changed. I had some health problems, which were probably work related. I'm fine now. I missed it terribly at first, and I've been offered some minor posts since, as a token gesture. I don't want that. I don't want a consolation prize. I had what I wanted. I thought it was time to give it up. And I enjoy practicing law. I've been asked several times to become a magistrate, a judge, but I would find that boring. It's more fun to be a lawyer than a judge. For me anyway. Although I'm planning to retire from that this year too.'

'Why?' She looked concerned for him. He was a man who needed to work. Even at sixty-eight, he had the drive and energy of a much younger man. She had seen it again when they were questioning her. He had been positively buzzing with electricity, like a live wire. It wasn't healthy for a man like him to retire. It was enough that he'd given up the ministry, it didn't seem wise to her for him to give up law as well.

'I'm old, my dear. It's time to do other things.

Write, read, travel, think, discover new worlds. I'm planning to do some travel in Southeast Asia.' He'd been to Africa the year before. 'I want to do things more slowly now, and savor them, before I can't do that anymore.'

'You have years ahead of you to do that. You're still a vital, youthful man.'

He laughed at her choice of words. 'Yes, youthful, but not young. There is a difference. I want to enjoy my life, and the freedom I never had. I answer to no one now. There is a benefit to that, and a downside. My children are grown, even my grandchildren are grown.' He laughed. It was hard to imagine, but she realized it was true. 'Arlette is gone. No one cares where I am or what I do, which is sad to admit, but true. I might as well take advantage of it while I can, before my children start calling the house to ask the maid if I ate my lunch or wet my bed.' He was a long way from there, and the picture he painted of his future touched her heart. In a way, she was there now too. Her children were much younger than his. She knew his oldest son must be well into his forties, and not much younger than she. He had married young and had children early, so he wasn't tied to relatively young children, as she was. But even hers were out of college, allegedly grown up, and lived in other cities. Without Stevie to keep her company every day, her house would have been a tomb. There was no man in her life, no children at home, no one to answer to or spend time with, or take care of, no one who cared what time she ate dinner, or if. She was nearly twenty years younger than he was, but she was unfettered now too. It was what had led her to pursue the book, and the trip roaming around Europe, to find the answers that had eluded her till then.

'What about you?' He turned to her, with the same questions in his eyes that he saw in hers. 'You haven't made a movie in a long time. I think I've seen them all.' He smiled again. It had been his treat to himself, to sit in a darkened theater, watching her and listening to her. He had seen some of them three and four times, and then watched them again on TV. His wife had never commented, and left the room quietly when

Carole was on the screen. She knew. Right till the end. It was a subject they no longer touched on in the last years of their life together. She accepted his love for Carole, and the fact that he had never loved her in the same way, and never would. His feelings for his wife had been very different. They were about duty, responsibility, companionship, and respect. His feelings for Carole had been born of passion, desire, dreams, and hope. He had lost the dreams, but not the hope or the love. They were his forever, and he kept them locked in his heart, like a rare, precious jewel in a safe, out of harm's way, and out of sight. Carole could feel the emotions he still had for her, as they sat in her hospital room and talked. The room was alive with all that was unsaid, and still felt, by him at least.

'I haven't liked the scripts in the past few years. I don't want to do stupid roles, unless I do something really funny, which I've thought about lately too. I've always wanted to do comedy, and I might one of these days. I don't know how funny I am, but I'd love to give it a try and play with it. At this point, why not? Otherwise, I want to do roles that are meaningful to me and make a difference to the people who see the films. I can't see the point of just keeping my face on screen, so people don't forget who I am. I want to be really careful about what parts I accept. The role has to matter to me, or it's not worth doing. There aren't a lot of parts like that around, particularly at my age. And I didn't want to work for the year my husband was sick. Since then I haven't seen a single script I liked. It's all junk. I never did junk, and I don't want to start now. I don't need to do that. I've been trying to write a book,' she confessed to him with a smile. They had always had interesting conversations, about movies, politics, their work, views about the human condition, and life. He was an extremely cultured, well-read, philosophical person, with master's degrees in literature, psychology, and art and a doctorate in political science. He had many facets and a razor-sharp mind.

'Are you writing a book about your life?' He looked intrigued.

'Yes and no.' She smiled sheepishly. 'It's a

novel, about a woman coming of age and examining her life after her husband dies. I've had about a dozen false starts on it. I've written several chapters, from different angles, and I always get stuck at the same place. I can't figure out what the purpose of her life is, once he's gone. She's a brilliant neurosurgeon, and she couldn't save him from a brain tumor, in spite of all her knowledge. She's a woman accustomed to power and control, and her failure to alter destiny brings her to a crossroads in her life. It's about acceptance and surrender and understanding herself and what life is really about. She's made some important decisions in her past, which still impact her. She leaves her practice and goes on a journey, trying to find the answers to her own questions, the keys to the doors that she has left locked for most of her life, while she was moving forward. Now she has to go back, before she can go forward again.' She surprised herself with the recalled memories of her book.

'It sounds interesting,' he mused, looking pensive. He understood perfectly that it was about her, and the decisions she had made, and so did she. The choices, and the forks in the road she had taken, and not least of it, the decision she had made about him, to leave France, and the relationship she had seen as a dead end for her.

'I hope so. Maybe even a movie someday, if I ever write it. That's a part I'd like to play!' They both knew she already had. 'I like writing the book though. It gives me the narrative voice, which is all-knowing, all-seeing, not just dialogue between characters, and facial expressions on a screen in film. The writer knows everything, or is supposed to, I think. As it so happens, I discovered that I didn't. I couldn't find the answers to my own questions, so I came to Europe to find them, before I go on with the book. I hoped it would open some doors for me, and unblock my writing.'

'And did it?' He looked intrigued, and she smiled ruefully.

'I don't know. It might have. I went to see our old house the day I arrived in Paris, and I had some ideas. I was going back to the hotel to do some writing, and the tunnel happened between the house and the hotel. And it all blew out of my head, along with everything that's ever been in it. It's very strange not knowing who you are, or where you've been, what mattered to you. All the people and places and events you had collected disappear, and you're left standing alone in silence, with no idea what your history is, or who you've been.' It was the ultimate nightmare, and he couldn't imagine it as he looked at her. 'It's coming back now, in bits and pieces. But I don't know what I've forgotten. Most of the time, I see pictures and faces and remember feelings, and I'm not sure how they fit into the scheme of things, or the jigsaw puzzle of my life.' She remembered more of him than of anyone else, which seemed odd to her. She remembered more about Matthieu than about her own children, which made her sad. And she remembered almost nothing of Sean, except what she'd been told, and a few high points of their eight years. Even the memory of his death was vague. And she was able to recall Jason least of all, although she knew she loved him in a kind, brotherly way. She had different feelings about

342

Matthieu. Her memories of him made her uncomfortable and brought back the memory of intense joy and pain. Mostly pain.

'I think your memory will come back. Probably fully in the end. You have to be patient. Maybe it will give you greater insights than you would have had otherwise.'

'Maybe.'

The doctors had been encouraging, but they couldn't promise full recovery yet. She was doing better, and moving forward quickly, but there were still times when she came to a dead stop. There were words, places, incidents, and people that had disappeared right out of her head. She didn't know if she would ever find them again, although the therapists were helping her. She was relying on others to share their history with her, and jog her memory, as Matthieu had. And in his case, she was not yet sure if it was a blessing or not. What he had shared so far had made her sad for what they'd lost, even a child. 'If my memory doesn't come back,' she said practically, 'I'm going to have a hell of a time working in future. It may be all over for me now. An actress who can't remember lines isn't likely to get a lot of work, although I've worked with a lot of those,' she said, and laughed. She had been an amazingly good sport about the loss she had sustained, and was far less depressed than her doctors and family had feared. She still had hope. And so did he. She seemed remarkably alive and alert to him, given what had happened, and the impact to her brain.

'I used to love watching you film your movies. I went to England every weekend, when you were doing the one after *Marie Antoinette*. I can't remember the name now. Steven Archer was in it, and Sir Harland Chadwick.' He tried to jog his memory, and without even trying, Carole blurted out the name of the film.

'*Epiphany*. Christ, what an awful picture that was,' she said, grinning, and then looked stunned that she had remembered the name, and the movie itself. 'Wow, where did that come from?'

'It's all in there somewhere,' Matthieu said gently. 'You'll find it. You just have to look.'

'I think I'm afraid of what I'll find,' she said

honestly. 'Maybe it's easier like this. I don't remember the things that hurt me, the people I hated, or who hated me. The events and people I must have wanted to forget . . . I don't remember the good ones either though,' she said, looking wistful. 'I wish I remembered more about my children, particularly Chloe. I think I hurt her with my career. I must have been very selfish when she and Anthony were children. He seems to have forgiven me, or he says there was nothing to forgive, but Chloe is more honest about it. She seems angry, and so hurt. I wish I'd been smarter then and spent more time with them.' With memory had come guilt.

'You did spend time with them. A lot of time. Too much, I thought sometimes,' Matthieu reassured her. 'You took them everywhere with you, and with us. Chloe was never out of your sight when you weren't working, and she was on the set with you when you were. You didn't even want to put her in school. She was a very needy little girl. Whatever you gave her, she wanted something different, or more. She was a hard child to please.'

'Is that true?' It was interesting seeing it through the lenses of his eyes, since her own were so cloudy, and she wondered if he was right, or biased by the gender and cultural difference between them.

'I thought so. I never spent as much time with my children as you did, and neither did their mother, and she didn't work like you. You were constantly glued to Chloe and worried about her. And Anthony too. I had an easier time with him. He was older, and more accessible for me, because he was a boy. We were great friends when you were here. And in the end, he hated me, as you did. He saw you crying all the time.' He looked guilty and uncomfortable when he said it.

'Did I hate you?' she asked, looking puzzled. What she remembered, or sensed from the memories she had retrieved, was agony not hatred, or perhaps they had been the same. Disappointment, deception, frustration, anger. Hatred seemed such a strong word. She didn't hate him as he sat next to her. And Anthony had been angry when he saw him, like a child who had been bitterly disappointed, or betrayed. In the end, Matthieu had betrayed not only them, but himself.

'I don't know,' he said, thinking about it before he answered. 'Perhaps you should have hated me, if you didn't. I let you down terribly. I was wrong. I engaged in commitments to you that I couldn't fulfill. I had no right to make the promises I did to you. I believed them then, but when I've looked back, and I have a lot, I know that I was dreaming. I wanted to make it real, and couldn't. My dream became a nightmare for you. And for me, in the end.' He was trying to be honest with her, and himself. He had wanted to say these things to her for years, and it was a relief to do so, although painful for both of them. 'Anthony wouldn't even say goodbye to me when you left. He felt his father had betrayed all of you, and then I added to it. It was a terrible blow for you and your children and for me as well. I think it was the first time in my life when I truly saw myself as a bad man. I was a prisoner of circumstance.' She nodded, absorbing what he had said. She couldn't confirm or deny the truth of what he said, but it made sense. And as she listened, she felt compassion for him, knowing he must have suffered too.

'It must have been a hard time for both of us.'

'It was. And for Arlette. I never thought she loved me, until you came along. Maybe she only discovered it then herself. I'm not sure it was really love. But she felt I had an obligation to her, and I suppose she was right. I've always thought of myself as a man of honor, and I wasn't honorable to any of you then. Or myself. I loved you, and stayed with her. Perhaps it would have been different if I hadn't stayed in the government. My second term changed everything, and your fame. Having a mistress wouldn't have been such a huge shock, others have done it before and since in France, but because it was you, the scandal would have been incredible, for all of us, and it would have destroyed your career, and mine, I think. Arlette benefited from that,' he said honestly.

'And took full advantage of it, as I recall,' Carole said, looking suddenly tense. 'She said she was going to call the studio on me, and the press, and then threatened suicide.' The memory of it came back to her in a rush, and Matthieu looked embarrassed.

'These things happen in France. It is much more common for women to threaten suicide here than in the States, especially in matters of the heart.'

'She had you by the ass, and me too,' Carole said bluntly, and he laughed.

'You might say that, although I would say a different part of the anatomy, in my case. But she had me by my children too. I truly thought they'd never speak to me again if I left her. She had my oldest son talk to me, as a spokesman for the family. She was very clever about that. I can't blame her. I was so sure she'd agree to a divorce. We didn't love each other, and hadn't in years by then. I was naïve in believing she would readily agree to let me go. And my naïveté caused me to mislead you.' He said it with an air of sorrow, as Carole met his eyes.

'We were both in a difficult position,' she said generously.

'Yes,' he agreed, 'trapped by our love for each

other, and held hostage by her, and the Ministry of the Interior, and my duties there.' Carole realized as he said it that he had had choices, hard ones maybe, but choices nonetheless. He had made his, and she had made hers when she left. She remembered fearing that it was too soon to throw in the towel, she had wondered for years if she should have stayed, if things would have ended differently if she had, if she might have won him in the end. She had finally let it go when she met Sean and got married. Until then she had blamed herself for leaving Matthieu too soon, but two and a half years seemed long enough for him to do what he had promised, and she had become convinced he never would. There had always been some excuse, which wasn't believable after a while. He believed them, but Carole no longer could. She had given up. And his gift to her, when they spoke of it since her accident, was to tell her she had been right. Even with her scrambled memory, it was an enormous relief to hear him finally admit that to her. Before, in conversations on the phone the year after she left, he always blamed her for leaving too soon. It wasn't, she knew now. It was right. Even fifteen years later she was grateful to know that, just as she was for the things Jason had told her about their marriage. She was beginning to wonder if, in some odd way, the tunnel bombing had been a gift. All of these people had come to her from her past, and opened their hearts. She would never have known any of this otherwise. It was exactly what she had needed for her book, and her life.

'You should rest,' Matthieu finally said to her, as he saw her eyes grow tired. The police investigation had drained her, and talking about their past was taxing for her too. And then he asked her a question that had haunted him since he had found her again. He had drifted in to see her several times, seemingly casual and politely concerned, but his interest in seeing her was far less offhand than it seemed. And now that she was fully conscious and remembered what they had once meant to each other, he respected the fact that she had a choice. 'Would you like me to come and see you again, Carole?' He held his breath as he asked, and she hesitated for a long time. At first seeing him had confused and unnerved her, but now there was something comforting about having him nearby, like a looming guardian angel who protected her with his wide wings and intensely blue eyes, the color of sky.

'Yes, I would,' she said finally, after an interminable pause. 'I like talking to you.' She always had. 'We don't have to talk about the past anymore.' She knew enough, she wasn't sure she wanted to know more. There was too much pain there, even now. 'Maybe we can be friends. I'd like that.' He nodded, still wanting more, but he didn't want to scare her, and knew he might. She was still fragile after everything that had happened to her, and so much time had passed since their affair. It was probably too late, much as he hated to admit it to himself. He had lost the love of his life. But she had come back now, in a different guise. Perhaps, as she said, it would be enough. They could try.

'I'll come to see you tomorrow,' he promised, standing up, as he looked down at her. She looked frail as she lay beneath the covers. She barely made a ripple in the bed. He bent to kiss her forehead. She smiled peacefully as she closed her eyes and spoke in a dreamy whisper.

''Bye, Matthieu . . . thank you . . .' He had never loved her more.

14

Stevie showed up at the hospital late that afternoon with a small overnight bag, and asked the nurse to set up a cot in Carole's room. She was planning to spend the night. When she walked in, Carole was just waking up from a long nap. She had slept for hours after Matthieu left, exhausted by the morning she'd had, and then talking to him. It had taken her full concentration to manage both.

'I'm moving in,' Stevie said, setting down her bag. Her eyes still looked watery, and she had a red nose and a cough. But she was taking the antibiotics and said she was no longer contagious. Carole's cold was better too. 'So what mischief did you get into today?' Carole told her about the police coming to see her, and Stevie was pleased to see the two CRS guards at her door, although their machine guns looked unpleasant, as they would to any would-be assailants too.

'And Matthieu stayed after they left. He was here when I talked to the police,' Carole added, looking pensive, as Stevie looked at her with narrowed eyes.

'Should I be worried?'

'I don't think so. That was all such a long time ago. I was a kid, younger than you are now. We agreed to be friends, or try to be. I think he means well. He looks like an unhappy man.' He had the same intensity she remembered even in their days of passion, but there was a depth of sadness in his eyes that hadn't been there before, except after his daughter died. 'I'll be going home soon anyway. It's kind of nice to put old ghosts to rest, and make friends with them. It takes away their power.'

'I'm not sure anything could take away that

guy's power,' Stevie said sensibly. 'He comes in here like a tidal wave, and everybody jumps about ten feet when they see him.'

'He was a very important man, and still is. He called the Minister of the Interior about me. That's how we got the guards at the door.'

'I don't mind that. I just don't want him upsetting you,' Stevie said protectively. She didn't want anything hurting Carole, ever again if possible. She'd been through far too much. Her recovery was hard enough. She didn't need to deal with emotional issues too, particularly Matthieu's. He'd had his chance, and blown it, as far as Stevie was concerned.

'He doesn't upset me. The things I remember about him do sometimes, but he's been very nice. He asked my permission to visit me again.' That had impressed her. He hadn't just assumed it, he had asked.

'And did you give it to him?' Stevie asked with interest. She still didn't trust the guy. He had scary eyes. But not to Carole. She knew him better than that, or had once upon a time.

'Yes. I think we can be friends now. It's worth a try. He's a very interesting man.'

'So was Hitler . . . and Stalin . . . I don't know why, but I get the feeling this guy would stop at nothing to get what he wants.'

'That's how it was before. It's different now. We're different. He's old. It's over.' Carole sounded sure of it, Stevie wasn't.

'Don't bet on that. Old loves die hard.' Theirs certainly had. She had thought about him for years, and loved him for a long time. It had kept her from loving anyone till Sean. But Carole said nothing and only nodded.

Stevie made herself comfortable on the cot they brought in, and later in the evening put on pajamas, and said they were having a slumber party. Carole felt guilty for having her assistant stay with her instead of at the Ritz. But after the boy-with-the-knife incident, Stevie no longer felt comfortable being far from Carole. She had also promised Jason she'd stay close. He had called a dozen times, shaken by the attack. Carole's children had called her too. They had guards with machine guns outside the room now, and

Stevie to protect her inside. It touched Carole that Stevie cared that much about her. And they giggled and chatted like two kids late into the night, while the nurse stood outside and talked to the guards.

'This is fun,' Carole said at one point, laughing. 'Thank you for staying with me.'

'I was lonely at the hotel too,' Stevie admitted. 'I'm really starting to miss Alan.' She had been gone for weeks, even over Thanksgiving. 'He's been calling a lot. He's actually beginning to sound like a grown-up, which is pretty goddamn good news since he turned forty last month. He's definitely a late bloomer.' Neither of them had ever been married, and lately he'd been talking about it, and long-term plans for their future. 'He invited me to Christmas dinner at his parents'. Up till now, we always spent the holidays separately. Spending them together seemed like too much of a commitment, to both of us. I guess that's progress, but toward what? I like what we've got.' His talking long term made her nervous.

'What would you do if you got married?' Carole asked cautiously, from her bed, with a night-light on nearby. The room was almost dark, which lent itself to confidences and questions they might not have dared ask each other otherwise, although they were always fairly candid with each other. But some topics were taboo, even between them. This was a question Carole had never asked her before, and hesitated even now.

'Kill myself,' Stevie said simply, and then laughed. 'About what? I don't know . . . nothing . . . I hate change. Our apartment is comfortable. He hates my furniture, I don't care. Maybe I'd repaint the living room, and get another dog.' Stevie couldn't see why anything would change, but it might. Marriage would give Alan a far greater claim on her life, which was why she didn't want to marry him. She liked her life just the way it was.

'I mean about your job.'

'My job? What does marriage have to do with that, unless I marry you? I guess then I'd move in.' They both laughed at that.

'You work a lot of hours, you travel with me. We're gone a lot. And anytime I get blown up in

359

a tunnel, you could get stuck in Paris for a hell of a long time,' Carole explained with a smile.

'Oh that. Shit, I don't know. I never thought about it. I think I'd give up Alan before I'd give up my job. In fact, I know it. If my work with you is an issue to him, he can take a long hike, into oblivion. I'm not giving up this job. Ever. You'd have to kill me first.' It was comforting for Carole to hear it, although sometimes things changed unexpectedly. She worried about that. And she wanted Stevie to have a good life, not just a job.

'How does Alan feel about it? Does he ever complain?'

'Not really. He whines sometimes, if I'm gone a long time, and says he misses me. I figure it's good for him, unless he finds another roommate. But he's very much steady-eddie, and he's pretty busy himself. He actually travels more than I do, although he doesn't go as far.' Most of his trips were in California, while hers with Carole were abroad. As far as I know, he's never cheated on me. I think he used to be fairly wild when he was younger. I'm the first woman he's ever lived with.

It's worked out pretty decently so far. Which is another thing, why fix what ain't broke?'

'Has he asked you to marry him, Stevie?'

'No, thank God. I just worry that he will. He never used to talk about marriage at all. Now the subject does come up. A lot lately. He says he thinks we should get married. But he's never proposed. I'd be upset if he did. I guess he's thinking that it must be some kind of midlife crisis, which is depressing too. I hate to think we're that old.'

'You're not. It's nice that he's feeling responsible about you. I'd be more upset if he weren't. Are you going to his parents' for Christmas?' Carole was curious, and Stevie groaned from her cot across the room.

'I guess. His mother is a real pain in the ass. She thinks I'm too tall and too old for him. Nice. But his father is cute. And I like both of his sisters. They're smart, like him.' It all sounded healthy to Carole, and reminded her to call Chloe the next day. She wanted to invite her to come to California a few days before the others, so they'd have some time alone. She thought it would be good for both of them.

She lay in the dark for a few minutes, thinking about what Matthieu had said about her, and how difficult and needy Chloe had been even as a little girl. It absolved Carole a little, and relieved her, but she still wanted to try to make up to her for what Chloe felt she had missed. Neither of them had anything to lose, and both had everything to win.

She was nearly asleep when Stevie spoke to her again. It was another of those easier-in-the-dark questions. They couldn't see each other from their beds. It was like confession. The question took Carole by surprise.

'Are you still in love with Matthieu?' Stevie had been wondering for days, and was worried about it. Carole took a long time to answer, pondering it, and then said what was closest to the truth.

'I don't know.'

'Do you think you'd ever move back here?' Stevie was worried about her job, just as Carole worried about losing her. This time Carole answered quickly, with no hesitation in her voice.

'No. Not for a man anyway. I like my life in L.A.' Even with Anthony and Chloe gone, she liked the house, the city, her friends, and the weather. Gray Paris winters no longer appealed to her, no matter how beautiful the city was. She had been there, done that, years before. She had no desire to move. 'I'm not going anywhere,' she reassured her assistant.

They both fell asleep shortly after, comfortable that nothing in their lives was going to change. The future was sure, as much as it ever was.

When Carole awoke the next morning, Stevie was already awake, up, dressed, and her bed had been made. A nurse was walking into the room with Carole's breakfast tray, and the neurologist was close on her heels.

The doctor came to stand beside Carole's bed, with a warm smile. She was their star patient and had made a recovery thus far that exceeded all their expectations. She said as much to Carole, while Stevie stood nearby, like a proud mother hen. They had much to be thankful for.

'There are still so many things I can't remember. My phone number, my address. What my house looks like from the outside. I know what my bedroom looks like, and the garden, and even my office. I can't visualize the rest of my house. I can't remember my housekeeper's face or name. I don't remember my children growing up . . . I can hear my father's voice, but I can't see him in my mind . . . I don't know who my friends are. I hardly remember anything about either of my marriages, particularly my last one.' It was an endless litany as her doctor smiled.

'The last item you mentioned could be a blessing. I remember far too much about both my marriages! Ah, to forget them both!' the doctor said as all three women laughed, and then grew serious again. 'You must be patient, Carole. It will take months, maybe a year, even two. Some things may never come back, small things probably. You can do things to push yourself, photographs, letters, rely on friends to tell you things. Your children will fill you in. Your brain had a tremendous shock, now it's doing its job again. Give it some time to recover. It's like when

364

a film breaks at a movie. It takes a little time to thread it back on the reel again and get it running smoothly. It jumps and skips for a while, the picture is blurry, the sound is too fast or too slow, and then the film rolls on again. You must be patient during this process. Stamping your feet or throwing popcorn at the screen won't make it go any faster. And the more impatient you get, the harder it will be for you.'

'Will I remember how to drive?' Her motor skills and coordination had already improved but weren't perfect yet. The physical therapists had been pushing her hard, with good results. Her balance was better, but every now and then the room reeled around her, or her legs felt weak.

'Perhaps not at first. It will probably come back. In each case, you have to remember what you once knew without a second thought. The dishwasher, the washing machine, your car, your computer. Everything you've ever learned has to be entered into the computer in your head again, or brought back if it was saved. I think more of it has been saved than you know. A year from now you may have no evidence of the accident at all. Or even in six months. Or there may always be some small thing that is harder for you now. You'll need a physical therapist in California, one who is familiar with brain trauma. I was going to suggest a speech therapist, but I don't think that's an issue for you.' After her initial difficulty at finding words, she seemed to have full access to her vocabulary, and had for a while. 'I have the name of an excellent neurologist in Los Angeles, who can follow your case. We'll send all your records to him after you arrive in L.A. I suggest that you see him every two weeks at first, but that's for him to decide. Later, you can see him once every few months, if you're not having any problems. I want you to be aware of headaches and report them to him immediately. Don't wait for your next visit. And any problems with balance. That could be a problem for a while. We're going to do some scans today, but I'm extremely pleased with your progress. You are our miracle child here at La Pitié.'

Others who had survived the bombing hadn't done as well, and many had died, even after the first days, most of them from burns. Carole's arms had healed well, the burn on her face had been superficial, and she was getting used to the scar. The doctor had been impressed at her lack of vanity. She was a sensible woman. Carole had been far more worried about her brain than her face. She hadn't decided yet whether to have surgery, to get rid of the scar, or live with it for a while and decide how she felt about it later. She was worried about the possible effect of anesthesia on her brain and so were they. The scar could wait.

'I still don't want you to fly for a few more weeks. I know you want to be home for the holidays, but if you could wait till the twentieth or twenty-first, I'd be pleased. Providing you have no complications between now and then. That could change plans considerably. But as things stand now, I think you'll be home for Christmas.' There were tears in Carole's eyes as she listened, and Stevie's too. For a while there, it looked as if she'd never go home again, or wouldn't recognize it if she did. It was going to be a great Christmas this year, with both her children around the tree, and Jason too. He hadn't spent holidays with them in years. The kids were thrilled he was coming, and so was she.

'When can I go back to the hotel?' Carole asked. She was safe and comfortable in her hospital cocoon, and a little frightened about leaving, but she liked the idea of spending her final days in Paris at the Ritz. They had already agreed to send a nurse with her.

'Let's see how your scans look today. Perhaps you can go back to the hotel tomorrow or the next day.' Carole beamed, although she was going to miss the feeling of safety she derived from being there, with medical care close at hand. The CRS guards were going to the Ritz with her, that had already been arranged, and hotel security would be tightened once she returned. They were planning for it. 'How would you feel about my sending a physician on the flight to California with you? I think it might be a good idea, and reassuring for you. The pressure might cause some changes that could alarm you, although I don't think you'll have a problem by then. It's just a precaution, and another element of comfort for you.' Carole and Stevie both liked that idea. Stevie hadn't mentioned it, but she was worried about the trip, and the pressure, as the doctor said.

'That would be great,' Carole said quickly, as Stevie nodded her approval.

'I have a young neurosurgeon who has a sister in Los Angeles, and he's dying to make the trip to spend the holidays with her. I'll let him know. He'll be thrilled.'

'Me too,' Stevie said with relief. She'd been panicking about the responsibility of being alone with Carole on the flight, in case anything went wrong when they were in the air. It was an eleven-hour flight, a long time to worry about her, and have no medical advice or support after all she'd been through. They had talked about chartering a plane, but Carole wanted to go commercial. Chartering seemed an unnecessary expense to her, and she was ambulatory after all, just frail. She wanted to go back as she had come, on Air France, with Stevie next to her, and now the young doctor with the sister in L.A. Stevie felt infinitely better now about the trip.

She could even sleep, with a doctor close at hand, a neurosurgeon yet.

'I think everything's in order then,' the doctor said, smiling again. 'I'll let you know how the tests look later on. I think you can start packing up soon. You'll be drinking champagne at the Ritz in no time.' She was teasing, they knew, as Carole had already been told she shouldn't drink alcohol for a while. She seldom drank anyway, so she didn't care.

She got out of bed and showered after the doctor left. Stevie helped her wash her hair, and this time Carole took a long look in the mirror at the scar on her cheek.

'Not too pretty, I must say,' she said, frowning at it.

'It looks like a dueling scar,' Stevie said blithely. 'I'll bet you can cover it with makeup.'

'Maybe. Maybe it's my badge of honor. At least my mind's not completely shot,' Carole said, walking away from the mirror with a shrug, drying her hair with a towel. She mentioned to Stevie again that it was a little scary leaving the hospital. It was like leaving the womb. She was glad she was taking a nurse back to the hotel.

She called Chloe in London after her hair was dry, and told her she'd be back at the hotel soon, and on her way to Los Angeles by Christmas. She assumed, as they all did, that her scans would be fine, or at least no worse than they'd been before. There was nothing to suggest otherwise.

'I was wondering if you'd like to come out a few days early,' Carole offered her daughter, 'before the others. Maybe the day after I get home myself. You can help me get ready for Christmas. We can do a little shopping together. I don't think I bought anything before I left L.A. I was thinking it might be a nice time for us to spend together, and maybe we can plan to take a trip together in the spring, someplace you'd really like to go.' Carole had thought about it for days, and liked the idea herself.

'Just us?' Chloe sounded stunned.

'Just us.' Carole smiled as she held the phone, and met Stevie's eyes, who gave her a thumbs-up. 'I think we have some mother–daughter time to make up for. I'm game if you are.'

'Wow, Mom . . . I never thought you'd do that.' Chloe sounded awed.

'I'd love it. It would be a treat for me, if you can take the time.' She remembered what Matthieu had said, about how needy and demanding she'd been as a child. But even if she had been, if that was what she needed, why not give it to her? Everyone's needs were different, and perhaps Chloe's were greater than most, for whatever reason, whether her mother's fault or not. Carole had the time. Why not use it to bring happiness to her daughter? Wasn't that what mothers were for? Just because Anthony was more independent and self-sufficient, it didn't make Chloe's needs wrong. Just different. And Carole wanted to spend time with him too. She wanted to share the gift that had been given to her, her life. They were her children after all, even if adults with their own lives. Whatever they needed from her now, she wanted to try to give them, in honor not only of the past, but the present, and future. One day they would have lives and families of their own. Now was the time for her to spend special moments with them, before it was too late. It was the eleventh hour for her, and she was just squeaking in under the wire. 'Why don't you think about where you'd like to go? Maybe this spring. Anywhere in the world.' It was an amazing offer, and as always, Stevie was impressed by her employer and friend. She always came through, for all of them. She was an extraordinary woman, and a pleasure to know and love.

'What about Tahiti?' Chloe said in a single breath. 'I can take my vacation in March.'

'Sounds great to me. I've never been there. At least I don't think so. And if I have, I don't remember it, so it'll be new to me.' They both laughed at what she said. 'We'll figure it out. Anyway, I'm hoping to get back to L.A. on the twenty-first. Maybe you want to arrive on the twenty-second. The others aren't coming till Christmas Eve. It's not a lot of time, but it's a start. I'll be in Paris till then.' But she knew Chloe had to catch up on her work at British *Vogue,* and even work weekends, to make up for the time she'd been away, so Carole didn't expect to see her till just before Christmas in L.A. She wasn't well enough yet to fly over to London to see her. She wanted to take it easy until her flight back to L.A., a trip that would be something of a challenge. Less so now with a neurosurgeon traveling with them.

'I'll come on the twenty-second, Mom. And thank you,' Chloe said. Carole could tell it was heartfelt. If nothing else, Chloe appreciated the effort her mother was making. Maybe she always had made the effort, Carole told herself, and maybe her daughter had never noticed it before, or been old enough to understand it and be grateful. They were both making an effort now, and aware enough to be kind to each other. That alone was an enormous gift, for both of them.

'I'll let you know when I'm back at the hotel. Tomorrow or the day after. I'll call you,' Carole said calmly.

'Thanks, Mom,' Chloe said in a loving tone, and they both hung up after saying that they loved each other.

Carole's next call was to Anthony in New York. He was at the office and sounded busy, but he was pleased to hear her. She told him about going back to the hotel, and how much she was looking forward to seeing him at Christmas. He sounded in good spirits, although he warned her about befriending Matthieu again. It was a recurring theme in every call.

'I just don't trust him, Mom. People don't change. I remember how miserable he made you before. All I remember about our last days in Paris was you crying all the time. I don't even remember what it was about. I just know how sad you were. I don't want that to happen to you again. You've been through enough hard times. I'd rather see you back with Dad.' It was the first time he had said that to her, and it startled her. She didn't want to disappoint him, any more than she wanted to hurt Jason, but she was not going back to him.

'That isn't going to happen,' she said calmly. 'I think we're better as friends.'

'Well, Matthieu is no friend,' her son growled at her. 'He was a real bastard to you when you lived with him. He was married, wasn't he?' His recollections were fuzzy now, only the negative impression had remained, and it was extreme. He would have done anything to protect his mother from that grief again. Even the memory of it hurt him now. She deserved so much better than that, from any man.

'Yes, he was married,' she said quietly. She didn't want to be put in the position of defending him.

'I thought so. Why did he live with us then?' He had been there most of the time.

'People make arrangements like that in France. They have mistresses as well as wives. It's not a great situation for anyone, but they seem to accept it here. It was a lot harder to get divorced in those days. So people lived that way. I wanted him to get divorced, but his daughter died, and then his wife threatened suicide. He was too high up in the government to get out of his marriage without it causing a major incident in the press. It sounds crazy, but it was considered less shocking to do what we did. He said he'd get divorced, and we were going to get married. I think he really believed we would, there was just never a good time for him to get out. So we left,' she said with a sigh. 'I didn't want to go, but I didn't want all of us living that way forever. It didn't seem right. For you, or for me. I'm too American for that. I didn't want to be someone's mistress permanently, and lead a secret life.'

'What happened to his wife?' Anthony asked, sounding stern.

'She died. Last year apparently.'

'I'm going to be very upset if you get involved with him again. He's just going to hurt you. He did before.' He sounded more like a father than a son.

'I'm not involved with him,' she said, trying to reassure him and calm him down.

'Is it a possibility? Be honest, Mom.' She loved the sound of 'Mom.' It still sounded new to her, and filled with love. Every time one of her children said it, it gave her a thrill.

'I don't know. I can't see that happening. That was all a long time ago.'

'He's still in love with you. I could see it the minute he walked in.'

'If so, he's in love with the memory of who I was then. We've all gotten old.' She sounded tired as she said it. So much had happened to her since she got to France. She had so much to recover from, relearn, and digest. It was overwhelming to think about.

'You're not old. I just don't want you to get hurt.'

'Neither do I. I can't even think about something like that right now.' He was comforted by what she said.

'Good. You'll be home soon. Just don't let him start something before you go.'

'I won't, but you have to trust me on that,' she said, feeling like a mother as she said it. No matter how much her son loved her, she had a right to make her own decisions and lead her own life. She wanted to remind him of that.

'I just don't trust him.'

'Why don't we give him the benefit of the doubt, for now? He wasn't a bad man, his situation was just a mess, and as a result, so was mine. I was foolish to get into it, but I was young, hardly older than you are now. I should have realized what would happen. He's French. In those days, Frenchmen didn't get divorced. I'm not sure they do even now. Having a mistress is a national tradition here.' She smiled, and at his end Anthony shook his head.

'If you ask me, it sucks.'

'Yeah, it did,' she admitted. She remembered that clearly now.

They changed the subject then, and he told her it was snowing in New York. And when he said it, the image of snow came to her mind, and she suddenly remembered taking them skating in Rockefeller Center when they were small, when the big Christmas tree was up, and it was snowing. It was just before they went to Paris, and everything was still right in their world. Jason had come to pick them up and had taken them all out for ice cream. She remembered them as the happiest days of her life. Everything had seemed so perfect, even if it wasn't.

'Bundle up,' Carole said to him, and he laughed.

'I will, Mom. You take care too. Don't do anything crazy when you get back to the Ritz, like go dancing.' She hit a blank spot, and didn't know if he meant it.

'Do I like to dance?' she asked, sounding puzzled.

'Like a lunatic. Best dancer on the floor. I'll remind you when I come out for Christmas. We'll put on some music, or I can take you to a club.'

'That sounds like fun.' If she didn't lose her balance and fall over, she thought to herself, dismayed that there were still so many things about herself she didn't know. At least there was someone to remind her.

They chatted for a few more minutes and hung up, after she told him she loved him too. And then Jason called her. He had walked into their son's office just as Anthony was hanging up, and he said his mother sounded pretty good. Carole was touched that Jason called.

'I hear it's snowing in New York,' she said to Jason.

'Like crazy. Four inches in the last hour. They said we'll have two feet of snow by tonight. Lucky for you you're going back to L.A. and not coming here. I heard it's seventy-five degrees there today. I can't wait to come out for Christmas.'

'I can't wait for all of us to be together,' she

said with a warm smile that matched the feeling in her heart. 'I was just remembering when I took the kids skating at Rockefeller Center and you took us out for ice cream. It was so nice.'

'Now you're remembering things even I don't recall,' he said with a smile. 'We used to take the kids sledding in the park. That was fun too.' And the carousel, and model sailboat pond. The zoo. There were a lot of things they had done together, and that she had done with her children between making movies. Maybe Matthieu was right and she wasn't the neglectful mother that she feared she had been. Chloe had made it sound like she was never there. 'When are you getting out of the hospital?' Jason asked.

'Tomorrow, I hope. I'm waiting to hear today.' And then she told him a doctor was flying back to L.A. with her, and he sounded relieved.

'That's smart. Don't do anything crazy before you leave. Just take it easy, and eat a lot of pastries at the hotel.'

'The doctor says I should walk. Maybe I'll do some Christmas shopping.'

'Don't worry about that. We all have the only

Christmas gift we wanted. You.' It was a sweet thing to say, and she was touched by him again. No matter how hard she dredged in her memory bank, she couldn't come up with any romantic feelings for him, but she loved him like a brother. He was her children's father, a man she had loved and been married to for ten years, and who was forever woven into the fabric of her heart, but in a different way than he once had been. Their relationship and attachment to each other had changed over the years. For her anyway. It was different with Matthieu. She had far fewer comfortable feelings about him, and sometimes he made her uneasy. Jason never did. Jason was a spot of warm sunlight where she felt comfortable and safe. Matthieu was a mysterious garden where she was afraid to go, but she still remembered its beauty, and its thorns. 'See you in L.A.,' Jason said cheerily, and then hung up. A little while later, the doctor came in with the results of her scans. They showed that she had improved.

'You're on your way,' the doctor beamed at her. 'You're going home . . . or back to the Ritz for now. You can leave the hospital tomorrow.'

They were actually sad to see her go, but happy for her. And so was she. It had been an extra-ordinary month.

Stevie packed her things for her that afternoon, and notified hotel security that they'd be arriving the next day. The head of security advised bringing her in through the rue Cambon door, on the back side of the hotel. They would open it for her. Most of the press and paparazzi lay in wait in the Place Vendôme. Carole wanted to come in with as little fuss as possible, although she knew that sooner or later they would take photographs of her. She wanted a breather for now. It was going to be her first time out of the hospital in a month, after being at death's door. Stevie wanted to give her time to get on her feet, before the press attacked her. Carole Barber getting out of the hospital in Paris was going to make the front page in newspapers all over the world. There was nothing easy about being a star. And certainly no privacy. Dead or alive, the public thought they owned her. And it was Stevie's job to shield her from prying eyes. The doctors had saved her life. And it was up to the CRS and hotel security to keep her alive. Given that, Stevie figured hers was the easiest job.

Matthieu called her that night to see how she was. He was in Lyon overnight on business for the law firm. He had a case pending there.

'I'm going home!' she chortled happily, and there was a silence at the other end.

'To Los Angeles?' he asked, sounding crestfallen, and she laughed.

'No, to the hotel. They want me here for two more weeks before I fly, to make sure I'm okay. They're sending a doctor home on the plane with me, and I'm taking a nurse to the hotel. I'll be fine. The doctor will come and check on me there. As long as I don't do anything crazy or stupid, and no one tries to kill me again, I'll be fine. I have to walk around to get my legs back. Maybe I can get my exercise at the jewelers in the Place Vendôme.' She was teasing, since she never bought jewelry for herself, but she was in high spirits, and he was relieved to hear that she was only going as far as the hotel, for now. He wanted to spend some time with her before she left. It was too soon to lose her again.

'We can go to Bagatelle and walk,' he said, and when he said the word she remembered being there with him before. And the Luxembourg Gardens and the Bois de Boulogne. There were a multitude of places to go for walks in Paris. 'I'll be back tomorrow. I'll call you. Be careful, Carole.'

'I will. I promise. It's a little scary leaving the hospital. I feel like my head is made of glass now.' Not quite, but she was well aware of her fragility and her own mortality as never before. She didn't want to challenge it again. Being away from the doctors who had saved her life was frightening. She was relieved to be taking a nurse to the hotel, and Stevie had gotten an adjoining room to her suite, so she'd be sleeping nearby if Carole had a problem, which no one expected. But they worried anyway, and Matthieu sounded concerned as well.

'Are you sure you should fly so soon?' He had a vested interest in her staying, but he was genuinely worried about her, even as a friend.

'They said it's fine, as long as nothing weird

happens in the next two weeks. And I want to be home for Christmas with my kids.'

'They could celebrate it with you at the Ritz,' he said hopefully.

'That's not the same.' Besides, Paris had an unhappy connotation for all of them now. It would be a while before her children would feel comfortable at the Ritz again, without thinking of the agonizing days they had spent there waiting to see if she would survive. It was going to be good to get home, especially for her.

'I understand. If you feel up to it, I'd like to visit you at the hotel tomorrow when I get back.'

'That would be fine,' she said calmly. She was looking forward to seeing him, and even to going for walks with him.

That seemed harmless enough, even for her.

'See you tomorrow,' he said, thinking about her, as he hung up at his end. He was dreading the day she would leave him again, this time perhaps forever.

15

Getting Carole ready to leave the hospital was more arduous than Stevie had expected. Carole was tired when she woke up the next day, and nervous about leaving the cocoon they had provided for her. She had to turn from caterpillar into butterfly once again. Stevie helped her wash her hair, Carole put on makeup for the first time, and covered the scar on her cheek surprisingly well. Stevie helped her put on jeans, a black sweater, a pea jacket she'd had at the hotel, and a pair of flat black suede loafers. Her signature diamond stud earrings were on her ears, and her hair was pulled back in the familiar sleek ponytail. She looked like Carole Barber again, instead of a patient in a hospital gown, and even after the ordeal she'd been through, her natural beauty was striking. She looked very thin and a little frail as she got into a wheelchair, and nurses and doctors came to say goodbye to her. The nurse who was coming to the Ritz with them had her coat on and pushed the wheelchair, as the two CRS guards assigned to them walked on either side of Carole with stern looks, holding their machine guns. Stevie was carrying Carole's bag and her own. They felt like a motley crew.

They made their way down in the elevator and across the lobby with hospital security surrounding them, and the head of the hospital came out to shake her hand and wish her well. It was a touching departure. Her own doctor saw them to the car, which the Ritz had sent for her, a long Mercedes limousine. Both CRS guards, the nurse, Stevie, and Carole disappeared rapidly inside. She lowered the window and waved at the crowd of well-wishers on the sidewalk, while Stevie marveled at the good luck that no photographers had been on hand to impede their way. With luck, they would get into the hotel as easily, on the Cambon side, and into Carole's suite without incident. She already looked tired from the shock of being up, dressed, and outside again. It was a big change for her.

The limousine slid easily down the rue Cambon and stopped at the back entrance of the Ritz that had been opened especially for her, and on slightly wobbly legs she stood up, looked up at the sky, and smiled, while the CRS guards stood tightly at her side. She walked toward the hotel entrance under her own steam, smiling, just as four photographers leaped into view between the hotel door and her. Carole hesitated for an instant and then continued walking, smiling. Someone had tipped them off after all. The CRS guards waved them away, and the paparazzi stepped aside, shooting frame after frame of her, shouting her name, as one of them yelled 'Brava!' and threw her a rose. She caught it, turned, and smiled at him, and then disappeared gracefully into the hotel.

The manager was waiting inside for her, and escorted her to her suite. Just getting that far was harder work for Carole than she had expected. Security guards lined the halls, and she looked strained by the time she got to her suite, but thanked the manager for the enormous bouquet of roses that stood four feet tall on a table, welcoming her back to the Ritz. A few minutes later he left the room, and the CRS guards positioned themselves outside, as hotel security clustered around them. Stevie set down Carole's bag, and gave her a stern look.

'Sit down. You look beat.' She was worried about her friend. Carole's face was the color of snow.

'I am,' Carole admitted, lowering herself into a chair, feeling about a hundred years old, as the nurse helped her take off her coat, and then removed her own and put it aside. 'I can't believe how tired I am. All I did was get out of bed, and ride over here in a car. I feel like I was hit by a bus,' she complained to Stevie, looking exhausted.

'You were, a month ago. Give yourself a break.' Stevie was still annoyed that someone had warned the press that Carole was arriving. It was inevitable, but they would be all over her now, and waiting at every exit to the hotel. Whenever she wanted to get out, she would have to make her way past them. Stevie was contemplating the service exit as an option. It had worked for them before, although it wasn't far from the Cambon door, and they'd be watching it too. It just added more strain to Carole's existence, which she didn't need at the moment. It would have been nice if no one had known she'd made the move from hospital to hotel. That was too much to hope for, with maids cleaning her room, room service waiters bringing her food, and all the internal gossip in a big hotel, even a great one like the Ritz. Someone had been bound to tell the press. They got paid handsomely to do it.

Without asking, Stevie handed her a cup of her tea, and Carole took it gratefully. She felt as though she'd already climbed Everest that morning. And given what she'd been through, she had. 'Do you want anything to eat?'

'No, thanks.'

'Why don't you go lie down for a while? I think you just had your morning exercise.'

'Shit, am I ever going to feel normal again? I wasn't this tired in the hospital. I feel like I died.'

'You did,' Stevie confirmed. She could see that Carole was discouraged, but what she was going through was normal. The change from hospital to real world, however gently handled and carefully masterminded, was like being shot out of a cannon for her. 'You'll feel better in a day or two, or maybe even before that. You need to get used to your surroundings, and not being wrapped in cotton wool at the hospital. When I had my appendix out two years ago, I felt about ninety years old when I got home. Five days later I was dancing my ass off at a club. Give it time, kid. Give it time,' Stevie reassured her as Carole sighed. It discouraged her to feel so shaken and weak.

Carole walked slowly into her bedroom, and stood looking around with amazement. She looked at the desk and saw her computer and handbag on it. She felt as though she had left the room hours before to go on her fateful walk. When she turned to Stevie there were tears in her eyes.

'It's such a strange feeling knowing that when I left this room, I almost died a few hours later. It's kind of like dying and being reborn, or getting another chance or something.' Stevie nodded and hugged her friend.

'I know. I thought of it too. Do you want to switch rooms?' Carole shook her head. She didn't want to be indulged or babied. She just needed time to adjust to all that had happened, not only physically, but psychologically as well. She lay down on the bed, and looked around, as Stevie brought her the rest of her tea. She felt better already, lying down. It had been stressful for her seeing the press, although it didn't show. It never did. She looked like a queen as she waved graciously, smiled at them, and walked past, with her long blond hair, and diamond studs sparkling on her ears.

Stevie ordered lunch for them eventually, and Carole felt better after she ate. She luxuriated in a hot tub, in the giant bathtub in the pink marble bathroom, and then lay on her bed again in the heavy pink terry-cloth robe provided by the hotel. It was four o'clock when Matthieu called, and by then she'd had a nap, and felt more herself.

'How is it being back at the hotel?' he asked kindly.

'It was harder than I thought it would be getting here,' she admitted to him. 'I was wiped out when we arrived, but I'm feeling better now. I can't believe what a jolt it was. And we ran into some paparazzi at the back door. I probably looked like the Bride of Frankenstein getting out of the car. I could hardly walk.'

'I'm sure you looked beautiful. You always do.'

'One of the paparazzi threw me a rose, which was sweet. It almost knocked me down. The expression "you could have knocked me over with a feather" seems to have taken on new meaning.' He laughed at what she said.

'I was going to ask you to take a walk with me, but it doesn't sound like you're up to it. Would you like a visit instead? Maybe we can go for a walk tomorrow. Or a drive, if you prefer.'

'Would you like to come to tea?' she offered. She didn't feel up to having him to dinner, and wasn't sure she should anyway. Their relationship was tenuous, heavily impacted by the sorrows of the past, as well as the love they'd shared.

'That sounds perfect. Five o'clock?' he suggested, grateful that she was willing to see him.

'I'm not going anywhere,' she assured him. 'I'll be here.'

He was there an hour later, in a dark business suit, and his gray topcoat. It had gotten bitter cold that afternoon, and his cheeks were pink from the wind. Carole was wearing the same black sweater and jeans she had worn leaving the hospital, the black suede loafers and diamond studs on her ears. She looked exquisite to him, although very pale. But her eyes were bright, and she felt better as they sat down to tea, pastry, and *macarons* from La Durée, which the hotel had sent her. He'd been pleased to see the guards on duty outside her room, and noticed hotel security in the hall around the floor. They were taking no chances with her, as well they shouldn't. The incident at the hospital had put everyone on warning that she was at risk.

'How was Lyon?' she asked with a quiet smile. She was happy to see him.

'Tiresome. I had a court appearance I couldn't put off. And I almost missed my train back. The trials and tribulations of an ordinary citizen and lawyer.' He laughed at himself, and was obviously happy to see her too.

She seemed to come alive again as they sat and chatted, and became more animated and more herself. She ate half a dozen *macarons*, he noticed with pleasure, and shared a coffee éclair with him. He hoped her appetite had returned, she was looking very thin, but not quite as pale as when he walked in. Considering how far she had come in recent weeks, it was remarkable to see her sitting there in diamond earrings and jeans. She'd had her nails done in the room that afternoon. They were a clear pale pink, which was the only color she'd worn for years. He silently admired her long graceful fingers as she sipped her tea. Stevie had left them alone, and retired to her own room with the nurse. Stevie was satisfied that Carole was comfortable alone with him. She had looked at her questioningly before she left the room, and Carole smiled and nodded, letting her know it was all right.

'I was afraid I'd never see this room again,' Carole admitted to him, as they sat in the living room of the suite.

'I was afraid you wouldn't either,' he confessed, with a look of relief. He was aching to take a walk with her, and get her out of the hotel, but she was obviously not ready to venture so far afield, although she would have liked it too.

'I always seem to run into trouble in Paris, don't I?' she said with a mischievous grin, as Matthieu laughed at her.

'I'd say this time was a bit extreme, wouldn't you?' he commented and she nodded, and then they started talking about her book.

She'd had some ideas for it in the past few days, and hoped she could get back to work once she was back in L.A. He admired her for it. Publishers were always asking him to write his memoirs, but he hadn't done it yet. There were a lot of things he said he wanted to do, which was why he was planning to retire in the coming year, to do the things he dreamed of, before it was too late. His wife's death had reminded him that life was short and precious, particularly at his age. He was going skiing with his children at Val d'Isère over Christmas. Carole said regretfully that her skiing days were over. The last thing she needed was another bump on her head, and he agreed. It reminded them both of the fun they'd had skiing together during her time in France. They had gone several times, and taken her kids. He had been a fabulous skier, and so was she. He had been on a national racing team in his youth.

They talked about a multitude of things as darkness fell outside. It was nearly eight o'clock when he got up, feeling guilty for keeping her up for so long. She needed rest. He had stayed quite a while, and she looked tired but relaxed. And then she exclaimed as she looked out the long-curtained windows as they stood up. It was snowing outside, and she opened the window and put her hand outside, reaching toward the snowflakes as he watched her. She turned to look at him with the wide eyes of a child.

'Look! It's snowing!' she said happily. He

nodded and smiled at her, as she looked into the night and felt gratitude overwhelm her. Everything had new meaning to her, and the smallest pleasures brought her joy. She was the greatest joy of all for him. She always had been. 'It's so beautiful,' she said in wonder, as he stood just behind her but didn't touch her. He was basking in her presence and trembling inside.

'So are you,' he said softly. He was so happy to be there with her, and that she was allowing him to spend time with her. It was a precious gift.

She turned to look at him again then, with the snow falling behind her, her face turned up to his. 'The night I moved into the house here, it was snowing . . . you were there with me . . . we touched the snowflakes, and kissed . . . I remember thinking I would never forget that night, it was so beautiful . . . we went for a long walk along the Seine, with the snow falling around us . . . I wore a fur coat with a hood . . .' she whispered.

'. . . You looked like a Russian princess . . .'

'That's what you said to me.' He nodded, as they both thought back to the magic of that night, and then standing in the open window at the Ritz, they moved imperceptibly toward each other and kissed as time stood still.

16

Carole looked worried when Matthieu called her at the Ritz the next morning. She was feeling better and her legs were stronger, but she had lain awake thinking about him for hours the night before.

'That was a silly thing to do last night . . . I'm sorry . . .' she said as soon as she answered the phone. It had troubled her all night. She didn't want to go there with him again. But the memories of that long-ago night had been so powerful, they had swept her away. It had had the same effect on both of them, just as it had then. They had an overwhelmingly intoxicating effect on each other.

'Why was it silly?' he asked, sounding disappointed.

'Because things are different. That was then. This is now. You can't go backward in time. And I'm leaving soon. I didn't mean to confuse you.' And she didn't want him to confuse her. After he had left, her head was spinning. It wasn't from her injury. It was him, and the reawakening of all she had felt for him before.

'You didn't confuse me, Carole. If I'm confused, it's of my own doing, but I don't think I am.' There was nothing confused about his feelings for her. He knew he was in love with her all over again, and always had been. Nothing had changed for him. It was Carole who had shut the door, and was trying to again.

'I want to be friends,' she said firmly. But nothing more.'

'We are.'

'I don't want to do that again,' she said, referring to their kiss. She was trying to sound strong but feeling frightened. She knew the effect he had on her, and had felt it like a tidal wave the night before.

'Then we won't. I give you my solemn word.' He promised, but she knew what promises meant to him. He never kept them. Or never had.

'We know what that's worth.' The words slipped out, and she heard him gasp. 'I'm sorry. I didn't mean to say that.'

'Yes, you did. And I deserved it. Let's just say that my word is worth more than it was before.'

'I'm sorry.' She was embarrassed by what she'd said. She didn't have her usual control, but it was no excuse, whether he deserved it or not. He didn't seem to hold it against her.

'It's all right. What about our walk? Do you feel up to it?' The snow had already melted from the previous night. It had just been a brief flurry, but it was cold outside. He didn't want her to get sick. 'You'll need to wear a heavy coat.'

'I have one . . . or actually, I did.' She remembered that she'd been wearing it that night in the tunnel, and along with everything else she'd been wearing, it had disappeared, blown right off her back. She had been wearing rags when the ambulance picked her up. 'I'll borrow Stevie's coat.'

'Where do you want to go?'

'Bagatelle?' She looked pensive.

'Excellent. I'll arrange to have your guards follow us in another car.' He wasn't taking any chances, which sounded fine to her. The trick would be getting out of the hotel. She suggested meeting him in front of the Crillon, and switching from her car to his. 'Sounds like espionage to me.' He smiled. That was familiar to him, they had been cautious in the old days too.

'It is espionage,' she laughed. 'What time shall we meet?' She sounded happier and more at ease than a few minutes before. She was trying to set boundaries with him.

'What about two o'clock? I have meetings before that.'

'See you at the Crillon at two. By the way, what does your car look like? I'd hate to get into the wrong car.' He laughed at the idea, although he was sure the driver would have been pleased.

'I have a navy blue Peugeot. I'll be wearing a gray hat, carrying a rose, and wearing one shoe.' She laughed. She remembered his humor now too. She had had fun with him, as well as grief.

She was still annoyed at herself for kissing him the night before. They wouldn't do it again. She had made up her mind.

She asked Stevie to make the arrangements for her, for the car, and they had lunch on trays in her room. She ate a club sandwich, which tasted heavenly to her, and the hotel's chicken soup.

'Are you sure you're up to going out?' Stevie was worried about her. She looked better than she had the day before, but going out for a walk was a big step, and possibly too much for her so soon. She didn't want Matthieu to wear Carole out or upset her. She had looked worn out and distracted when he left the night before.

'I'll see how I feel. If I'm too tired, I can come back.' Matthieu was being cautious with her too, and wouldn't let her overdo it.

She borrowed Stevie's coat, and her assistant walked her to the car waiting on the rue Cambon side. She had the hood of the coat pulled up over her head, and dark glasses on. She was wearing the same outfit as the previous day, with a heavy white sweater this time. There were two paparazzi waiting outside, who took her photograph getting into the car. Stevie came with her for two blocks, and then walked back to the hotel, and Carole had both of her guards with her.

Matthieu was waiting outside the Crillon, precisely where he said he would, and she slipped unnoticed from her car into his. No one had followed her. She was breathless when she got into the car with him, and a little dizzy.

'How do you feel?' he asked with a look of concern. She was still very pale, but she looked very pretty, as she pushed the hood off and took off her dark glasses. She still took his breath away.

'Pretty good,' she said in answer to his question. 'A little wobbly. But it's nice to get out of the hotel.' She was already getting tired of being stuck in her room, and she said she was eating too many pastries, for lack of something better to do. 'It sounds stupid, but it's nice to go for a walk. It's the most exciting thing I've done in a month.' Except kiss him. But she wouldn't allow herself to think of it now. He could see in her eyes that her guard was up, and she wanted to keep him at a distance, although she had kissed his cheek when she got in. Old habits died hard, even after fifteen years. She had a habit patterned in her somewhere of intimacy with him. It was buried, but not gone.

They drove to Bagatelle, and the sun was shining. It was cold and windy, but they were both warmly dressed, and she was surprised at how good it felt to be out in the air. She tucked her hand in his arm to steady herself, and they walked slowly for a long time. She was winded when they got back to his car. The guards had stayed far enough away to give them privacy, but close enough to keep her safe.

'How do you feel?' he asked her again, checking on her. He was afraid they'd gone too far. He reproached himself for it, but her company was too inebriating to give up.

'Wonderful!' Her cheeks were bright, after their walk in the cold, and her eyes sparkled as she answered. 'It feels good to be alive.'

He would have liked to take her out somewhere, but he didn't dare. He could see that she was tired, but relaxed. She chatted animatedly on their way back to the hotel. Despite their plans for 'espionage,' he drove her back to the Ritz in his car, with hers behind them. They both forgot to stop at the Crillon. They were at the Ritz on the Vendôme side, the main entrance to the hotel. She reminded herself that they had nothing to hide. They were nothing more than old friends now, and both of them widowed. It seemed odd to her that they now had that in common. In any case, they were free and un-attached, and he was only a lawyer, not a minister of France.

'Do you want to come upstairs?' she asked, as she turned to him, and put her hood up again. She didn't bother with the dark glasses. She could see no paparazzi waiting for her or anyone else.

'Are you up to it? You're not too tired?' he asked, sounding concerned.

'It'll probably hit me later. I feel fine right now. The doctor said I should go on walks.' He was just afraid they'd walked too far, but she looked very much alive. 'We could have tea again, without the kiss,' she reminded him, and he laughed.

'That certainly makes things clear. All right, we'll have tea without the kiss. Although I must admit, I enjoyed it,' he said honestly.

'So did I.' She smiled shyly. 'But that's not on the regular menu. It was some kind of one-time special yesterday.' It had been a slip, no matter how sweet it tasted at the time.

'What a shame. Why don't you go up with your guards? I'll park my car and come up in a minute.' That way, if a lurking paparazzo got her, she wouldn't have to explain him.

'See you soon,' she said, and slipped out of his car, as her guards hopped out of hers and fell into step behind her. A moment later there were a series of flashes in her face, and she looked surprised at first, and then smiled and waved. As long as they had her, there was no point looking unpleasant. She had learned that years before. She walked quickly into the hotel, through the lobby, and took the elevator up to her room. Stevie was waiting for her in the suite, although Carole had told her she could go out. Stevie had just gotten back herself. She had worn a windbreaker she had with her instead of the coat Carole had borrowed, and had taken a nice walk along the rue de la Paix. It felt good to get some air.

'How was it?' Stevie asked politely, and Carole nodded.

'It was fine.' She was proving to herself that they could be friends.

Matthieu reached the room a minute later, and Stevie ordered sandwiches and tea for them, which Carole devoured as soon as they came. Her appetite had improved, and Matthieu could see that the walk had done her good. She looked tired but happy as she stretched her legs out and they talked, as they always did, about a variety of things, philosophical as well as practical. In the old days, he had loved talking politics with her, and valued her opinions. She wasn't up to that yet, nor was she current on French politics.

He didn't stay as long this time, and as promised, there was no kiss. The snow of the night before had brought back an avalanche of memories, and with them feelings that had surprised her and lowered her guard. Her boundaries were back in place now, and he respected her for it. The last thing he wanted to do was hurt her. She was vulnerable and frail, and only newly returned to life. He didn't want to take advantage of her, just be with her, in any way she would allow. He was grateful for what they had. It was hard to believe there was anything left, after the scorched earth of the past.

'Another walk tomorrow?' he asked before he left, and she nodded, looking pleased. She was enjoying the time she spent with him too. She stood in the doorway of the suite, as he looked down at her with a smile.

'I never thought I'd see you again,' he said, savoring the moment.

'Neither did I,' she agreed.

'I'll see you tomorrow,' he said softly, and then let himself out of her suite. He greeted the two guards on the way out, and walked out of the Ritz with his head down, thinking of her, and how nice it had been just to walk beside her, with her hand tucked into his arm.

The next day he met her at three. They walked for an hour, and then drove till six. They parked for a while in the Bois de Boulogne, and talked about their old house. He said he hadn't seen it in years, and they agreed to drive by on the way back to the hotel. It was a pilgrimage she had already made, but now they would make it together.

The door to the courtyard was open again, and with the guards waiting discreetly outside, they walked inside side by side. Instinctively, they both looked up to where their bedroom had been, looked at each other, and held hands. They had shared so much here, hoped for so many things, and then lost their dreams. It was like visiting a cemetery where their love had been buried. And inevitably, she thought of the baby she had lost, and looked at him with damp eyes. In spite of herself, she felt closer to him than ever.

'I wonder what would have happened if we'd had him,' she said softly, and he knew what she meant, and sighed. It had been a terrible time after she fell off the ladder, and all that had happened after that.

'I suppose we'd be married by now,' he said, with a deep tone of regret.

'Maybe not. Maybe even then, you wouldn't have left Arlette.' There were plenty of children born out of wedlock in France. It had been a tradition even with the kings of France.

'It would have killed her if she'd known.' He turned to Carole sadly. 'Instead it nearly killed you.' It had been a tragedy for them both.

'It wasn't meant to be,' Carole said philosophically. She still went to church every year on that date, the day their baby died. She realized the date was coming soon, and pushed it from her mind.

'I wish it had been,' he said quietly, and had to fight himself not to kiss her again. Instead, remembering his promise to her, he took her in his arms and held her for a long time, as he felt her warmth next to him, and thought of how happy they had been in that house for what seemed like a long time. In the scheme of a life-time, two and a half years was nothing, but at the time it had been their entire world.

This time it was Carole who turned her face to his, and kissed him first. He was startled, and hesitated, and then let his own resolve dissolve as he kissed her back, and then kissed her again. Afterward he was afraid she would be angry at him, but she wasn't. She was so overwhelmed by her feelings for him that nothing could have stopped it. She felt swept away by a current.

'Now you're going to tell me that I didn't keep my word,' he scolded her, looking worried. He didn't want her to be angry at him, but he was relieved to see she didn't look it.

'I didn't keep mine,' she said calmly, as they walked out of the courtyard, back toward his car. 'Sometimes I feel as though my body remembers you better than I do,' she said in a small voice. And surely her heart did. 'Just being friends isn't as easy as I thought it would be,' she said honestly, as he nodded his head.

'It isn't for me either, but I want to do what you want.' He owed her that now at least. But she always took him by surprise.

'Maybe we should just enjoy it for the next two weeks, as a tribute to history, and kiss it goodbye when I leave.'

'I don't like that plan,' he said as they got back into his car. 'What would be wrong with seeing each other again? Maybe we were meant to find each other. Maybe this is God's way of giving us another chance. We're both free now, we're not hurting anyone. We don't have to answer to anyone but ourselves.'

'I don't want to get hurt again,' she said clearly, as he started the car and turned to look at her. 'The last time hurt too much.' He nodded. He couldn't deny that.

'I understand.' And then he asked her a question that had haunted him for years. 'Did you ever forgive me, Carole? For letting you down, and not doing what I said I would do? I meant to, but it never happened the way I wanted it to. I couldn't do it in the end. Did you forgive me for that, and hurting you so much?' He had no right to it, he knew, but hoped she had. He wasn't sure. Why should she? He didn't deserve it.

She looked at him with wide honest eyes. 'I don't know. I can't remember. All of that is gone. I remember the good part, and the pain. I don't know what happened after that. All I know is that it took a long time.' It was the best answer he was going to get. It was remarkable enough that she was willing to spend time with him, in these extraordinary circumstances. Forgiveness was too much to ask, and he knew he had no right to that.

He dropped her off at the hotel, and promised to come the next day, to take her for another walk. She wanted to go back to the Luxembourg Gardens, where she had gone so often with Anthony and Chloe while they lived there.

All he could think about was her lips on his, as he drove back to his house. He let himself in with his key, walked through the hallway into his study, and sat down in the dark. He had no idea what to say to her, or if he would ever see her again when she left. He suspected she didn't know either. For the first time, they had no history, no future, all they had was each day as it came. There was no way of knowing what would happen after that.

17

Walking in the Luxembourg Gardens with Matthieu brought back a flood of memories for Carole, of all the times she'd been there with her children, and with him. She had come here with him the first time, and a hundred times with Anthony and Chloe after that.

They laughingly remembered silly things the kids had done, and other times that had escaped her until then. Walking around Paris with him was bringing back many things she wouldn't have remembered otherwise, most of them good times, and tender moments they had shared. The pain he had caused her seemed a little dimmer now, in contrast to the happiness that came to mind.

They were still chatting easily and laughing when they got out of his car at the Ritz. She had invited him up for dinner in her suite, and he had agreed to come. He was handing his car keys to the *voiturier,* with her arm tucked into his, when a photographer snapped their picture with a flash of light in their faces. Both of them looked up, startled, and Carole smiled the second time, while Matthieu looked dignified and stern. He didn't like having his photograph taken at the best of times, but particularly not by paparazzi for the gossip press. They had always been careful when they lived together, but now they had far less at risk. They had nothing to hide. It was just unpleasant to be photographed and talked about, and not his style. He was complaining about it as they walked into the hotel. They were using the front door these days, it was easier than having the rue Cambon side opened for her every time. She had been wearing gray slacks and Stevie's coat when they photographed her, with her dark glasses in her hand. They recognized her, obviously, but seemed not to know who Matthieu was.

She mentioned it to Stevie when they went upstairs.

'They'll figure it out' was all Stevie said. She was worried about the time Carole was spending with Matthieu. But they looked happy and relaxed, as Carole regained her strength day by day. Spending time with him was not hurting her at least.

Stevie ordered dinner from room service for them. Carole ordered sautéed foie gras, and Matthieu ordered steak. Stevie ate in her room with the nurse. They both commented that Carole was doing well. She was visibly stronger and her color had returned. And more than that, Stevie realized that she looked happy.

Matthieu stayed, talking to her, until ten o'clock that night. They always had a lot to say to each other, and never ran out of topics that interested them both. She had been contacted by the police again, for a further statement about the tunnel bombing. They wanted to know if she remembered anything more, but she didn't.

She had been unconscious very quickly, as soon as the car next to her exploded. But they had a mountain of statements from others. The police seemed to feel that, with the exception of the boy who'd come to the hospital, all of the bombers had died. There were no other suspects.

Matthieu told her about the cases he was working on at the law firm, and he still insisted he wanted to retire. She thought it was a poor decision, unless he found something else to keep him busy.

'You're too young to retire,' she insisted.

'I wish I were, but I'm not. What about your book?' he asked. 'Have you thought any more about it?'

'I have,' she admitted, but she wasn't ready to go back to work yet. She had other things on her mind, him for instance. He was beginning to fill her head day and night. She was trying to resist it. She didn't want to become obsessed by him, just enjoy him until she left. She realized it was a good thing she was leaving soon, before things got out of hand between them, as they had before.

They kissed again before he left that night. It was as much about the past as the present. It was habit mixed with longing, joy and sadness, love and fear.

The rest of the time they talked of his work, her book, her career, their respective children, and whatever else came to mind. They never seemed to stop talking, and both of them loved their exchanges of ideas. It challenged her to speak intelligently to him, and forced her to stretch her mind to what it once had been. She still had to struggle for a word or a concept sometimes. And she had not yet figured out how to work her computer. The secrets to her book were still locked in it. Stevie had offered to help her, but she insisted she wasn't ready. It required too much concentration.

Stevie brought her the newspapers the next morning over breakfast. She had a stack of them. Carole was on the front page with Matthieu in each one, and all of them had recognized him and identified him by name. He looked grim and startled in the picture. Carole looked lovely, with a wide, easy smile. They had used the second photograph, where she was smiling. She looked pretty, the scar on her cheek showed slightly, but not enough to upset her. And the *Herald Tribune* had done their homework. Not only had they identified Matthieu as the former Minister of the Interior, but it had obviously sparked the curiosity of some zealous young reporter, or maybe an old one. They had gone back into their archives during the time she had lived in France, and checked to see if there were any photographs of them together then. They had found a good one, taken at a charity event at Versailles. Carole remembered it. They had been careful not to go to the party together. Arlette had been there with him, and Carole had gone with a movie star she had made a picture with, who was an old friend and visiting Paris at the time. They had made a dazzling couple, and had been photographed constantly, and although his fans didn't know it, he was secretly gay. He had been a perfect beard for Carole.

She and Matthieu had met in the garden for a few minutes, late in the evening. They were talking quietly, when a photographer spotted them and took their picture. All it said in the papers the next day was 'Matthieu de Billancourt, Minister of the Interior, confers with American film star Carole Barber.' They had been lucky. No one guessed, although his wife had been irate when she saw the papers the next day.

The two photographs, from Versailles, and in front of the Ritz the day before, had a different caption. 'Then, and Now. Did We Miss Something?' It raised the question. Carole knew they would never have the answer. They had covered their tracks well. It would have been different if she'd had his baby, if he'd left Arlette for her, filed for divorce, or resigned from the ministry, but none of that had happened. And now they were just two people walking into a hotel, old friends perhaps, or more. He was retired from the ministry, and they were both widowed. It was difficult to make much of it, particularly after her being wounded in the bombing. She had a right to see old friends she had known while she lived in Paris. But the way the *Tribune* captioned it posed an interesting question, to which no one but

Matthieu and Carole had the answer.

He called her as soon as he saw it. He was annoyed, it was the kind of innuendo that bothered him. But Carole was accustomed to it. She had lived with it all of her adult life.

'How stupid of them,' he said, growling.

'No, actually, very smart. They must have had to really dig to find that picture. I remember when it was taken. Arlette was there with you, and you hardly spoke to me all evening. I was already pregnant.' There was an edge to her voice as she said it, of resentment, anger, and sorrow. They'd had a fight afterward, which was the first of many. He had given her a thousand excuses by then, and she was accusing him of stalling. Their life together began to unravel over the next months, particularly after she lost the baby. She had had a rotten evening the night the photograph at Versailles was taken. He remembered it too, and felt guilty about it, which was part of why seeing the photograph in the *Herald Tribune* had upset him. He hated to be reminded of the grief he'd caused her. And he knew she'd be upset too, unless she had forgotten. She hadn't. 'It's not worth getting upset over,' she said finally. 'There's nothing we can do about it.'

'Do you want to be more careful?' he asked, sounding cautious.

'Not really,' she said quietly. 'It doesn't matter now. We're both free people. And I'll be gone soon.' She was leaving in ten days. 'We're not hurting anyone. We're old friends, if anyone wants to know.' Which of course later that morning, they did. *People* magazine called to ask if they'd ever been involved.

'Of course not,' Stevie answered for Carole, who didn't take the call. She went on to tell them how well Carole was doing, hoping to distract them, and told Carole about it after she hung up.

'Thanks,' Carole said calmly, finishing her breakfast, as Stevie helped herself to a croissant.

'Are you worried about the press figuring it out?' Stevie asked with a look of concern.

'There's nothing to figure out. We really are just friends. We kiss once in a while, but that's about it.' She wouldn't have said that to anyone but Stevie, especially her kids.

'What happens next?' Stevie asked with a look of concern.

'Nothing. We go home,' Carole said, meeting her assistant's eyes. Stevie could see that Carole believed that, but she herself wasn't as convinced. She could see the love in Carole's eyes. Matthieu had brought something magical in her back to life.

'And then what?'

'The book is closed. It's just a gentler epilogue to a story that ended badly a long time ago.' She sounded firm, and as though she were trying to convince herself.

'No sequel to the book?' Stevie asked, and Carole shook her head.

'Okay, if you say so. It doesn't look like that to me though, for what it's worth. He still looks madly in love with you.' And Carole didn't seem indifferent to him by any means, despite what she said to Stevie, and herself.

'Maybe so,' Carole said with a sigh, 'but *madly* is the operative word. We were both crazy then. I think we've grown up and gotten sane. We never had a chance.'

'It's different now,' Stevie pointed out. She had slowly changed her opinion of Matthieu and she saw how much Carole cared for him. He obviously felt just as strongly about her. Stevie liked the way he protected Carole. 'Maybe it wasn't the right time.'

'That's for sure. I don't live here anymore. I have a life in L.A. It's too late,' Carole said, looking determined. She knew she loved him but didn't want to step backward in time.

'Maybe he'd be willing to move,' Stevie said hopefully, and Carole laughed.

'Stop it. I'm not going there again. He was the love of my life. That was then. This is now. You can't carry that forward fifteen years.'

'Maybe you can. I don't know. I just hate to see you alone. You deserve to be happy again.' Stevie had felt sorry for her since Sean had died. She had practically been a recluse. And whatever had happened between them before, the time she spent with Matthieu was bringing her back to life.

'I am happy. I'm alive. That's enough. I have my kids and my work. That's all I want.'

'You need more than that,' Stevie said wistfully.

'No, I don't,' Carole said firmly.

'You're too young to fold up the show.'

Carole looked her squarely in the eye. 'I've had two husbands and a great love. What more do you want?'

'I want you to have a happy life. You know, "happily ever after" and all that shit. Maybe the happily ever after took a long time to come in this case.'

'You can say that again. Fifteen years. A *very* long time. Believe me, it would make a mess. I loved it here then. I don't now. I live in L.A. We have totally different lives.'

'Really? You two never stop talking when you're together. You look more alive than you've been in years. I haven't seen you like this since Sean.' She didn't want to convince her, but she had to admit she liked the guy, even if he was a little austere, and very French. It was obvious that he still loved her. And his wife was gone now. At least he was eligible this time, and single. So was Carole.

'He's an intelligent, interesting man. Brilliant even. But he's French,' Carole insisted. 'He'd be miserable anywhere else, and I don't want to live here anymore. I'm happy in L.A. What about Alan, by the way? What's new with him?' It was obvious that she wanted to change the subject, and as soon as she asked, Stevie looked like she had swallowed the proverbial canary along with the croissant.

'Alan? Why?' She looked guilty and vague.

'What do you mean, "why"? I just was asking how he was.' And then she smiled at Stevie. 'Okay. Cough it up. What's going on?'

'Nothing. Absolutely nothing.' She was blushing. 'He's fine. Great actually. He said to say hi.'

'You are so full of shit you're turning brown,' Carole said, laughing at her. 'Something is going on.' There was a pregnant silence in the room. Stevie could never keep a secret of her own. Only Carole's.

'Okay, okay. I didn't want to tell you till I got home. And I haven't made up my mind. I have to talk to him, and see what the conditions are.'

'What conditions?' Carole looked mystified, as

Stevie collapsed into a chair like a deflated balloon, with a sigh.

'He asked me to marry him last night,' Stevie confessed with an embarrassed smile.

'On the phone?'

'He couldn't wait. He even bought a ring. But I haven't said yes.'

'Take a look at the ring first,' Carole teased, and Stevie groaned. 'Make sure you like the ring.'

'I don't know if I want to get married. He swears he won't screw up my job. He said it will be just like it is now, only better, with papers and a ring. If I do it, would you be my best man, or whatever you call it?'

'I think it's called a matron of honor, if I remember correctly. I'd be honored. I think you should say yes,' Carole volunteered.

'Why?'

'I think you love him,' Carole said simply.

'So? Why do we have to get married?'

'You don't. But it's a nice commitment to make. I felt the same way you do when I married Sean. Jason had dumped me for a younger woman. Matthieu lied to me and himself, and wouldn't leave his wife or his job, and broke my heart. The last thing I wanted was to get married again, or even fall in love. Sean talked me into it, and I never regretted it for a minute. It was the best thing I ever did. Just make sure Alan is the right guy.'

'I think he is,' Stevie sounded glum as she said it.

'Then see how you feel when you go back. You can have a long engagement.'

'He wants to get married on New Year's Eve in Vegas. How tacky is that?'

'Very. But it might be fun. The kids will be in St. Bart's with Jason. I could fly up,' Carole volunteered, and Stevie came over to hug her.

'Thank you. I'll let you know. I'm scared I'm going to say yes.'

'Maybe you're ready,' Carole said, looking at her with affection, trying to reassure her. 'I think you are. You've been talking about it a lot lately.'

'That's because he has. He's obsessed with it.'

'Thank you for telling me,' Carole said warmly.

'You'd better be there to hold my hand if I do

it,' Stevie said ominously, but she was smiling and looked happy.

'You bet,' Carole promised. 'I wouldn't miss it.'

Carole had dinner with Matthieu again that night. For the first time, they went out. They went to L'Orangerie on the Île Saint Louis, in the Seine, and she wore the only skirt she'd brought. Matthieu wore a dark suit and had had a haircut. He looked very proper, and extremely handsome, although he was still furious about the comments in the *Herald Tribune*. He was righteous indignation itself.

'For heaven's sake,' Carole said, laughing at him. 'They're right. It's true. How can you be so outraged?' He was like a whore pretending to be a virgin, although she didn't say that to him.

'But no one knew!' He had been so proud of that, and it always irked her. She had hated being hidden and not sharing his life.

'We were lucky.'

'And careful.' He was right, they had been.

They both knew they could have turned into a full-blown scandal at any moment. It was a miracle that they hadn't.

They talked about other things over dinner, and the food was delicious. He waited until dessert to open a delicate subject with her. Their future. He had been awake the night before, thinking about it. And the insinuation in the paper did it for him. It was time. They had been clandestine for too long in the past, and deserved respectability at least now, at their age. He said as much to her as they shared a *tarte tatin* with caramel ice cream that melted in her mouth.

'We are respectable,' Carole pointed out. 'Extremely respectable. At least I am. I don't know what you've been up to lately. But I am a very proper widow.'

'So am I,' he said primly. 'I haven't been involved with anyone since you left,' he added, and looking at him, she believed him. He had always claimed that she was the only woman he'd been involved with, other than his wife. 'The piece in the *Tribune* makes us look dishonest and sly,' he complained.

'No, it doesn't. You are one of the most respected men in France, and I'm a movie star. What do you expect them to say? Has-been actress and washed-up politician seen going for a walk like two old farts? That's what we are.'

'Carole!' He laughed at what she said, looking shocked.

'They have to sell newspapers, so they tried to make us look more interesting than we are. And they made a lucky guess, or raised a lucky question. Unless you or I tell them, they'll never know for sure.'

'We know. That's enough.'

'Enough for what?'

'Enough to build the life we should have had years ago, and didn't, because I couldn't get out of my own way, and do what I promised.' He admitted it readily now, but hadn't then.

'What are you saying?' She looked worried.

He went right to the point. 'Will you marry me, Carole?' He took her hand as he asked the question and looked deep into her eyes. She sat in silence for a long moment, and then shook her head. It took a superhuman effort to do it.

'No, Matthieu, I won't.' She sounded certain, and his face fell. He had been afraid that she would say that, and that it was too late.

'Why not?' He looked sad, but hoped he could change her mind.

'Because I don't want to be married,' she said, sounding tired. 'I like my life the way it is. I was married twice. That's enough. I loved my late husband. He was a wonderful man. And I had ten good years with Jason. Maybe that's all you get. And I loved you with all my heart, and lost you.' It had nearly killed her, but she didn't say it. He knew it anyway, and had regretted it for fifteen years. She had gotten over it eventually. He never had.

'You didn't lose me. You left,' he reminded her, and she nodded.

'I never had you,' she corrected. 'Your wife did. France did.'

'Now I'm widowed, and retired,' he pointed out.

'Yes, you are. I'm not. Widowed. But not retired. I want to make some more movies, if I get decent parts.' She was excited about that again. 'I could be traveling all over the place, just like I did when I was married to Jason, and even when I was with you. I don't want someone at home complaining about it, or maybe even following me around. I want my own life. And even if I don't go back to making movies, I want to be free to do what I want. For me, the UN, the causes I believe in. I want to spend time with my children, and write this book, if I can ever get my computer turned on again. I wouldn't be a good wife.'

'I love you just the way you are.'

'And so do I, love you, I mean. But I don't want to be tied down, or make that kind of commitment. And more than anything, I don't want my heart broken again.' That was the essence of it for her, more than her career and her causes. She was too afraid. She already knew she was in love with him again. It was dangerous for her. She didn't want to abandon herself to him now. It had been too painful last time, although he was no longer married.

'I wouldn't break your heart this time,' he said, looking guilty.

'You might. People do that to each other. That's what love is all about. Being willing to risk a broken heart. I'm not. I've had one. I didn't like it. I don't want another one, particularly delivered by the same man who gave me the first one. I don't want to hurt that much again, or love that much again. I'm fifty years old, I'm too old to start that.' She didn't look it, but she felt it, particularly since the bombing.

'That's ridiculous. You're a young woman. People older than we are get married all the time.' He was desperate to convince her, but he could see he wasn't succeeding.

'They're braver than I am. I lived through you, Sean, and Jason. That's enough. I don't want to do it again.' She was adamant about what she was saying, and he knew she meant it. And he was equally determined to change her mind. They were still arguing about it when they left the restaurant, and he had gotten nowhere with her. This wasn't the way he wanted it to turn out. 'And I like my life in L.A. I don't want to live in France again.'

'Why not?'

'I'm not French. You are. I'm American. I don't want to live in someone else's country.'

'You did before. You loved it here,' he insisted, trying to remind her, but she remembered it only too well. That's why he scared her. She was more afraid of herself than him this time. She didn't want to make a bad decision.

'Yes, I did. But I was happy when I got home. I realized then that I didn't belong here. That was part of the trouble with us. Cultural differences, you used to call them. That made it okay for you to live with me and be married to her, and even have our baby out of wedlock. I don't want to live somewhere where they think that differently than I do. In the end, you get hurt trying to be something you're not in a place you don't belong.' He could see now that the pain he had caused her had wounded her so deeply that even fifteen years later, the scars were still raw, even more so than the one on her cheek. The ones he had inflicted had gone too deep. It had even affected how she felt about France and the French. All she wanted was to go home, and live out the rest of her years alone in peace. He

438

wondered how Sean had convinced her to marry him. And then she was abandoned again when he died. Now she had closed the doors to her heart.

They talked about it all the way back to the hotel, and said goodnight in his car. She didn't want him to come upstairs this time. She kissed him lightly on the lips, thanked him for dinner, and slipped out of the car quickly.

'Will you think about it?' he begged her.

'No, I won't. I thought about it fifteen years ago. You didn't. You lied to me, Matthieu, and to yourself. You stalled for almost three years. What do you want from me now?' Her eyes were wide and sad, and he could see that it was hopeless, but didn't want to believe it.

'Forgive me. Let me love you and take care of you for the rest of my life. I swear I won't let you down this time.' She could see that he meant it.

'I can take care of myself,' she said sadly, looking at him through the open car window after she got out. 'I'm too tired to take a risk like that again.' She turned away then and hurried up the steps of the Ritz, with the CRS guards behind her. Matthieu watched until she was gone, and drove away. There were silent tears running down his cheeks as he drove home. He knew now what he had feared all this time, and hoped wasn't true. He had lost her.

18

Carole was unusually quiet as she sat across the breakfast table from Stevie the next morning, as Stevie ate a chanterelle omelette and several pains au chocolat.

'I'm going to weigh three hundred pounds by the time we go home,' Stevie complained, as Carole read the newspaper in silence. Stevie was wondering if Carole was feeling all right. She had hardly said a word since she got up.

'How was dinner last night?' Stevie asked her finally, as Carole set the paper down. She sat back in her chair and sighed.

'It was fine.'

'Where'd you go?'

'L'Orangerie, on the Île Saint Louis. Matthieu and I used to go there all the time.' It was one of his favorite restaurants, and had become hers, along with Le Voltaire.

'Are you feeling okay?'

Carole nodded in answer to her question. 'Just tired. The walking has been doing me good.' She'd been out with Matthieu every day, and they walked for hours as they chatted.

'Was he upset about the thing in the *Herald Tribune*?'

'A little. He'll get over it. I don't know how he can be righteous about it. They were right. It's a wonder no one figured it out before, although we were pretty careful in those days. He had a lot at stake, and so did I. He forgets.'

'It'll probably just slip away,' Stevie reassured her. 'No one can prove anything now anyway. It's been way too long.' Carole nodded again. She agreed. 'Did you have fun?' This time Carole shrugged. And then looked across the table at her assistant and friend.

'He proposed.'

'He *what*?'

'He proposed. As in marriage.' Her face was blank. Stevie looked stunned, and then delighted, but Carole didn't.

'Holy shit! What did you say?'

'I said no.' Her voice was painfully calm, as Stevie stared.

'You did? I've been getting the feeling that you two were still in love with each other, and I thought he was trying to get things going again.'

'He is. Or was.' Carole was wondering if he would speak to her again. He was probably hurt by the night before.

'Why did you say no?' Although he had worried her at first, now Stevie was disappointed.

'It's too late. Too much water under the bridge by now. I still love him, but he hurt me too much. It was too hard. And I don't want to get married again. I told him that last night.'

'I can understand the first two reasons, about your being hurt. But why don't you want to get married again?'

'Been there. Done that. Divorced. Widowed. Broken heart in Paris. Why do I need to risk all

443

that again? I don't. My life is easier like this. I'm comfortable now.'

'You sound like me.' Stevie sounded dismayed.

'You're young, Stevie. You've never been married. You should at least do it once, if you love the guy enough to make that kind of commitment.' She was speaking about Alan. 'I loved the men I was married to. Jason left me. Poor Sean died, way too young. I don't want to start all over again, especially with a guy who already broke my heart once. Why take the chance?' She loved him, but this time she wanted her head to rule her heart. It was safer.

'Yeah, but he didn't start out to be a shit to you, from what I understand. At least according to what you told me. He got himself tangled up in his own mess. He was afraid to leave his wife, he was a high-up government official, and he got appointed to another term, which complicated things further. But now he's retired from the ministry, and she's dead, he's not likely to make the same mess again. And he makes you happy, or he seems to. Am I right?'

'Yes,' Carole said honestly, 'he does. But even

if he doesn't make a mess of it again, then what? He dies and leaves me heartbroken again.' She looked bleak as she said it. 'I just don't want to put my heart on the line again. It hurts too much.' It had been hard enough losing Sean, and trying to bounce back again. It had been two years. And five years of misery after she left Matthieu in Paris. Every day, she hoped he'd call to say he'd left his wife, and he never did. He stayed. Until she died.

'You can't give up like that,' Stevie said, looking sad for her. She hadn't realized Carole felt that way to that degree. 'It's not like you to quit.'

'I didn't even want to marry Sean. He talked me into it. But I was your age then. I'm just too old to do it now.'

'At fifty? Don't be ridiculous. You look thirty-five.'

'I feel ninety-eight. And my heart is three hundred and twelve. Believe me, it's been around the block more than a couple of times.'

'Come on, Carole. Don't give me that. You're tired now because you've been through a terrible ordeal. I saw your face when we came back to

Paris to close the house. You loved this man.'

'That's my point. I don't want to feel like that again. I was devastated. I thought I'd die when I flew out of here and said goodbye to him. I cried over him every night for three years. Or two at least. Who needs that? What if he leaves me or dies?'

'What if he doesn't? What if you're happy with him, for real this time, not stolen or borrowed, or hiding out? I mean really happy, in a grown-up partnership and life. Do you want to risk missing that?'

'Yes.' There was no doubt in Carole's voice.

'Do you love him?'

'Yes. I do. Amazing as that is, even to me, after all this time. I think he's wonderful. But I don't want to be married to him, or anyone else. I want to be free to do whatever I want. I know how selfish that sounds. Maybe I've always been selfish. Maybe that's what Chloe's pissed about, and why Jason left me for someone else. I was so busy pursuing my career and being a movie star, maybe I missed the important stuff. I don't think I did, but you never know. I raised my kids, loved my husbands. I never left Sean for a minute before he died. Now I want to do what I want to do, without worrying if I'm offending somebody, letting them down, pissing them off, or supporting a cause they don't like. If I want to get on a plane and go somewhere, I can. If I don't want to call home, I won't. And it won't upset anyone. There's no one at home anyway now. Besides, I want to write my book, without worrying about whether I'm disappointing someone, or they think I should be somewhere else, doing what suits them. Eighteen years ago, I would have laid down and died for Matthieu. I would have given up my career for him, if he'd asked me to. Or Jason for that matter. I wanted to have babies with Matthieu and be his wife. But that's a long time ago. Now I'm not so anxious to give it all up. I have a house I like, friends I like, I see my kids whenever I can. I don't want to sit here in Paris, wishing I were somewhere else. Worse yet, with a man who might hurt me, and already has in the past.'

'I thought you liked Paris.' Stevie looked stunned by her speech. Maybe it really was too late. She hadn't believed that, but Carole had almost convinced her.

'I do like Paris. I love it. But I'm not French. I don't want to be told what's wrong with my country, how obnoxious Americans are, or that I don't understand anything because I come from a different country, which is uncivilized anyway. Matthieu put half our problems down to "cultural differences" because I expected him to get divorced in order to live with me. Call it old-fashioned or puritanical, I just didn't want to sleep with someone else's husband. I wanted my own. I figured he owed me that. But he stayed with her.' It had been more complicated than that, particularly because of his position in the government, but his insistence about it being okay to have a mistress had been typically French, and always upset her deeply.

'He's free now. You wouldn't have to deal with that. If you love him, I don't understand what's stopping you.'

'I'm too chicken,' Carole said miserably. 'I don't want to get hurt again. I'd rather walk away before that happens. It always does.'

'That's sad,' Stevie said unhappily, looking at her friend.

'It is sad. It was sad fifteen years ago when I left him. It was sad as hell. We were both devastated. We both cried at the airport. But I just couldn't stay anymore, the way things were. And maybe now it would be something else. His kids, his work. His country. I can't see him living outside France. And I don't want to live here, not full-time anyway.'

'Can't you two compromise in some way?' Stevie asked, and Carole shook her head.

'It's simpler not doing it all. No one will get disappointed, or feel they got less than they deserved. We won't hurt each other, or insult each other, or disrespect each other. I think we're both too old.' She had made up her mind and nothing was going to change it. Stevie knew how she was when she got that way. Carole was stubborn as a mule.

'So you're going to be alone for the rest of your life, with your memories, seeing your kids a few times a year? What happens when they have lives and kids of their own, and hardly have time to see you anymore? Then what? You do a movie every few years, or give it up? Write a book, make a speech now and then for some cause you may not even care about by then? Carole, that's the dumbest thing I've ever heard.'

'I'm sorry you feel that way. It makes sense to me.'

'It won't ten or fifteen years from now, when you're lonely as hell and have missed all these years with him. He may even be gone by then, and you'll have missed your chance to be with a guy you've already loved for nearly twenty years. What you two have has already stood the test of tragedy and time. You still love each other. Why not grab it while you can? You're still young, and beautiful, and have some life left in your career. But when that goes, you'll be all alone. I don't want to see that happen to you.' Stevie was deeply sad for her.

'So what am I supposed to do? Give up everything for him? Stop being who I am? Give up doing movies entirely? Give up the work I do for UNICEF? And sit there, holding hands with him? That's not who I want to be when I grow up. I have to respect myself, and honor what I believe in. If I don't, who will?'

'Can't you have both?' Stevie said, looking frustrated. She wanted Carole to have more in her life than her charity work, making the occasional movie, and holiday visits with her kids. She deserved to be loved and happy too, and have companionship for the rest of her days, or however long it lasted. 'Do you have to be Joan of Arc, and take a vow of celibacy to be true to yourself?'

'Maybe I do,' Carole said through clenched teeth. Stevie was upsetting her, which was exactly what she hoped to do, but she didn't think she was getting through to her.

The two women went back to reading the newspapers, frustrated with each other. It was rare for them to disagree to that extent. Neither of them spoke to each other until the doctor came to see Carole at noon.

She was pleased with Carole's progress, and with all the walking she said she'd done. The muscle tone in her legs was better, her balance was good now, and her memory was improving exponentially. The doctor was confident Carole would be able to go back to Los Angeles when she'd planned to. There was no medical reason why she couldn't. The doctor said she'd come back to see her again in a few days, and told her to continue what she was doing. She said a few words to the nurse, and then left to go back to the hospital.

Stevie ordered lunch for Carole after the doctor left, but she left her alone at the table, and ate lunch in her own room. She was too upset by what Carole had said to her to be able to make chitchat with her over lunch. She thought Carole was making the biggest mistake of her life. Love didn't come along every day, and if it had landed in Carole's lap again, Stevie thought it was a crime to waste it. Worse yet, to run away because she was afraid to get hurt again.

Carole got bored alone at the lunch table. Stevie had said she had a headache, which Carole suspected wasn't true. She didn't challenge her about it, and after pacing around the living room of the suite for a while, she finally called Matthieu in his office. She thought he might be out to lunch, but called him anyway. His secretary put her through to him immediately. He was eating a sandwich at his desk, and had been in a rotten mood all day. He had bitten his secretary's head off twice, and slammed the door to his office after talking to a client who had annoyed him. He was obviously not having a good day. She had never seen him like that. And she was cautious when she told him who was on the phone. He picked up the call immediately, hoping Carole had changed her mind.

'Are you too mad to talk to me?' Carole asked in a soft voice.

'I'm not mad at you, Carole,' he said sadly. 'I hope you called to tell me you had a change of heart. The offer still stands.' He smiled. It would stand forever, for as long as he was alive.

'I didn't. I know I'm right. For me. I'm too scared to get married again. For now anyway. And I just don't want to. I talked to Stevie about it this morning, and she tells me in ten or fifteen years I'll change my mind.'

'By then I'll be dead,' he said matter-of-factly as Carole shuddered.

'You'd better not be. What was that? A short-term offer, or a long-term one?'

'Long-term. Are you playing with me?' He knew he deserved it. He deserved everything she dished out to him now, after what he'd done to her in the past.

'I'm not playing with you, Matthieu. I'm trying to find myself, and honor what I believe in and who I am. I love you, but I have to honor myself, if not, who am I? That's all I have.'

'You always did honor yourself, Carole. That's why you left me. You had too much respect for yourself to stay. That's why I love you.' It was a catch-22 for both of them, for him then, and her now. They were always trapped between impossible choices that had to do with respecting both others and themselves, sometimes both at the same time.

'Will you have dinner with me tonight?' she asked him.

'I'd love to.' He sounded relieved. He'd been afraid she wouldn't see him again before she left.

'The Voltaire?' she asked him. They had been there a hundred times. 'Nine o'clock?' It was the standard Paris dinner hour, even a little early.

'Perfect. Do you want me to pick you up at the hotel?'

'I'll meet you there.' She was far more independent than she had been in the old days, but he loved that about her too. There was nothing about her he didn't love. 'One condition,' she added suddenly.

'What's that?' He wondered what she had come up with.

'You won't propose to me again.'

'Not tonight. But I won't agree to that long-term.'

'All right. That's fair.' Her answer led him to hope that he might convince her someday. Maybe after she'd recovered fully from her accident, or after she finished her book. He was going to propose to her again one day, and hoped that eventually she'd accept. He was willing to wait, they already had for fifteen years, a little longer couldn't hurt. Or even a lot longer. He refused to give up, no matter what she said.

She arrived at Le Voltaire promptly at nine o'clock, on the Quai Voltaire. The guards were in the car with her, and Matthieu was standing in the doorway of the restaurant when she arrived. It was a crystal clear night with a chill December wind blowing around them. He kissed her on the cheek when she walked up to him, and she looked up at him and smiled. All he wanted to do was tell her he loved her. He felt as though he had waited for her all his life.

They sat in a corner booth, and the restaurant was busy. A waiter brought crudités to the table and hot toasted bread and butter.

They made it all the way to dessert without touching on sensitive subjects for either of them. And after dessert, as they nibbled chocolate mocha candies that she said would keep her up all night, he finally broke down. He had had an idea after he spoke to her that afternoon. If she wasn't willing to agree to marriage, he had another plan.

'Long ago, when I met you, you told me you didn't believe in people living together. You believed in the full commitment of marriage. And I agreed with you. Apparently, you don't feel that way anymore. How would you feel about some sort of loose living arrangement, where you are free to come and go? An open-door policy of sorts.' He smiled at her, as she continued to eat the mocha beans. She had already had enough to keep her awake into the following week, and he had too. But who needed sleep when love was up for grabs? And maybe a lifetime.

'What exactly does that mean?' She looked at him with interest. He was creative, if nothing else, stubborn, and determined, and so was she. It was what had kept them together years ago. That and the fact that they loved each other.

'I don't know. I thought maybe we could come up with something that works for both of us. I'd rather be married to you, to be honest. It fits my notions of propriety, and besides I've always wanted to be married to you. I love the idea of your being my wife, and I know you did too. Maybe we don't need the paperwork or titles now, if that's too restricting for you. What if you live with me in Paris for six months, and I live with you in California for the other six months a year? You could come and go as you please, travel, do your projects, make movies, write, see your children. I'll be waiting for you whenever you want. Would that suit you better?'

'It doesn't sound fair to you,' she said honestly. 'What would you get out of it? You'd be alone a lot of the time.' She looked worried as she asked the question, and he patted her hand.

'I get you, my love. That's all I want. And whatever time together you can spare.'

'I'm not sure living together sounds right to me, even now, although we were happy when we did. But it felt too awkward not being married to you, and it still might now.' Besides which, the arrangement he was suggesting wouldn't protect her heart from getting hurt again, or either of them from leaving each other. But there was no way to guarantee that. There were no guarantees. If she was going to risk her heart, she would have to risk it, however they chose to live. But the things Stevie had said to her that morning hadn't fallen on deaf ears.

'What is it you want?' he said simply.

'I'm scared to get hurt.'

'So am I,' he confessed. 'There's no way to be sure we won't. Maybe if we love each other, we have to take that chance. What if we just come and go for a while, and see how that works? I could come to visit you in Los Angeles after the holidays.' She knew he was going away with his children, and she wanted to be with hers. And with luck, she'd be going to Stevie's wedding in Las Vegas on New Year's Eve. 'I could come out on January first, if that works for you,' he suggested politely. 'I could stay for however long you like. And then you could come to Paris to visit me in the spring. Why don't we try to go back and forth for a while, depending on our schedules, and see how that works?' Knowing he had been prepared to marry her, she didn't feel he was 'trying her out.' He was doing his best to try to accommodate her, and give her the room she wanted to be herself. 'How does that sound?'

'Interesting.' She smiled at him. She wasn't ready to commit to anything. But just looking at him told her she loved him. More than she ever had, just more sanely. She was protecting herself this time. Not doing that created the mess she was in with him last time.

'Would you like to do that?' he pressed, and she laughed.

'Maybe.' She smiled again and ate another handful of mocha beans. He watched her do it and chuckled. She had always been unable to resist their mocha beans. It reminded him of old times. Afterward she had kept him up all night.

'You're going to be awake for weeks,' he warned. He was only sorry she wouldn't be keeping him up that night.

'I know.' She smiled happily. She liked his idea. She didn't feel as though she was selling her soul, or taking too great a risk. She could still get hurt because she loved him, but she wanted to ease into it, and see how it worked for both of them.

'May I come to see you in January?' he asked again, as they smiled at each other. Things were going much better than they had the night before. He realized now that he had moved too fast. After all the pain he'd caused her before, he knew now that he had to move slowly, and win her confidence in him again. He also knew how important it was to her to respect herself. It had always been that way. She wasn't willing to sell herself out this time, for his convenience, or to accommodate his life. She was taking care of herself. *And* she loved him.

'Yes,' she said softly. 'I'd love you to come out. How long could you stay? Weeks? Days? Months?'

'I could probably arrange to stay for a couple of months, but I don't have to stay that long. It's up to you.'

'Let's see how it goes,' she said, and he nodded. She wanted to keep the doors open, in case she wanted to back out.

'That sounds fine,' he said, wanting to reassure her. He didn't want to make any fast moves and frighten her again. He reminded himself too that she had just been through a terrible ordeal and nearly died, which had left her feeling vulnerable and scared.

'I could come to Paris with you in March, after I go to Tahiti with Chloe. And maybe stay here through the spring, depending on what else is going on in my life,' she was quick to add.

'Of course.' She was the busier of the two now,

particularly if he retired from his law firm. He was going to take a leave of absence for the time being. The timing was ideal for him. He was finishing most of his projects in the next few weeks, and hadn't taken on any new ones. It was as though he had sensed she was coming back into his life.

He paid the check for dinner, and they were the last to leave the restaurant. It was late, but they had covered a lot of ground. He had suggested something that she could live with. Her heart wouldn't be protected from potential injuries, but she wasn't giving up her life for him. That was important to her now, even more so than it had been then.

He drove her back to the hotel, with her car following them. He almost drove her through the fateful tunnel near the Louvre, and then swerved away at the last minute. It was open again, but he didn't want to take her through it. He had almost forgotten, but she hadn't. Her eyes were wide with terror as he turned away.

'I'm sorry,' he said apologetically, looking at her with loving eyes. He didn't want to do anything to upset or frighten her, in any way.

'Thank you,' she said, leaning over to kiss him. She liked the plans they had just made, and so did he. It wasn't exactly what he wanted yet, but he knew he had to earn her trust again, come to understand what her needs were, and how her life had changed. He was willing to do that for her. All he wanted was to make her happy.

They were back at the hotel five minutes later, and he took her in his arms and kissed her before she got out of the car.

'Thank you, Carole, for giving me a chance again. I don't deserve it. But I promise you I won't disappoint you this time. I give you my solemn vow.' She kissed him again, and he walked her into the hotel, holding her hand.

'See you tomorrow?' She looked at him with a peaceful smile.

'I'll call you in the morning. After I call Air France.'

Her guards accompanied her to her room, and he was smiling as he got back in his car. He was a happy man. And he wasn't going to blow it this time, of that he was sure.

* * *

Stevie woke up at four o'clock, and saw lights in Carole's room. She approached on tiptoe, to check if she was all right. She was startled to see her sitting at the desk, hunched over the computer. She had her back to Stevie and didn't hear her come in.

'Are you okay? What are you doing?' It struck Stevie then that Carole hadn't been able to use the computer since the accident, and she was working fast and furiously on it now.

'Working on my book.' She looked over her shoulder with a grin. Stevie hadn't seen her look like that since before Sean got sick. Happy, working, and alive. 'I figured out how to get the computer going, and how to rework the story. I'm going to start all over again and chuck the stuff I had. I know where I'm going now.'

'Wow!' Stevie smiled at her employer. 'You look like you're going about a hundred miles an hour.'

'I am. I ate two bowls of chocolate mocha beans at Le Voltaire. I ate enough to keep me awake for years.' They both laughed, and then Carole turned to look at her with a grateful expression. 'Thanks for what you said this morning. Matthieu and I figured out what we want to do tonight.'

'You're getting married?' Stevie looked at her excitedly, and Carole laughed.

'No. Not yet anyway. Maybe one day, if we don't kill each other first. He's the only person I know who's more stubborn than I am. We're going to travel back and forth for a while, and see how that goes. Eventually, he'd be willing to live in California half the time. We're going to live in sin for now.' She laughed, thinking of the irony that now she didn't want to get married, and he did. The tables had turned.

'That'll work,' Stevie said happily. 'I hope you do marry him one day. I think he's the right guy for you. You must have thought so too or you wouldn't have put up with all that shit years ago.'

'Yeah. I think so too. I just need time. It was a rough ride.'

'Some things are, but they're worth it in the

end.' Carole nodded, and Stevie yawned. 'How's the book coming?'

'I like it so far. Go back to bed, I'll see you in the morning.'

'Get some sleep eventually,' Stevie said as she padded back to her own room. It didn't look like that was going to happen for a while. Carole was up and running again.

19

Carole and Matthieu spent her last night in Paris having dinner at a new restaurant he had heard about and wanted to try. The food was excellent, the atmosphere was romantic and intimate, and they had a lovely time. He had made his plans by then, and was coming to Los Angeles on January second. He was returning from his ski vacation in Val d'Isère with his children the day before. They talked about their respective plans for the holidays, and she told him about spending some extra time with Chloe before Christmas. It wasn't much, but it was a start.

'You really didn't cheat her out of anything,

you know,' he reassured her. He still thought Chloe's resentment of her mother was unreasonable, given what he'd seen when she was a child. But Chloe's impressions of that time were different.

'She thinks I did. Maybe that's all that matters. Neglect is in the eye of the beholder, or the heart. I've got the time to spend with her, so why not?' Although they only had a short time before her father and brother arrived.

There was nothing sad about their evening together, because Carole knew Matthieu was coming to California in two weeks. She was looking forward to spending Christmas with her children and Jason. And she was hoping to go to Las Vegas over New Year's for Stevie's wedding. In spite of that, Stevie had already said she would come to Paris with her in March or April. Alan was fully prepared to be understanding. And at some point, Carole intended to try to do without her for a while. Maybe she and Matthieu would take some trips in Italy and France. She was hoping to have made good inroads on her book by then.

When dessert arrived, he pulled something out of his pocket and handed her a Cartier box. It was a Christmas gift that he'd had made for her.

She opened the box carefully, relieved to see that it wasn't a ring box. There was nothing formal about their arrangement yet. They were trying it on for size. When she opened the box, she saw that it was a beautiful gold bangle bracelet. It was totally simple with the exception of three diamonds on it. He had had an inscription engraved inside, which he said was the best part. She held it close to the candle on the table so she could read it, and as she did, tears came to her eyes. It said 'Honor Thyself. I love you, Matthieu.' She kissed him and put it on. It was his way of saying that he approved of what she was doing and loved her just as she was. It was a sign of respect as well as love.

She had brought him a present too, and he smiled when he saw that it came from the same store. He opened it as cautiously as she had hers, and saw that it was an elegant gold watch. She had given him one years before that he still wore.

Arlette had known it was from her, and had refrained from comment. It was the only jewelry he wore, and she knew it would be meaningful to him. Carole had had her gift to him engraved too. On the back it said 'Joyeux Noël. Je t'aime. Carole.' He was as pleased with her gift as she had been with his.

The restaurant was close to the hotel and they walked back to the Ritz slowly, with the guards behind them. Carole was used to them by now and so was Matthieu. They stopped in front of the Ritz and kissed as a flash went off in their faces. They turned, and Carole whispered to him quickly, 'Smile.' He did, and then they both laughed and the paparazzi got them again. 'As long as they've got you, you might as well smile pretty for the camera,' she said, looking up at him, and he laughed again.

'I always look like an ax murderer when photographers get me by surprise.'

'Remember to smile next time,' Carole said as they walked into the lobby. They didn't care if they were in the papers. They had nothing to hide.

He walked her back to her room and kissed her again in the living room of her suite. Stevie had already gone to bed, after packing up the last of their things. Carole's computer was still on the desk, but she wasn't planning to work that night.

'I'm still addicted to you,' he said passionately, as he kissed her again. He was looking forward to the discoveries they were going to make when he came to California to stay with her. He remembered only too well how wonderful that had been before.

'Don't be,' Carole said softly, in response to his comment. She didn't want the craziness of what they'd shared in the past. She wanted something peaceful and warm, not the agonizing passion they had experienced before. But looking at him, she was reminded that this wasn't Sean. It was Matthieu. He was a powerful, passionate man, always had been, and still was, despite his age. Nothing about Matthieu was quiet or lukewarm. Sean hadn't been either, but he had been a different kind of man. Matthieu was a driving force, and a perfect match for her. Together their energy could light the world. It was what had frightened her at first, but she was growing used to it again.

They were both wearing their Christmas presents from each other, and they sat in the living room of the suite for a long time and talked. It was one of the things they did best, and the rest would come soon enough. Neither of them had dared to brave any greater physical involvement. She had been too recently injured, and the doctor had suggested she wait, which seemed wiser to both of them. He didn't want to do anything to put her at risk, and he was worried about the flight.

Matthieu was coming to take her to the airport in the morning. They were leaving at seven, and she had to check in by eight o'clock for a ten o'clock flight. The neurosurgeon who was traveling with them had promised to be at the Ritz at six-thirty, to check her before they left. He had made the arrangements with Stevie and told her that he was excited about the trip.

Matthieu left her room finally just after one o'clock. Carole looked peaceful and happy as she brushed her teeth and put her nightgown on.

She was excited about his coming to California, and everything she was planning to do before he arrived. She had a lot to look forward to in the weeks to come. It was a whole new life.

Stevie woke her at six the next morning. Carole was already dressed and at breakfast when the young doctor arrived. He looked like a kid. She had said goodbye to her own neurologist the day before, and given her a Cartier watch as well, a practical one in white gold, with a second hand. The doctor had been thrilled.

Matthieu arrived promptly at seven. He was wearing a suit and tie as always, and commented that Carole looked like a young girl in jeans and a loose gray sweater. She wanted to be comfortable for the flight. And in case photographers caught her, she had put makeup on. She was wearing his bracelet, and the diamonds on it sparkled on her arm. Matthieu was proudly wearing his new watch, and announced the time to anyone who cared to listen, while Carole laughed. They both looked happy and relaxed.

'You guys are cute,' Stevie commented, as the bellman came to take their bags. As always, she had everything organized. She had left tips for room service and the maids, the concierges who had helped her, and two assistant managers at the front desk. This was what she did. Matthieu was impressed as she shepherded the doctor from the room, carried Carole's computer case and heavy handbag, managed her own hand luggage, dismissed the nurse, and spoke to the guards.

'She's very good,' he said to Carole as they took the elevator to the lobby.

'Yes, she is. She's been with me for fifteen years. She'll be back when I come next spring.'

'Her husband won't mind?' Carole had told him Stevie might be getting married.

'Apparently not. I'm part of the deal.' She grinned.

They went to the airport in two cars, Carole in Matthieu's, Stevie, the doctor, and the guards in the rented limousine. And the now familiar photographers took pictures of Carole as she got into Matthieu's car. She stopped for a minute to smile and wave. She looked every inch a movie star with her brilliant smile, long blond hair, and diamond earrings. No one would ever have imagined that she'd been injured or sick. And Matthieu could hardly see the fading scar on her cheek, with artful makeup.

They chatted easily on the way to the airport, and Carole couldn't help thinking of the last time he had gone to the airport with her, fifteen years before. It had been a devastating morning for both of them. She couldn't stop sobbing on the trip out. She believed then she'd never see him again. In spite of vague assurances she made, she knew she wasn't coming back, and so did he. This time she was all smiles when she got out of the car at the airport, went through security, and went to the first-class lounge with Matthieu, while Stevie checked their bags. Air France had arranged for him to go through security with her, because of who he was.

The doctor took her vital signs discreetly half an hour before the flight. They were fine. He was looking forward to the flight in first class.

Matthieu walked her to the gate when they announced the flight, and she stood talking to him until the last minute and then he took her in his arms.

'It's different this time,' he said, acknowledging what she had remembered that morning.

'Yes, it is.' They were both grateful for a second chance. 'That was one of the worst days of my life,' Carole said softly, looking up at him.

'Mine too,' he said, and held her close.

'Take care of yourself when you get back. Don't push too hard. You don't have to do everything all at once,' he reminded her. She had started doing more and moving faster in the past few days. She was beginning to feel like her old self.

'The doctor says I'm fine,' she countered.

'Don't push your luck,' he chided her, as Stevie came to remind her that it was time to get on the plane. Carole nodded and looked up at Matthieu again. His eyes mirrored the same joy that she felt.

'Have fun with your children,' he told her.

'I'll call as soon as I arrive,' she promised. Stevie had given him the details of their flight.

They kissed, and this time there were no photographers to interrupt them. Carole could hardly tear herself away. Only days before she had been frightened to open her heart to him again, and now she could feel herself moving closer day by day. She was sad to leave Matthieu, but happy to be going back to L.A. as well. She could easily have never come home from this trip. They were all aware of it, as she pulled herself away at last, and walked slowly toward the plane. She stopped, turned, and looked back at him with a broad smile, which was the one he had always remembered. It was the movie star smile that made fans swoon all over the world. She stood looking at him for a long moment, mouthed the words '*je t'aime*,' and then with a wave, she turned and walked on to the plane. It had been a miraculous journey, and she was going home, with Matthieu in her heart. This time with hope, not heartbreak.

20

The flight to L.A. was blissfully uneventful. The young neurosurgeon took her vital signs several times, but Carole had no problem whatsoever. She ate two meals, watched a movie, and then turned her seat into a bed, cuddled up under the blanket and comforter, and slept the rest of the way. Stevie woke her up before they landed, so she could do her makeup and brush her teeth and hair. There was a strong possibility that there would be press to meet the plane. The airline had offered her a wheelchair, but she had declined it. She wanted to walk off under her own steam. She much preferred the story of a miraculous recovery to the vision of her return as an invalid, which she wasn't. Despite the long flight, she felt stronger than she had in weeks. Part of it was the excitement of the fresh hope she was sharing with Matthieu, but much of it was simply her own sense of gratitude and peace. She had not only survived the tunnel bombing, but refused to be defeated.

She looked out her window in silence, seeing the buildings, the swimming pools, the familiar sights and landmarks of L.A. She saw the Hollywood sign, smiled, and glanced at Stevie. There was a time when she thought she would never see those things again. There were tears in her eyes. So much had happened in the last two months. It was dizzying to think about as the landing gear touched the runway and the plane taxied to a stop.

'Welcome home,' Stevie said with a broad grin, as Carole looked at her and nearly burst into tears of relief. The young doctor was ecstatic to be in L.A. His sister was picking him up and he was spending a week with her before going back to Paris.

Carole and her two companions were among the first to disembark. A VIP person from Air France was waiting for them to whisk them through customs. Carole had nothing to declare, except the bracelet from Matthieu. And she finally accepted a wheelchair to get her through the long hike to immigration. The walk was too long for her. Customs had already been warned that she was coming through. She had her declaration ready, they told her the amount she owed, and she wrote a check within minutes. And once she handed them the check, an officer checked their passports and waved them through.

'Welcome back, Miss Barber.' The customs officer smiled at her as she stepped out of the wheelchair then, in case there were photographers waiting for her when she came through the doors. She was glad she did, because there was a wall of them there, shouting and calling her name as their flashes went off in her face. There was literally a cheer as they spotted her and she waved, walked steadily past them, and looking radiant and strong.

'How do you feel? . . . Is your head okay? . . .

What happened? . . . How does it feel to be back?' They shouted questions at her.

'Great! Just great!' She beamed as Stevie took her arm and helped her push her way through them. They waylaid her for a full fifteen minutes, taking photographs of her.

She looked tired when they got into the limousine waiting for them outside. And Stevie had hired a nurse to stay with her at the house. She didn't need medical care, but it seemed wiser for her not to be alone right at first. Carole had suggested letting her go as soon as the kids arrived, or at least when Matthieu came out. It was just comforting to have someone there at night, and Stevie was going home to her own man, life, and bed. She'd been gone for a long time and was happy to be back too. Particularly given Alan's proposal while she was gone. She wanted to celebrate that with him now.

Matthieu was the first to call Carole, literally as they came through the door. He had been worried about her all day and night. It was ten o'clock at night in Paris when she got home, and one o'clock in L.A.

'Was it all right?' he asked, sounding worried. 'How do you feel?'

'Absolutely fine. There was no problem at all, even on takeoff and landing.' Her doctor had been somewhat concerned that the changes in pressurization might do damage or give her a severe headache, but they hadn't. 'All the doctor did was eat and watch movies.'

'Good. I'm glad he was there anyway,' Matthieu said, relieved.

'So was I,' she admitted. She had been somewhat worried too.

'I already miss you,' he complained, but he sounded in good spirits, and so was she. They were going to see each other in no time at all, and their life together, whatever form it took, would start again. She had a lot to look forward to.

'Me too.'

'What are you going to do first?' He was excited for her. He knew how much it must mean to her to be back, after all she'd been through.

'I don't know. Just walk around and look, and thank God I'm here.' He was thankful too. He remembered how shocked he'd been when he saw her first, on the respirator at La Pitié Salpêtrière. She looked dead. And nearly was. Her recovery was like being born again. And now they had each other too. It was like a dream for both of them.

'My house looks beautiful,' she said, glancing around, still on the phone with him. 'I'd forgotten how nice it is.'

'I can't wait to see it.'

They hung up after a few more minutes, and Stevie settled her in. The nurse arrived ten minutes later, and was a pleasant woman who was excited to meet Carole. Like everyone else who had read about it, she'd been horrified by her accident in France, and said it was miraculous she was alive.

Carole wandered into her bedroom then and looked around. She remembered it perfectly now, and had for a while. She looked out at the garden, and then walked into her office, and sat down at her desk. Stevie had already set her computer up for her. And the nurse went to make lunch. Stevie had asked the cleaning person to order groceries for them. As usual, she had thought of everything, down to the last detail. There was nothing Stevie didn't do.

Stevie sat down and had lunch with her in the kitchen, as they so often did. Carole was halfway through a turkey sandwich when she started to cry.

'What's wrong?' Stevie asked gently, but she knew. It was an emotional day for Carole, and even for her.

'I can't believe I'm here. I never thought I'd come back again.' She could finally admit to the terrible fear she'd experienced. She didn't have to be brave anymore. And even once she'd survived the bomb, the last terrorist had come to kill her. It was more than any one human being should have had to live through.

'You're okay,' Stevie reminded her, and gave her a hug, and then handed her a tissue to blow her nose.

'I'm sorry. I don't think I realized how rattled I was. And even Matthieu . . . that was so emotional for me.'

'You're entitled,' Stevie reminded her. 'You can

stand here and scream if you want. You've earned it.'

The nurse cleared away their lunch dishes, and Carole and Stevie sat at the kitchen table for a while. And then Stevie made her a cup of vanilla tea and handed it to her.

'You should go home,' Carole reminded her. 'Alan must be anxious to see you.'

'He's picking me up in half an hour. I'll call and let you know what happens.' Stevie looked nervous and excited.

'Just enjoy him. You can tell me tomorrow.' Carole felt guilty for how much of her time and life she had taken. Stevie had always given her way beyond the call of what was normal, or could be considered 'duty.' She gave herself body and soul to her employer and her job, beyond what any human being would.

Stevie left half an hour later, when Alan honked twice outside, and as she raced out the door, Carole wished her luck. The nurse helped her unpack, and then she went to sit in her office and stared out the window. The computer was waiting for her, but she was too tired to touch it.

By then it was three o'clock, which was midnight in Paris. She was wiped out.

She walked out into her garden that afternoon, and called both her children. Chloe was arriving the next day, and she said she could hardly wait to see her mom. Carole wanted to rest up for her that night, but she wanted to get on L.A. time, so she didn't go to bed until nearly ten o'clock. It was morning in Paris by then. Carole was asleep the minute her head hit the pillow, and stunned that Stevie was already there when she got up the next day at ten-thirty. She woke up when Stevie peeked into her room with a big smile.

'Are you awake?'

'What time is it? I must have slept twelve or thirteen hours.' Carole lay in bed, stretched, and yawned.

'You needed it,' Stevie said as she pulled back the curtains. Carole saw instantly that there was a small diamond on her left hand.

'So?' she said, sitting up with a sleepy smile. She had a headache, and an appointment with both the neurologist and a neuropsychologist that morning. They worked as a team with

486

patients who'd suffered brain injuries. She figured the headache was probably normal after the time change and the flight. She wasn't worried.

'Are you still free on New Year's Eve?' Stevie asked, nearly crowing with excitement, and Carole beamed.

'Are you going to do it?'

'Yes,' Stevie said, looking faintly panicked, and held out the ring for inspection. It was a small but exquisite antique diamond ring that suited her hand. Stevie was thrilled, and Carole was happy for her. She deserved all the joy life gave her, for the love and comfort she gave others, particularly her boss. 'We're flying to Las Vegas on the morning of New Year's Eve. Alan booked rooms at the Bellagio for us, and you too.'

'I'll be there. With bells on. Oh my God, we have to go shopping. You need a dress.' Carole started to come alive as she said it. She was excited for her friend.

'We can go with Chloe. You should rest today. You had a long day yesterday.'

Carole got out of bed slowly, and felt better when she had a cup of tea and some toast. Stevie went to the doctor with her, and they talked about the wedding on the way. The neurologist had said she was fine, and told her to take it easy. He was stunned as he glanced through her records, and read the doctor's report from Paris. She had done a final summary in English for him.

'You're one lucky woman,' he told her. He predicted that she would have memory lapses for six months to a year, which was what they had told her in Paris too. She wasn't crazy about the doctor, she liked the one in Paris better. But she didn't have to see him again for another month, just to check in. They were going to do another CT scan then, just to keep an eye on her. And physical therapists were going to continue to work with her.

The doctor who impressed both Carole and Stevie was the neuropsychologist Carole saw in the same office immediately after the neurologist, who had been methodical, precise, and very dry. The neuropsychologist was a woman, who bounced into the examining room to see Carole like a ray of sunshine. She was tiny, elfin, with huge blue eyes, freckles, and bright red hair. She looked like a pixie, and was very sharp.

She smiled at Carole as soon as she walked in, and introduced herself as Dr. Oona O'Rourke, and was as Irish as a leprechaun, with a brogue. It made Carole smile just looking at her, as the doctor hopped up on the table like a sprite in her white coat, and smiled at the two women sitting across from her in chairs. Stevie had been in the examining room with Carole for moral support and to help fill in details she might have forgotten or didn't know.

'So, I hear you did some flying around a tunnel in Paris. Pretty impressive. I read about it. How was it?'

'Not as much fun as it was cracked up to be,' Carole commented. 'It wasn't what I had planned for my trip to Paris.' Dr. O'Rourke glanced at her chart then and commented on the memory loss, and wanted to know how it was going.

'Much better,' Carole said openly. 'It was pretty weird in the beginning. I had no idea who

I was, or who anyone else was. My memory was completely gone.'

'And now?' The bright blue eyes saw all, and her smile was warm. She was an added feature they hadn't had in Paris, but Carole's new L.A. neurologist thought the psychological factor was important, and at least three or four meetings with her were required, although Carole was doing well.

'My memory is much better. I still have some holes, but they're nothing compared to when I first woke up.'

'Have you had any anxiety attacks? Trouble sleeping? Headaches? Strange behavior? Depression?' Carole answered no to all of the above, with the exception of the mild headache she'd had that day when she woke up. Dr. O'Rourke agreed with Carole that she was doing extremely well. 'It sounds like you were very lucky, if you can call it that. That kind of brain injury can be very hard to predict. The mind is a strange and wondrous thing. And sometimes I think what we do is more art than science. Are you planning to go back to work?'

'Not for a while. I'm working on a book, and I thought I'd start looking at scripts in the spring.'

'I wouldn't rush it. You may be tired for a while. Don't push. Your body will tell you what it's ready to do, and it may bite back if you push too hard. You could get some memory lapses again if you overdo it.' The prospect of that impressed Carole, and Stevie gave her a warning look. 'Anything else you're concerned about?' she asked, and waited for Carole's response.

'Not really. Sometimes it scares me how close I came to dying. I still have nightmares about it.'

'That's reasonable.' Carole told her about the attack in the hospital then, by the remaining suicide bomber who had come back to kill her. 'Sounds like you've really been through it, Carole. I think you should take it easy for a while. Give yourself a chance to heal from the emotional shock as well as the physical trauma. You've been through an awful lot. Are you married?'

'No, I'm widowed. My children and ex-husband are coming out for Christmas.' She looked happy as she said it, and the doctor smiled.

'Anyone else?'

Carole smiled. 'I rekindled an old flame in Paris. He's coming out right after the holidays.'

'Good. Have some fun, you've earned it.'

They sat and talked for a while, and she suggested some exercises to sharpen Carole's memory, which sounded interesting and fun. The doctor was bright and lively and full of life. And Stevie and Carole commented on it when they left the office.

'She's cute,' Stevie remarked.

'And smart,' Carole added. 'I like her.' She felt as though she could ask or tell her anything if something unusual came up. She had even inquired about having sex with Matthieu, and Dr. O'Rourke had said it was fine and then warned her to use condoms, which made Carole blush. It had been a long time since she'd had to worry about that. Dr. O'Rourke commented with her impish grin that she didn't need to get an STD on top of everything else she'd been through. Carole agreed and laughed, feeling almost girlish again.

She felt relieved as she left the office that she had a doctor she could talk to, in case she felt the effects of the accident differently now that she was home. But so far she was doing well and felt fine. She was looking forward to the holidays with her family and to Stevie's wedding, both of which sounded like fun.

Carole insisted on stopping at Barney's for Stevie's dress on the way back from the doctor's office. Stevie tried on three dresses and fell in love with the first one. Carole bought it for her as a wedding present, and they found white satin Manolos on the main floor. The dress was long and showed off Stevie's statuesque figure. She was getting married in white. They had found a dark green dress for Carole. It was short, strapless, and the color of emeralds. She said she felt like the mother of the bride.

Chloe wasn't arriving till seven that night, so they had the afternoon to putter around the house and get things ready for her. Stevie was going to pick her up, and at the last minute, Carole decided to go with her. They left the house at six. Her florist had delivered a fully decorated Christmas tree at five, and the house suddenly looked like Christmas.

They talked about the wedding again on the way to the airport. Stevie was so excited, and Carole was too.

'I can't believe I'm doing this,' she said for the hundredth time that day, as Carole smiled at her. They both knew it was the right thing, and Carole said so again. 'You don't think I'm crazy, do you? What if I hate him in five years?' Stevie was a maelstrom of emotions.

'You won't, and if you do, we'll talk about it then. And no, I don't think you're crazy. He's a good man, and he loves you, and you love him. Is he okay about not having kids?' Carole asked, looking concerned.

'He says he is. He says I'm enough for him.'

'That'll do,' Carole said.

As they got out of the car, Carole's cell phone rang. It was Matthieu. 'What are you up to?' he asked with a happy voice.

'I'm picking up Chloe at the airport. I saw the doctor today, and he says I'm fine. And we found a wedding dress for Stevie on the way back.' It was fun sharing her activities with him. After the nightmare in Paris, every minute seemed like a gift.

'Now you have me worried. You're doing far too much. Did the doctor say you could, or are you supposed to rest?'

It was nearly four in the morning in Paris. He had woken up, and decided to call her. She seemed much too far away. He loved hearing her voice. She sounded excited and young.

'He said I don't have to see him again for a month.' As she said it, she was suddenly reminded of when she was pregnant with his baby, and she pushed the thought from her mind. It made her too sad. He had always wanted doctor's reports from her then too, and kissed her belly as it grew. He had come to one of her appointments, to listen to the baby's heartbeat. They had been through a lot together, especially after the miscarriage and when his daughter died. She and Matthieu had history that bound them to each other, even now.

'I miss you,' he told her again as he had the day before. She had been out of his life for fifteen years, and now that she was back, each day seemed interminable without her. He could hardly wait to come. He was leaving the next day to go skiing with his children, and promised to call her from there. He wished that she could join them on the trip, even if she couldn't ski. She had never met his children in the old days and he wanted her to now. She knew it would be bittersweet for her when she did. In the meantime, she was looking forward to spending time with her own.

She and Stevie waited for Chloe to come out of customs. She knew Stevie was coming to the airport, but she looked stunned when she saw her mother.

'You came?' she said, amazed, throwing her arms around her. 'Should you do that? Are you okay?' She looked worried, but thrilled, which made Carole doubly happy she had come. It had been well worth the effort to see that look on Chloe's face, of amazed delight and appreciation. She was reveling in her mother's love, which was just what Carole had wanted.

'I'm fine. I saw the doctor today. I can do

whatever I want, within reason. This seemed reasonable to me. I couldn't wait to see you,' she said as she put an arm around her daughter's waist, and Stevie went to get the car. Carole wasn't driving yet, and didn't plan to for a while. The doctors didn't want her to, and she didn't feel up to the pressure of L.A. traffic.

The three women chatted on the way back from the airport, and Carole told her about Stevie's wedding plans. Chloe was thrilled for her too. She had known Stevie almost all her life, and loved her like a big sister.

Stevie left them when they got home, and Chloe and her mother sat in the kitchen. She had slept on the flight so she was wide awake. Carole made her scrambled eggs, and they ate ice cream afterward. It was nearly midnight when they went to bed. And the next day they went Christmas shopping. Carole didn't have anything for anyone yet. She had two days to do it. It was going to be a skimpy Christmas this year. But a good one.

By the next day, she had gotten everything she needed at Barney's and Neiman's, for Jason,

Stevie, and both her children. They had just come through the door, when Mike Appelsohn called her.

'You're back! Why didn't you call me?' He sounded hurt.

'I just got in the day before yesterday,' she apologized. 'And Chloe arrived last night.'

'I called the Ritz and they said you checked out. How are you feeling?' He still sounded worried about her. She'd been at death's door a month before.

'Great. A little tired, but I would be anyway, with jet lag. How are you, Mike?'

'Busy. I hate this time of year.' He made social chitchat for a few minutes, and then got to the reason for his call. 'What are you doing next September?'

'Going to college. Why?' she teased him.

'You are?' He was surprised.

'No. How do I know what I'll be doing in September? I'm just happy to be here now. I damn near wasn't.' They both knew how true that was.

'Don't tell me. I know,' he said. She was still

touched by his trip to Paris to see her. No one else would have done that but him, on an overnight flight from L.A. 'Well, kid, I've got a part for you. A great one. If you don't do this picture, I quit.' He told her who was doing it, and who the stars were. She had a starring role with two major actors and a respected younger actress, and she was getting lead billing. It was a fabulous movie, with a big budget, and a director she'd worked with before and loved. She couldn't believe her ears.

'Are you serious?'

'Damn right I am. The director is starting another picture in Europe in February. He'll be there till July. And he can't start this one till September. He has to wrap up postproduction on the other one in August. So you'd have time off till then to write your book, if you're still doing that.'

'I am. I'm already working on it.' She was thrilled by what he had said.

'There'll be some location shooting in Europe. In London and Paris. They'll shoot the rest in L.A. How does that sound to you?'

'Tailor-made.' She hadn't told him about Matthieu yet. But what he had just said fit perfectly with her current plans, to spend time with Matthieu in Paris, and in L.A. London was the icing on the cake, and she could spend time there with Chloe.

'I'll send you the script. They want an answer by next week. They've got two other actresses lined up behind you, who would kill to do this. I'll messenger the script over to you tomorrow. I read it last night and it's great.' She trusted him. He always told her the truth, and they had similar taste in scripts. They usually liked the same ones.

'I'll read it right away,' Carole promised.

'How are you feeling, seriously? Do you think you'll be up to it by then?' He still sounded worried.

'I do. I'm feeling better every day. And the doctor here gave me a clean bill of health.'

'Don't push,' he reminded her, as Matthieu had. They both knew her too well. She always pushed, it was just her way. She drove herself hard, and had since the beginning of her career, although she had slowed down in recent years.

But she could feel her engines revving up again. She'd taken a long enough break. 'You'll regret it later,' he warned.

'I know. I'm not that stupid.' She was well aware of what she'd been through and how taxing it had been. She still needed time to convalesce. But she had no major plans for a while. She and Matthieu could take it easy too. And she was going to write the book at her own pace. She had eight months now before she had to go back to work.

'Well, kid. You're going to be back in business on this one.' He was thrilled for her.

'Sounds like it. I can't wait to read the script.'

'You'll go nuts,' he promised. 'I'll eat my shoes if you don't.' It was a tall order. He was a big man and wore a size fourteen.

'I'll call you the day after Christmas.' The next day was Christmas Eve, and Jason and Anthony were flying in from New York.

'Merry Christmas, Carole,' Mike said, sounding choked up. He couldn't even imagine it if she were no longer here, if they'd all been mourning her. It didn't bear thinking, and would have been a tragedy to him, and so many others.

'Merry Christmas to you too, Mike,' she said, and hung up.

She told Chloe about the script over dinner, and saw a shadow come over her face. It was the first time she had realized how much her daughter really resented her career.

'We'll be on location in London, if I do it. That would be great, I could spend that time with you. And you can hop over to Paris while we're there.' Chloe's face lightened at the words, she knew how hard her mother was trying, and it meant a lot to her. Whatever her sins of the past were, in Chloe's mind, she was atoning for them now.

'Thanks, Mom. That would be fun.'

They had dinner alone that night. They ordered Chinese takeout, and the nurse went to pick it up. Carole didn't want to waste a minute with her daughter. Chloe slept in her bed that night, and they giggled like two little kids. And the next day Chloe and her mother went to pick Jason and Anthony up at LAX. Mercifully, Stevie was off. It was Christmas Eve, and she'd earned it. She wasn't coming back to work till the day after Christmas.

The script Mike had told her about had arrived that afternoon. She had glanced at it, and it looked great so far, as good as he had promised. She was going to try to read it on Christmas night, after everyone went to bed. But she was already fairly sure she would like it. Mike was right. And the part they wanted her for was fantastic. She had told Matthieu about it on the phone. He was excited for her. He knew she wanted to go back to work. And this sounded like a perfect part for her.

Anthony and Jason were among the first off the plane. Chloe drove them home, and they all talked at the same time on the way back. There was giggling and laughing, and embarrassing stories from Christmases past. They talked about the year Anthony had accidentally knocked over the tree when he was five, trying to trap Santa as he slid down their chimney in New York. There were dozens of stories like that that touched Carole's heart and amused the others. She remembered almost all the stories now.

They ordered pizza when they got to the house, and after the kids went to their rooms, Jason wandered into the kitchen for something to drink and found Carole there.

'How are you feeling, really?' he asked her seriously. She looked better than when he had last seen her, but still pale. She'd done a lot since she got home. Probably too much, knowing her, he thought.

'Good, actually,' she said, looking surprised herself.

'You sure gave us a hell of a scare,' he said, referring to the bombing and its aftermath. He had been wonderful to her then, and she was still touched by all he had said.

'I gave myself a hell of a scare too. It was shit luck, but it turned out okay in the end.'

'Yes, it did,' he said, smiling at her. They talked for a little while, and then he went to bed, and Carole stopped in her office for a few minutes before she went to her room. She liked that time of night, when everything was quiet. She always had, especially when the kids were young. It was private time for her. She needed that.

She glanced at her watch and saw that it was just after midnight. It was nine o'clock in the morning in France. She could have called Matthieu, and she wanted to at some point, to wish him a Merry Christmas. But right now, she didn't. They had time now, lots of it, and he would be in L.A. with her soon enough. She was happy to have him back in her life. He was an unexpected gift. She sat down at her desk, glanced at her computer, and saw the last entries she'd made on her book. She had it sorted out in her head now, and knew what she wanted to write.

She looked out into the garden, with the fountain all lit up, and the pond. Her children were at home, in their rooms. Jason was there, like the loving friend and brother he had become. Their transition from past to present had been smooth. She had a movie to do. Stevie was getting married in a week. She had survived a terrorist bombing, and she had her memory back. Carole closed her eyes and silently thanked God for the blessings she had, and then opened them again and smiled. She had everything she had ever wanted and more. And best of all, she had herself. She hadn't compromised herself in the process or in the course of her life. She hadn't given up her ideals or her values, or the things that mattered to her. She had been true to herself and those she loved. She glanced at the bracelet Matthieu had given her, and read the inscription again. 'Honor Thyself.' To the best of her knowledge, she had. She hadn't told her family about Matthieu yet. But when the time was right she would. She knew Anthony would probably object at first, but hopefully he would calm down with time. He had a right to his opinions and concerns for her. And she had a right to her own life, and to make the choices that seemed best for her.

'What are you doing?' a voice behind her asked. It was Chloe, standing in her nightgown in the doorway. She wanted to sleep in her mother's bed again, and it was fine with Carole. It reminded her of when Chloe was a little girl. She had loved sleeping with her mother then too.

'I'm just thinking,' Carole said, turning to smile at her.

'About what?'

'About how much I have to be thankful for this year.'

'Me too,' Chloe said softly, and then came to give her mother a hug. 'I'm so glad you're here.' And then she scampered into the hall on her long graceful legs. 'Come on, Mom, let's go to bed.'

'Okay, boss,' Carole said, as she turned out the lights in her office, and followed her daughter down the hall to her own room. 'Thank you,' Carole whispered, glancing skyward with a grateful smile. It was indeed a merry Christmas that year, for them all.

THE END

A GOOD WOMAN
By Danielle Steel

*A spellbinding tale of war, loss,
history, and one woman's
unbreakable spirit*

Annabelle Worthington, born into a life of privilege,
was raised amid the glamour of New York society. But
everything changes on a cold April day in 1912, when
the sinking of the *Titanic* alters her world forever.

Finding strength within her grief, Annabelle throws
herself into volunteer work, nursing the poor and
igniting a passion for medicine that will shape the
course of her life. But a seemingly idyllic marriage
brings more grief and, pursued by a scandal she does
not deserve, Annabelle flees New York for war-ravaged
France. There she finds her true calling, working as an
ambulance medic on the front lines. When the war
ends, Annabelle begins a new life in Paris – now a
doctor and mother, her past almost
forgotten . . . until a fateful meeting opens her heart
to the world she had left behind.

9780593056776

BANTAM PRESS

BUNGALOW 2
By Danielle Steel

Beyond the dazzle of Hollywood . . .

As she checks into the lush Beverly Hills Hotel,
Tanya Harris dreads being away from her husband
and three teenage children. She is here to do a
major screenplay after years of always putting her
family first. Tanya is amazed at what she finds in
her luxury suite: lilies, orchids and roses, a pink
marble tub, her favourite chocolates, a cashmere
robe, and slippers that fit perfectly. Things are
going to be different in Bungalow 2.

From her first day on the set, Tanya is thrust into
an intoxicating new world. Suddenly she's
working with a Hollywood legend: Oscar-winning
producer Douglas Wayne . . . and he seems to
have his sights set on her. As her family needs her
less and less, Tanya watches helplessly as her old
life is pulled out from under her in the most
crushing of ways. Then she is offered another
dazzling opportunity – with an ending she never
could have written herself.

9780552151818

CORGI BOOKS

AMAZING GRACE
By Danielle Steel

On a warm May night in San Francisco,
a glittering, celebrity studded crowd gathers for a
charity event. Just minutes before midnight, the room
begins to sway. Glass shatters, the lights go out, and
people begin to scream . . .

In the earthquake's aftermath, the lives of four strangers
will converge:

Sarah Sloane, the beautiful wife of a financial star,
watches her perfect world fall to pieces.

Melanie Free, award-winning singer, comes to a turning
point in her career.

Everett Carson, a former war correspondent whose
personal demons have demoted him to covering society
parties, finds new purpose amid the carnage.

Sister Maggie Kent, a nun who does her best work in
jeans and trainers, searches through the rubble – and
knows instantly that there is much work to be done.

The city staggers back to life, and a chain reaction will
touch each of the survivors as they find the amazing grace
of new beginnings.

9780552154734

CORGI BOOKS

THE WEDDING
By Danielle Steel

Allegra Steinberg, entertainment lawyer to the stars,
is the daughter of one of the most respected couples in
Hollywood. Successful and happy, her career consumes so
much of her energy that she has little time for a private
life, and marriage is the last thing on her mind. However,
a chance encounter with a New York writer turns her life
upside down and she suddenly finds herself planning a
wedding at her parents' Bel Air home.

But in the chaos of last-minute arrangements, surprise
announcements and ever-increasing anxiety, family secrets
are revealed and the real meaning of Allegra's marriage
becomes apparent. It is a bridge between the past and the
future and an opportunity for reconciliation, forgiveness
and new hope.

Believe in Happy Endings

9780552141352

CORGI BOOKS

ANSWERED PRAYERS
By Danielle Steel

*A moving story of the second chances that
only come once in a lifetime.*

Faith Madison is the very picture of a sophisticated
New Yorker. Slim, blonde, stylish and married to a
successful merchant banker, she has a life many would
envy. But Faith has overcome a childhood marred by
tragedy, and has carried within herself a secret she
can divulge to no-one.

The death of her stepfather sets off a journey of
change and revelation. At the funeral, an old friend
re-enters Faith's life. Brad, a lanky boy from her
childhood days who had teased, tormented and
protected her, is now a lawyer in California.
Determined to have a career of her own, Faith
applies to law school against her husband's wishes,
igniting a barrage of anger and recrimination. As
she and Brad rediscover each other, Faith is finally
ready to face the most painful step of all: sharing
a secret that has long been haunting her, and
opening up her heart for the first
time in her life.

Believe in Happy Endings

9780552148542

CORGI BOOKS